Mrs. Molesworth

Nurse Heatherdale's Story and Little Miss Peggy

Mrs. Molesworth

Nurse Heatherdale's Story and Little Miss Peggy

ISBN/EAN: 9783743389977

Manufactured in Europe, USA, Canada, Australia, Japa

Cover: Foto ©Andreas Hilbeck / pixelio.de

Manufactured and distributed by brebook publishing software (www.brebook.com)

Mrs. Molesworth

Nurse Heatherdale's Story and Little Miss Peggy

NURSE HEATHERDALE'S STORY

AND

LITTLE MISS PEGGY

BY

MRS. MOLESWORTH

AUTHOR OF "CARROTS," "GRANDMOTHER DEAR," "TELL ME A STORY"

ILLUSTRATED BY LESLIE BROOKE AND WALTER CRANE

New York

MACMILLAN AND CO.

AND LONDON

1893

Education

GIFT

Norwood Press:
J. S. Cushing & Co. — Berwick & Smith.
Boston, Mass., U.S.A.

CONTENTS.

NURSE HEATHERDALE'S STORY.

315

CHAPTER VII.

CHAPTER VIII.

CHAPTER IX.

CHAPTER X.

CHAPTER XI.

CHAPTER XII.

CHAPTER XIII.

CONTENTS.

LITTLE MISS PEGGY.

CHAPTER I.

CONTENTS.

CHAPTER VII.

CHAPTER VIII.

CHAPTER IX.

CHAPTER X.

CHAPTER XI.

CHAPTER XII.

LIST OF ILLUSTRATIONS.

NURSE HEATHERDALE'S STORY.

LIST OF ILLUSTRATIONS.

LITTLE MISS PEGGY.

She was sitting in the Dame's old-fashioned armchair, in the window of the little room; the bright summer sunshine streaming in behind her. — page 27.

— Frontispiece.

NURSE·HEATHER=DALE'S·STORY·BY MRS·MOLESWORTH

ILLUSTRATED·BY L·LESLIE·BROOKE

MACMILLAN·&·CO

LONDON·MDCCCXCIII:

TO

𝔐𝔶 𝔉𝔞𝔯 𝔄𝔴𝔞𝔶 𝔟𝔲𝔱 𝔉𝔞𝔦𝔱𝔥𝔣𝔲𝔩 𝔉𝔯𝔦𝔢𝔫𝔡

GISÉLA

LINDFIELD, August 22, 1891

NURSE HEATHERDALE'S STORY.

CHAPTER I.

LOVE AT FIRST SIGHT.

I COULD fancy it was only yesterday! That first time I saw them. And to think how many years ago it is really! And how many times I have told the story — or, perhaps, I should say the *stories*, for after all it is only a string of simple day-by-day events I have to tell, though to me and to the children about me they seem so interesting and, in some ways, I think I may say, rather out of the common. So that now that I am getting old, or "beginning to think just a tiny bit about some day getting old," which is the only way Miss Erica will let me say it, and knowing that nobody else *can* know all the ins and outs which make the whole just as I do, and having a nice quiet time to myself most days (specially since dear tiresome little Master Ramsey is off to school with his brothers), I am going to try to put it down as well as I can. My "as well as I can" won't be anything very scholarly or fine, I know well; but if one knows what one wants to say it seems to me the words will come. And the story will be there for the dear children, who are never sharp judging of old Heather — and for their children after them, maybe.

I was standing at our cottage door that afternoon — a beautiful summer afternoon it was, early in June. I was looking idly enough across the common, for our cottage stood — stands still, perhaps — I have not been there for many a year — just at the edge of Brayling Common, where it skirts the pine woods, when I saw them pass. Quite a little troop they looked, though they were scarcely near enough for me to see them plainly. There was the donkey, old Larkins's donkey, which they had hired for the time, with a tot of a girl riding on it, the page-boy leading it, and a nursemaid walking on one side, and on the other an older little lady — somewhere about ten years old she looked, though she was really only eight. What an air she had, to be sure! What a grand way of holding herself and stepping along like a little princess, for all that she and her sisters were dressed as simple as simple. Pink cotton frocks, if I remember right, a bit longer in the skirts than our young ladies wear them now, and nice white cotton stockings, — it was long before black silk ones were the fashion for children, — and ankle-strap shoes, and white sun-bonnets, made with casers and cords, nice and shady for the complexions, though you really had

to be close to before you could see a child's face
inside of them.   And some way behind, another little
lady, a good bit shorter than Miss Bess — I meant to
give all their names in order later on, but it seems
strange-like not to say it — and looking quite three
years younger, though there was really not two between them.   And alongside of her a boy, thin and
pale and darkish-haired — that, I could see, as he had
no sun-bonnet of course, only a cap of some kind.
He too was a good bit taller than Miss ——, the
middle young lady I mean, though short for his age,
which was eleven past.   They were walking together,
these two — they were mostly always together, and I
saw that the boy was a little lame, just a touch, but
enough to take the spring out of his step that one
likes to see in a young thing.   And though I couldn't
see her face, only some long fair curls, long enough
to come below the cape of her bonnet, a feeling came
over me that the child beside him was walking slow,
keeping back as it were, on purpose to bear him
company.   There was something gentle and pitying-
like in her little figure, in the way she went closer
to the boy and took his hand when the nurse turned
round and called back something — I couldn't hear
the words but I fancied the tone was sharp — to the
two children behind, which made them press forward
a little.   The other young lady turned as they came
nearer and said something with a sort of toss-up of
her proud little head to the nurse.   And then I saw

that she held out her hand to her younger sister, who kept hold all the same of the boy's hand on the other side. And that was how they were walking when they went in among the trees and were lost to my sight.

But I still stood looking after them, even when there was nothing more of them to be seen. Not even the dog — oh, I forgot about him — he was the very last of the party — a brisk, shortish haired, wiry-looking rough terrier, who, just as he got to the entrance of the wood, turned round and stood for a moment barking, for all the world as if he might be saying, "My young ladies have gone a-walking in the wood now, and nobody's to come a-troubling of them. So I give you fair notice." He did think, did Fusser, that was *his* name, that he managed all the affairs of the family. Many a time we've laughed at him for it.

"Dear me," thought I to myself, "I could almost make a story out of those young ladies and gentleman, though I've only seen them for a minute, or two at the most."

For I was very fond of children even then, and knew a good deal about their ways, though not so much — no, nor nothing like — what I do now! But I was in rather a dreamy sort of humour. I had just left my first place, — that of nursery-maid with the family where my mother had been before me, and where I had stayed on older than I should have done by rights, because of thinking I was going to be

married. And six months before, my poor Charles
had died suddenly, or so at least it had seemed to us
all. For he caught cold, and it went to his chest,
and he was gone in a fortnight. The doctor said for
all he looked strong, he was really sadly delicate, and
it was bound to be sooner or later. It may have been
true, leastways the doctor meant to comfort me by
saying so, though I don't know that I found much
comfort in the thought. Not so much anyhow as in
mother's simple words that it was God's will, and so
it must be right. And in thinking how happy we
had been. Never a word or a coldness all the four
years we were plighted. But it was hard to bear,
and it changed all my life for me. I never could
bring myself to think of another.

Still I was only twenty-one, and after I'd been at
home a bit, the young ladies would have me back to
cheer me up, they said. I travelled with them that
spring; but when they all went up to London, and
Miss Marian was to be married, and the two little
ones were all day with the governess, I really couldn't
for shame stay on when there was no need of me.
So, though with many tears, I came home, and was
casting about in my mind what I had best do —
mother being hale and hearty, and no call for dress-
making of a plain kind in our village — that afternoon,
when I stood watching the stranger little gentry and
old Larkins's donkey and the dog, as they crossed the
common into the fir-wood.

It was mother's voice that woke me up, so to say.

"Martha," she called out in her cheery way, "what's thee doing, child? I'm about tidied up; come and get thy work, and let's sit down a bit comfortable. I don't like to see thee so down-like, and such bright summer weather, though mayhap the very sunshine makes it harder for thee, poor dear."

And she gave a little sigh, which was a good deal for her, for she was not one as made much talk of feelings and sorrows. It seemed to spirit me up somehow.

"I wasn't like that just now, mother," I said cheerfully. "I've been watching some children — gentry — going over the common — three little young ladies and a boy, and Larkins's donkey. They made me think of Miss Charlotte and Miss Marian when first I went there, though plainer dressed a good deal than our young ladies were. But real gentry, I should say."

"And you'd say right," mother answered. "They are lodging at Widow Nutfold's, quite a party of them. Their father's Sir ———; dear, dear, I've forgot the name, but he's a barrowknight, and the family's name is Penrose. They come from somewhere far off, near by the sea — quite furrin parts, I take it."

"Not out of England, you don't mean, do you?" I asked. For mother, of course, kept all her old country talk, while I, with having been so many years with Miss Marian and her sisters, and treated more like a friend than a servant, and great pains taken with my reading and writing, had come to speak less old-fashioned, so to say, and to give the proper meaning to my words. " Foreign parts really means out of this country, where they talk French or Italian, you know, mother."

But mother only shook her head.

"Nay," she said, "I mean what I say. Furrin parts is furrin parts. I wouldn't say as they come from where the folks is nigger blacks, or from old Boney's country neither, as they used to frighten us about when I was a child. But these gentry come from furrin parts. Why, I had it from Sarah Nutfold's own lips, last Saturday, as never was, at Brayling market, and old neighbours of forty years; it's not sense to think she go for to deceive me."

Mother was just a little offended, I could see, and I thought to myself I must take care of seeming to set her right.

"Of course not," I said. "You couldn't have it surer than from Mrs. Nutfold. I dare say she's pleased to have them to cheer her up a bit. They seem nice little ladies to look at, though they're on the outside of plain as to their dress."

"And more sense, too," said mother. "I always thought our young ladies too expensive, though where money's no consideration, 'tis a temptation to a lady to dress up her children, I suppose."

"But they were never *over*-dressed," I said, in my turn, a little ruffled. "Nothing could be simpler than their white frocks to look at."

"Ay, to look at, I'll allow," said mother. "But when you come to look *into* them, Martha, it was another story. Embroidery and tucks and real Walansian!" and she held up her hands. "Still they've got it, and they've a right to spend it, seein' too as they're generous to those who need. But these little ladies at Sarah's are not rich, I take it. There was a deal of settlin' about the prices when my lady came to take the rooms. She and the gentleman's up in London, but one or two of the children got ill and needed country air. It's a heavy charge on Sarah Nutfold, for the nurse is not one of the old sort, and my lady asked Sarah, private-like, to have an eye on her."

" There now," I cried, " I could have said as much ! The way she turned just now so sharp on the poor boy and the middle little lady. I could see she wasn't one of the right kind, though I didn't hear what she said. No one should be a nurse, or have to do with children, mother, who doesn't right down love them in her heart."

"You're about right there, Martha," mother agreed.

Just then father came in, and we sat round, the three of us, to our tea.

"It's a pleasure to have thee at home again, my

girl, for a bit," he said. And the kind look in his eyes made me feel both cheered and sad together. It was the first day I had been with them at tea-time, for I had got home pretty late the night before. "And I hope it'll be a longish bit this time," he went on.

I gave a little sigh.

"I'd like to stay a while; but I don't know that it would be good for me to stay very long, father, thank you," I said. "I'm young and strong and fit for work, and I'd like to feel I was able to help you and mother if ever the time comes that you're laid by."

"Please God we'll never need help of that kind, my girl," said father. "But it's best to be at work, I know, when one's had a trouble. The day'll maybe come, Martha, when you'll be glad to have saved a little more for a home of your own, after all. So I'd not be the one to stand in your way, a few months hence — nor mother neither — if a good place offers."

"Thank you, father," I said again; "but the only home of my own I'll ever care for will be here — by mother and you."

And so it proved.

I little thought how soon father's words about not standing in my way if a nice place offered would be put to the test.

I saw the children who were lodging at Mrs. Nutfold's several times in the course of the next week or two. They seemed to have a great fancy for the pine-woods, and from where they lived they could not, to get to them, but pass across the common within sight of our cottage. And once or twice I met them in the village street. Not all of them together — once it was only the two youngest with the nurse; they were waiting at the door of the post-office, which was also the grocer's and the baker's, while she was inside chattering and laughing a deal more than she'd any call to, it seemed to me. (I'm afraid I took a real right-down dislike to that nurse, which isn't a proper thing to do before one has any certain reason for it.) And dear little ladies they looked, though the elder one — that was the middle one of the three — had rather an anxious expression in her face, that struck me. The baby — she was nearly three, but I heard them call her baby — was a little fat bundle of smiles and dimples. I don't think even a cross nurse would have had power to trouble *her* much.

Another time it was the two elder girls and the lame boy I met. It was a windy day, and the eldest Missy's big flapping bonnet had blown back, so I had a good look at her. She was a beautiful child — blue eyes, very dark blue, or seeming so from the clear black eyebrows and thick long eyelashes, and dark almost black hair, with just a little wave in it; not so long or curling as her sister's, which was out-of-the-way beautiful hair, but seeming somehow just to suit her, as everything about her did. She came walking along with the proud springing step I had noticed that first day, and she was talking away to the others as if to cheer and encourage them, even though the boy was full three years older than she, and supposed to be taking charge of her and her sister, I fancy.

"Nonsense, Franz," she was saying in her decided spoken way, "nonsense. I won't have you and Lally treated like that. And I don't care — I mean I can't help if it does trouble mamma. Mammas must be troubled about their children sometimes; that's what being a mamma means."

I managed to keep near them for a bit. I hope it was not a mean taking-advantage. I have often told them of it since — it was really that I did feel such an interest in the dear children, and my mind misgave me from the first about that nurse — it did so indeed.

"If only — " said the boy with a tiny sigh. But again came that clear-spoken little voice, "Nonsense, Franz."

I never did hear a child of her age speak so well as Miss Bess. It's pretty to hear broken talking in a child sometimes, lisping, and some of the funny turns they'll give their words; but it's even prettier to hear clear complete talk like hers in a young child.

Then came a gentle, pitiful little voice.

"It isn't nonsense, Queen, darling. It's *howid* for Franz, but it wasn't nonsense he was going to say. I know what it was," and she gave the boy's hand a little squeeze.

" It was only — if aunty *was* my mamma, Bess, but you know she isn't. And *aunts* aren't forced to be troubled about not their own children."

"Yes they are," the elder girl replied. " At least when they're instead of own mammas. And then, you know, Franz, it's not only you, it's Lally too, and — "

That was all I heard. I couldn't pretend to be obliged to walk slowly just behind them, for in reality I was rather in a hurry, so I hastened past; but just as I did so, their little dog, who was with them, looked up at me with a friendly half-bark, half-growl. That made the children smile at me too, and for the life of me, even if 'twas not good manners, I couldn't help smiling in return.

" Hasn't . her a nice face ? " I heard the second little young lady say, and it sent me home with quite a warm feeling in my heart.

It was about a week after that, when one evening as we were sitting together — father, mother, and I — and father was just saying there'd be daylight enough to need no candles that night — we heard the click of the little garden gate, and a voice at the door that mother knew in a moment was Widow Nutfold's.

"Good-evening to you, Mrs. Heatherdale," she said, " and many excuses for disturbing of you so late, but

"Hasn't her a nice face?"—p. 12.

I'm that put about. Is your Martha at home? — thank goodness, my dear," as I come forward out of the dusk to speak to her. " It's more you nor your good mother I've come after; you'll be thinking I'm joking when you hear what it is. Can you slip on your bonnet and come off with me now this very minute to help with my little ladies? Would you believe it — that their good-for-nothing girl is off — gone — packed up this very evening — and left me with 'em all on my hands, and Miss Baby beginning with a cold on her chest, and Master Francis all but crying with the rheumatics in his poor leg. And even the page-boy, as was here at first, was took back to London last week."

The good woman held up her hands in despair, and then by degrees we got the whole story — how the nurse had not been meaning to stay longer than suited her own convenience, but had concealed this from her lady; and having heard by a letter that afternoon of another situation which she could have if she went at once, off she had gone, in spite of all poor Widow Nutfold could say or do.

" She took a dislike to me seein' as I tried to look after her a bit and to stop her nasty cross ways, and she told me that impertinent, as I wanted to be nurse, I might be it now. She has a week or two's money owing her, but she was that scornful she said she'd let it go; she had been a great silly for taking the place."

"But she might be had up and made to give back some of her wages," said father.

"Sir Hulbert and my lady are not that sort, and she knows it," said Mrs. Nutfold. "The wages was pretty fair — it was the dulness of the life down in Cornwall the girl objected to most, I fancy."

"Cornwall," repeated mother. "There now, Martha, if that isn't furrin parts, I don't know what is."

But I hadn't time to say any more. I hurried on my shawl and bonnet, and rolled up an apron or two, and slipped a cap into a bandbox, and there I was.

"Good-night, mother," I said. "I'll look round in the morning — and I don't suppose I'll be wanted to stay more than a day or two. My lady's sure to find some one at once, being in London too."

"I should think so," said old Sarah, but there was something in her tone I did not quite understand.

CHAPTER II.

WE hurried across the common — it was still day-light, though the sun had set some little time. The red and gold were still lingering in the sky and casting a beautiful glow on the heather and the gorse bushes. For Brayling Common is not like what the word makes most people think of — there's no grass at all — it's all heather and gorse, and here and there clumps of brambles, and low down on the sandy soil all sorts of hardy, running, clinging little plants that ask for nothing but sunshine and air. For of moisture there's but scanty supply; it no sooner rains than it dries up again. But oh it is beautiful — the colours of it I've never seen equalled — not even in Italy or Switzerland, where I went with my first ladies, as I said before. The heather seems to change its shade a dozen times a day, as well as with every season — according as the sky is cloudy or bright, or the sun overhead or on his way up or down. I cannot say it the right way, but I know that many far cleverer than me would feel the same; you may travel far before you'd see a sweeter piece of nature than our common, with its wonderful changefulness and yet always beautiful.

There's little footpaths in all directions, as well as a few wider tracks. It takes strangers some time to learn their way, I can tell you. The footpaths are seldom wide enough for two, so it's a queer sort of backwards and forwards talking one has to be content with. And we walked too fast to have breath for much, only Widow Nutfold would now and then throw back to me, so to say, some odds and ends of explaining about the children that she thought I'd best know.

"They're dear young ladies," she said, "though Miss Elisabeth is a bit masterful and Miss Baby — Augusta's her proper name — a bit spoilt. Take them all together, I think Miss Lally's my favourite, or would be if she was a little happier, poor child! I can't stand whiney children."

I smiled to myself — I knew that the good woman's experience of children was not great — she had married late and never had one of her own. It was real goodness that made her take such an interest in the little Penroses.

"Poor child," I said, "perhaps the cross nurse has made her so," at which Sarah gave a sort of grunt. "What is her real name — the middle young lady's, I mean?"

"Oh, bless you, I couldn't take upon me to say it — it's too outlandish. Miss Lally we call her —"

and I could hear that Mrs. Nutfold's breath was getting short — she was stout in her later years — and that she was a little cross. "You must ask for yourself, Martha."

So I said no more, though I had wanted to hear about the boy, who had spoken of their mother as his aunty, and how he had come to be so delicate and lame. And in a few moments more we found ourselves at the door of Clover Cottage; that was Mrs. Nutfold's house, though "Bramble Cottage" would have suited it better, standing where it did.

She took the key out of her pocket.

"I locked them in," she said, nodding her head, "though they didn't know it."

"Gracious," says I, "you don't mean as the children are all alone?"

"To be sure — who'd be with them? I wasn't going to make a chatter all over the place about that impident woman a-goin' off. And Bella, my girl, goes home at five. 'Twas after she left thére was all the upset."

I felt rather startled at hearing this. Suppose they had set themselves on fire! But old Sarah seemed quite easy in her mind, as she opened 'the door and went in, me following.

'Twas a nice roomy cottage, and so clean. Besides the large kitchen at one side, with a good back-kitchen behind it, and a tidy bedroom for Mrs. Nutfold, there was a fair-sized parlour, with casement windows and deep window-seats — all old-fashioned, but roomy and airy. And upstairs two nice bed-rooms and a small one. I knew it well, having been there off and on to help Mrs. Nutfold with her lodgers at the busy season before I went away to a regular place. So I was a little surprised when she turned to the kitchen, instead of opening the parlour door. And at first, what with coming out of the half-light and the red glow still in my eyes, and what with that there Fusser setting upon me with such a barking and jumping — all meant for a wel-come, I soon found — as never was, I scarce could see or hear. But I soon got myself together again.

"Down Fusser, naughty Fuss," said the children, and, "he won't bite, it's only meant for 'How do you do?'" said the eldest girl. And then she turned to me as pretty as might be. "Is this Martha?" says she, holding out her little hand. "I *am* pleased to see you. It's very good of you, and oh, Mrs. Nut-fold, I'm so glad you've come back. Baby is getting so sleepy."

Poor little soul — so she was. They had set her up on Sarah's old rocking-chair near the fire as well as they could, to keep her warm because of her cold, and it was a chilly evening rather. But it was past her bed-time, and she was fractious with all the upset. I just was stooping down to look at her when she gave a little cry and held out her arms to me. "Baby so tired," she said, "want to go to bed."

"And so you shall, my love," I said. "I'll have off my bonnet in a moment, and then Martha will put Miss Baby to bed all nice and snug."

"Marfa," said a little voice beside me. It was the middle young lady. "I like that name, don't you, Francie?"

That was the boy — they were all there, poor dears. Old Sarah had thought they'd be cosier in the kitchen while she was out. I smiled back at Miss Lally, as they called her. She was standing by Master Francis; both looking up at me, with a kind of mixture of hope and fear, a sort of asking, "Will she be good to us?" in their faces, which touched me very much. Master Francis was not a pretty child like the others. He was pale and thin, and his eyes looked too dark for his face. He was small too, no taller than Miss Bess, and with none of her upright hearty look. But when he smiled his expression was very sweet. He smiled now, with a sort of relief and pleasure, and I saw that he gave a little squeeze to Miss Lally's hand, which he was holding.

"Yes," he said, "it's a nice name. The other nurse was called 'Sharp;' it suited her too," with a twinkle in his eyes I was pleased to see. "Lally can't say her 'th's' properly," he went on, as if he was excusing her a little, "nor her 'r's' sometimes, though Bess and I are trying to teach her."

"It's so babyish at *her* age, nearly six, not to speak

properly," said Miss Bess, with her little toss of the head, at which Miss Lally's face puckered up, and the corners of her mouth went down, and I saw what Sarah Nutfold meant by saying she was rather a "whiney" child. I didn't give her time for more just then. I had got Miss Baby up in my arms, where she was leaning her sleepy head on my shoulder in her pretty baby way. I felt quite in my right place again.

"Come along, Miss Lally, dear," I said. "It must be your bed-time too, and if you'll come upstairs with Miss Baby and me, you'll be able to show me all the things — the baths, and the sponges, and everything — won't that be nice?"

She brightened up in a moment — dear child, it's always been like that with her. Give her a hint of anything she could do for others, and she'd forget her own troubles — fancy or real ones — that minute.

"The hot water's all ready," said Mrs. Nutfold. "I kep' the fire up, so as you shouldn't have no trouble I could help, Martha, my dear."

And then the three of us went upstairs to the big room at the back, where I was to sleep with Miss Baby in her cot, and which we called the night nursery. Miss Lally was as bright as a child could be, and that handy and helpful. But more than once I heard a sigh come from the very depths of her little heart, it seemed.

"Sharp never lettened me help wif Baby going to bed, this nice way," she said, and sighed again.

"Never mind about Sharp, my dear," I said. "She had her ways, and Martha has hers. What are you sighing about?"

"I'm so fwightened her'll come back and you go, Marfa," she said, nestling up to me. Baby was safe in bed by now, prayers said and all. "And—I'm sleepy, but I don't like going to bed till Queen comes."

"Who may she be, my dear?" I asked, and then I remembered their talking that day in the street. "Oh, it's Miss Bess, you mean."

"Yes—it's in the English history," said the child, making a great effort over the "r." "There was a queen they called 'Good Queen Bess,' so I made that my name for Bess. But mamma laughed one day and said that queen wasn't 'good.' I was so sorry. So I just call Bess 'Queen' for short. And I say 'good' to myself, for my Bess *is* good; only I wish she wouldn't be vexed when I don't speak words right," and again the little creature sighed as if all the burdens of this weary world were on her shoulders.

"It's that Miss Bess wants you to speak as cleverly as she does, I suppose. It'll come in time, no fear. When I was a little girl I couldn't say the letter 'l,' try as I might. I used to leave it out altogether —I remember one day telling mother I had seen such a sweet 'ittie 'amb'—I meant 'little lamb.'"

"Oh, how funny," said Miss Lally laughing. She

was always ready to laugh. "It's a good thing I can say 'l's,' isn't it? My name wouldn't be — nothing — would it? — without the 'l's.'"

"But it's only a short, isn't it, Missy?" I said.

"Yes, my *weal* name is 'Lalage.' Do you fink it's a pretty name?" she said. She was getting sleepy, and it was too much trouble to worry about her speaking.

"Yes, indeed, I think it's a sweet name. So soft and gentle like," I said, which pleased her, I could see.

"Papa says so too — but mamma doesn't like it so much. It was Francie's mamma's name, but she's dead. And poor Francie's papa's dead too. He was papa's brother," said Miss Lally, in her old-fashioned way. There was a funny mixture of old-fashioned-ness and simple, almost baby ways about all those children. I've never known any quite like them. No doubt it came in part from their being brought up so much by themselves, and having no other companions than each other. But from the first I always felt they were dear children, and more than common interesting.

A few days passed — very quiet and peaceful, and yet full of life too they seemed to me. I felt more like myself again, as folks say, than since my great trouble. It *was* sweet to have real little ones to see to again — if Miss Baby had only known it, that first evening's bathing her and tucking her up in bed brought tears of pleasure to my eyes.

"Come now," I said to myself, "this'll never do. You mustn't let yourself go for to get so fond of these young ladies and gentlemen that you're only with for a day or two at most," but I knew all the same I couldn't help it, and I settled in my own mind that as soon as I could I would look out for a place again. I wasn't afraid of what some would count a hardish place — indeed, I rather liked it. I've always been that fond of children that whatever I have to do for them comes right — what does try my temper is to see things half done, or left undone by silly upsetting girls who haven't a grain of the real nurse's spirit in them.

My lady wrote at once on hearing from Mrs. Nutfold. She was very angry indeed about Sharp's behaviour, and at first was by way of coming down immediately to see to things. But by the next day, when she had got a second letter saying how old Sarah had fetched me, and that I was willing to stay for the time, she wrote again, putting off for a few days, and glad to do so, seeing how cleverly her good Mrs. Nutfold had managed. That was how she put it — my lady always had a gracious way with her, I will say — and I was to be thanked for my obligingness; she was sure her little dears would be happy with any one so well thought of by the dame. They were very busy indeed just then, she and Sir Hulbert, she said, and very gay. But when I came to know her better I did her justice, and saw she was not the butterfly I was inclined to think her. She was just frantic to get her husband forward, so to speak, and far more ambitious for him than caring about anything for herself. He had had a trying and disappointing life of it in some ways, had Sir Hulbert, and it had not soured him. He was a right-down high-minded gentleman, though not so clever as my lady, perhaps. And she adored him. They adored each other — seldom have I heard of a happier couple: only on one point was there ever disunion between them, as I shall explain, all in good time.

A week therefore — fully a week — had gone by before my little ladies' mother came to see them. And when she did come it was at short notice enough — a letter by the post — and Mayne, the postman, never passed our way much before ten in the morning. So the dame told as how she'd be down by the first train, and get to Clover Cottage by eleven, or soon after. We were just setting off on our morning walk when Sarah came calling after us to tell. She was for us not going, and stopping in till her ladyship arrived; but when I put it to her that the children would get so excited, hanging about and nothing to do, she gave in.

"I'll bring them back before eleven," I said. "They'll be looking fresh and rosy, and with us out of the way you and the girl can get the rooms all tidied up as you'd like for my lady to find them."

And Sarah allowed it was a good thought.

" You've a head on your shoulders, my girl," was how she put it.

So off we set — our usual way, over the common to the fir-woods. There's many a pretty walk about Brayling, and a great variety; but none took the young ladies' and Master Francie's fancy like the fir-woods. They had never seen anything of the kind before, their home being by the seashore was maybe the reason — or one reason. For I feel much the same myself about loving fir-woods, though, so to say, I was born and bred among them. There's a charm one can't quite explain about them — the sameness and the stillness and the great tops so high up, and yet the bareness and openness down below, though always in the shade. And the scent, and the feel of the crisp crunching soil one treads on, soil made of the millions of the fir-needles, with here and there the cones as they have fallen.

" It's like fairy stories," Miss Lally used to say, with her funny little sigh.

But we couldn't linger long in the woods that morning, though a beautiful morning it was. Miss Bess and Miss Baby were in the greatest delight about " mamma " coming, and always asking me if I didn't think it must be eleven o'clock. Miss Lally was pleased too, in her quiet way, only I noticed that she was a good deal taken up with Master Francie, who seemed to have something on his mind, and at last they both called to Miss Bess, and said something to her which I didn't hear, evidently asking her opinion.

"Nonsense," said Miss Bess, in her quick decided way; "I have no patience with you being so silly. As if mamma would be so unjust."

"But," said Master Francis hesitatingly, "you know, Bess — sometimes — "

"Yes," put in Miss Lally, "she might think it had been partly Francie's fault."

"Nonsense," said Miss Bess again; "mamma knows well enough that Sharp was horrid. I am sure Francie has been as good as good for ever so long, and old Mrs. Nutfold will tell mamma so, even if possibly she did not understand."

Their faces grew a little lighter after this, and by the time we had got home and I had tidied them all up, I really felt that my lady would be difficult to please if she didn't think all four looking as bright and well as she could wish.

I kept myself out of the way when I heard the carriage driving up, though the children would have dragged me forward. But I was a complete stranger to Lady Penrose, and things having happened as they had, I felt that she might like to be alone with the children, at first, and that no doubt Sarah Nutfold would be eager to have a talk with her. I sat down to my sewing quietly — there was plenty of mending on hand, Sharp's service having been but eye-service in every way — and I won't deny but that my heart was a little heavy thinking how soon, how very soon, most likely, I should have to leave these children, whom already, in these few days, I had grown to love so dearly.

I was not left very long to my meditations, however; before an hour had passed there came a clear voice up the old staircase, " Martha, Martha, come quick, mamma wants you," and hastening out I met Miss Bess at the door. She turned and ran down again, I following her more slowly.

How well I remember the group I saw as I opened the parlour door! It was like a picture. Lady Penrose herself was more than pretty — beautiful, I have heard her called, and I think it was no exaggeration. She was sitting in the dame's old-fashioned armchair, in the window of the little room; the bright summer sunshine streaming in behind her and lighting up her fair hair — hair for all the world like Miss Lally's, though perhaps a thought darker. Miss Baby was on her knee and Miss Bess on a stool at her feet, holding one of her hands. Miss Lally and Master Francie were a little bit apart, close together as usual.

" Come in," said my lady. " Come in, Martha," as I hesitated a little in the doorway. "I am very pleased to see you and to thank you for all your kindness to these little people."

She half rose from her chair as I drew near, and shook hands with me in the pretty gracious way she had.

"I am sure it has been a pleasure to me, my lady," I said. "I've been used to children for so long that I was feeling quite lost at home doing nothing."

"And you are very fond of children, truly fond of them," my lady went on, glancing up at me with a quick observant look, that somehow reminded me of Miss Bess; "so at least Mrs. Nutfold tells me, and I think I should have known it for myself even if she had not said so. I have to go back to town this afternoon — supposing you all run out into the garden for a few minutes, children; I want to talk to Martha a little, and it will soon be your dinner time."

She got up as she spoke, putting Miss Baby down gently; the child began grumbling a little — but, "No, no, Baby, you must do as I tell you," checked her in a moment.

"Take her out with you, Bess," she added. I could see that my lady was not one to be trifled with.

When they had all left the room she turned to me again. "Sit down, Martha, for a minute or two. One can always talk so much more comfortably sitting," she said pleasantly. "And I have no doubt the children have given you plenty of exercise lately, though you don't look delicate," she added, with again the little look of inquiry.

"Thank you, my lady; no, I am not delicate; as a rule I am strong and well, though this last year has brought me troubles and upsets, and I haven't felt quite myself."

"Naturally," she said. "Mrs. Nutfold has told me about you. I was talking to her just now when I first arrived." Truly my lady was not one to let the grass grow under the feet. "She says you will be looking for a situation again before long. Is there any chance of your being able to take one at once, that is to say if mine seems likely to suit you."

She spoke so quick and it was so unexpected that I felt for a moment half stupid and dazed-like.

"Are you sure, my lady, that I should suit you?" I managed to say at last. "I have only been in one place in my life, and you might want more experience."

"You were with Mrs. Wyngate, in ——shire, I believe? I know her sister and can easily hear any particulars I want, but I feel sure you would suit me."

She went on to give me a good many particulars, all in the same clear decided way. "The Wyngates are very rich," she said, as she ended. "You must have seen a great deal of luxury there. Now we are not rich — not at all rich — though we have a large country place that has belonged to the family for many hundreds of years; but we are obliged to live plainly and the place is rather lonely. I don't want you to decide all at once. Think it all over, and consult your parents, and let me have your answer when I come down again."

"That will be the difficulty," I replied; "my

parents wanted me to stay on some time with them. There is nothing about the work or the wages I should object to, and though Mrs. Wyngate was very kind, I have never cared for much luxury in the nursery — indeed, I should have liked plainer ways; and I love the country, and as for the young ladies and gentleman, my lady, if it isn't taking a liberty to say so, I love them dearly already. But it is father and mother — "

" Well, well," said my lady, " we must see. The children are very happy with you, and I hope it may be arranged, but of course you must consult your parents."

She went back to London that same afternoon, and that very evening, when they were all in bed, I slipped on my bonnet and ran home to talk it over with father and mother.

CHAPTER III.

THERE were fors and againsts, as there are with most things in this world. Father was sorry for me to leave so soon and go so far, and he scarce thought the wages what I might now look for. Mother felt with him about the parting, but mother was a far-seeing woman. She thought the change would be the best thing for me after my trouble, and she thought a deal of my being with real gentry. Not but that Mrs. Wyngate's family was all one could think highly of, but Mr. Wyngate's great fortune had been made in trade, and there was a little more talk and thought of riches and display among them than quite suited mother's ideas, and she had some-times feared it spoiling me.

"The wages I wouldn't put first," she said. "A good home and simple ways among real gentlefolk — that's what I'd choose for thee, my girl. And the children are good children and not silly spoilt things, and straightforward and well-bred, I take it?"

"All that and more," I answered. "If anything, they've been a bit too strict brought up, I'd say. If I go to them I shall try to make Miss Lally brighten up — not that she's a dull child, but she has the look of taking things to heart more than one likes to see at her age. And poor Master Francis — I'm sure he'd be none the worse of a little petting — so delicate as he is and his lameness."

" You'll find your work to do, if you go — no fear," said mother. " Maybe it's a call."

I got to think so myself — and when my lady wrote that all she heard from Mrs. Wyngate was most satisfactory, I made up my mind to accept her offer, and told her so when she came down again for a few hours the end of the week.

We stayed but a fortnight longer at Brayling — and a busy fortnight it was. I had my own things to see to a little, and would fain have finished the set of shirts I had begun for father. The days seemed to fly. I scarce could believe it was not a dream when I found myself with all the family in a second-class railway carriage, starting from Paddington on our long journey.

It was a long journey, especially as, to save expense, we had come up from Brayling that same morning. We were not to reach the little town where we left the railway till nearly midnight, to sleep there, I was glad for the poor children's sake to hear, and start again the next morning on a nineteen miles' journey by coach.

" And then," said Miss Lally, with one of her deep sighs, " we shall be at home."

I thought there was some content in her sigh this time.

"Shall you be glad, dearie, to be at home again?" I said.

"I fink so," she answered. "And oh, I am glad you've comed wif us, 'stead of Sharp. And Francie's almost more gladder still, aren't you, dear old Francie?"

"I should just think I was," said the boy.

"Sharp,"— and the little girl lowered her voice and glanced around; we were, so to speak, alone at one end of the carriage,— Miss Lally, her cousin and I, for Miss Baby was already asleep in my arms and Miss Bess talking, like a grown-up young lady, at the other end, with her papa and mamma — "Sharp," said Miss Lally, "really *hated* poor Francie, because she thought he told mamma about her tempers. And she made mamma think he was naughty when he wasn't. Francie and I were frightened when Sharp went away that mamma would think it was his fault. But she didn't. Queen spoke to her, and Mrs. Dame" (that was her name for old Sarah) "did too. And you didn't get scolded, did you, Francie?"

"No," said Master Francie quietly, "I didn't."

He looked as if he were going to say more, but just then Miss Bess, who had had enough for the time, of being grown up — and indeed she was but a complete child at heart — got up from her seat and came to our end of the carriage. Sir Hulbert was reading his newspaper, and my lady was making notes in a little memorandum book.

"What are you talking about?" said the eldest little sister, sitting down beside me. "You all look very comfortable, Baby especially."

"We are talking about Sharp going away," replied Miss Lally, "and Francie thinking he'd be scolded for it."

"Oh! do leave off about that and talk of something nicer. Franz is really silly. If you'd only speak right out to mamma," she went on, "things would be ever so much better."

The boy shook his head rather sadly.

"Now you know," said Miss Bess, "they would be. Mamma is never unjust."

She was speaking in her clear decided way, and feeling a little afraid lest their voices should reach to the other end — I wouldn't have liked my lady to think I encouraged the children in talking her over — I tried to change the conversation.

"Won't you tell me a little about your home?" I said. "You know it'll all be quite new to me; I've only seen the sea once or twice in my life, and never lived by it."

"Treluan isn't quite close to the sea," said Master Francis, evidently taking up my feeling. "We can see it from some of the top rooms, and from one end of the west terrace at high tides, and we can hear it too when it's stormy. But it's really two miles to the coast."

" There are such dear little bays, lots of them," said Miss Bess. " We can play Robinson Crusoe and smugglers and all sorts of things, for the bays are quite separated from each other by the rocks."

" There's caves in some," said Miss Lally, " rather f'ightening caves, they're so dark ; " but her eyes sparkled as if she were quite able to enjoy some adventures.

" We shall be at no loss for nice walks, I see ; but how do you amuse yourselves on wet days ? "

" Oh ! we've always plenty to do," said Miss Bess. " Miss Kirstin comes from the Vicarage every morning for our lessons, and twice a week papa teaches Franz and me Latin in the afternoon, and the house is very big, you know. When we can't go out, we may race about in the attics over the nurseries. There's a stair goes up to the tower, just by the nursery door, and you pass the attics on the way. They're called the tower attics, because there are lots more over the other end of the house. Francie's room is in the tower."

It was easy to see by this talk that Treluan was a large and important place.

" I suppose the house is very, very old ? " I said.

" Oh yes ! thousands — I mean hundreds — of years old. Centuries mean hundreds, don't they, Franz ? " said she, turning to her cousin.

"Yes, dear," he answered gently, though I could see he was inclined to smile a little. "If you know English history," he went on to me, "I could tell you exactly how old Treluan is. The first bit of it was built in the reign of King Henry the Third, though it's been changed ever so often since then. About a hundred years ago the Penroses were very rich, very rich indeed. But when one of them died — our great, great grand-uncle, I think it was — and his nephew took possession, it was found the old man had sold a lot of the land secretly — it wasn't to be told till his death — and no one has ever been able to find out what he did with the money. It was the best of the land too."

"And they were so surprised," said Miss Bess, "for he'd been a very saving old man, and they thought there'd be lots of money over, anyway. Wasn't it too bad of him — horrid old thing?"

"Queen," said Miss Lally gravely. "You know we fixed never to call him that, 'cos he's dead. He was a — oh, what's that word? — something like those things in the hall at home — helmet — was it that? No — do tell me, Queen."

"You're muddling it up with crusaders, you silly little thing," said Miss Bess. "How could he have been a crusader only a hundred years ago?"

"No, no, it isn't that — I said it was *like* it," said Miss Lally, ready to cry. "What's the other word for helmet?"

"I know," said Master Francis, "*vizor* — and — "

"Yes, yes — and the old man was a *miser*, that's it," said the child. "Papa said so, and he said it's like a' illness, once people get it they can't leave off."

Miss Bess and Master Francis could not help laughing at the funny way the child said it, nor could I myself, for that matter. And then they went on to tell me more of the strange old story — how their great grandfather and their grandfather after him had always gone on hoping the missing money would sooner or later turn up, though it never did, till — putting what the children told me together with my lady's own words — it became clear that poor Sir Hulbert had come into a sadly impoverished state of things.

"Perhaps the late baronet and his father were not of the 'saving' sort," I said to myself, and from what I came to hear afterwards, I fancy I was about right.

After a while my lady came to our end of the carriage. She was afraid, she said, I'd find Miss Baby too heavy — wouldn't I lay her comfortably on the seat, there was plenty of room? — my lady was always thoughtful for others — and then when we had got the child settled, she sat down and joined in our talk a little.

"We've been telling Martha about Treluan and about the old uncle that did something with the money," said Miss Bess.

My lady did not seem to mind.

"It is a queer story, isn't it?" she said. "Worse than queer, indeed—" and she sighed. "Though even with it, things would not be as they are, if other people had not added their part to them."

She glanced round in a half impatient way, and somehow her glance fell on Master Francis, and I almost started as I caught sight of the expression that had come over her face — it was a look of real dislike.

"Sit up, Francis — do, for goodness' sake," she said sharply; "you make yourself into a regular humpback."

The boy's pale, almost sallow face reddened all over. He had been listening with interest to the talking, and taking his part in it. Now he straightened himself nervously, murmuring something that sounded like, "I beg your pardon, Aunt Helen," and sat gazing out of the window beside him as if lost in his own thoughts. I busied myself with pulling the rugs better over Miss Baby, so that my lady should not see my face just then. But I think she felt sorry for her sharp tone, for when she spoke again it was even more pleasantly than usual.

"Have you told nurse other things about Treluan, children?" she said. "It is really a dear old place," she went on to me; "it might be made *quite* delightful if Sir Hulbert could spend a little more upon it. I had set my heart on new furnishing your room this year, Bess darling, but I'm afraid it will have to wait."

" Never mind, dear," said Miss Bess comfortingly, in her old-fashioned way, " there's no hurry. If I could have fresh covers to the chairs, the furniture itself — I mean the *wood* part — is quite good."

"I did get some nice chintz in London," said her mamma; "there was some selling off rather cheap. But it's the getting things made — everything down with us is so difficult and expensive," and my lady sighed. Her mind seemed full of the one idea, and I began to think she should try to take a cheerier view of things.

" If you'll excuse me mentioning it," I said, "I have had some experience in the cutting out of chair-covers and such things. It would be a great pleasure to me to help to make the young ladies' rooms nice."

" That would be very nice indeed," said my lady; " I really should like to do what we can to brighten up the old house. I expect it will look very gloomy to you, nurse, till you get used to it. I do want Bess's room to look better. Of course Lally is in the nursery still, and won't need a room of her own for a long time yet."

Miss Lally was sitting beside me, and as her mamma spoke, I heard a very tiny little sigh.

" Never mind, Miss Lally dear," I whispered. " We'll brighten up the nurseries too, nicely."

These little scraps of talk come back to my mind now, when I think of that first journey down to Treluan so many years ago. I put them down such as they are, as they may help better than words of my own to give an idea of the dear children and all about them, as they then were.

We reached Treluan the afternoon of the next day. It was a dull day unfortunately, though the very middle of summer—rainy and gray. Of course every one knows that there's much weather of that kind in the west country, but no doubt it added to the impression of gloom with which the first sight of the old house struck me, I must confess. Gloom, perhaps, is hardly the word to use; it was more a feeling of desertedness, almost of decayed grandeur, quite unlike anything I had ever seen before. For in my former place everything had been bright and new, fresh and perfect of its kind. Afterwards, when I came to see into things better, I found there was no neglect or mismanagement; everything that *could* be done was done by Sir Hulbert outside, and my lady in her own department — uphill and trying work though it must often have been for them.

But that first evening, when I looked round the great lofty hall into which my lady had led the way, dusky and dim already with the rain pattering against the high arched windows and a chilly feeling in the air, the half dozen servants or so, who had come out

to meet us — evidently the whole establishment —
standing round, I must own that in spite of the
children's eager excitement and delight at finding
themselves at home again, my heart went down. I
did feel so very far away from home and father and
mother, and everything I had ever known. The first
thing to cheer me was when the old housekeeper —
cook-housekeeper she really was — Mrs. Brent, came
forward after speaking to my lady, and shook me
kindly by the hand.

"Welcome to Treluan, Nurse Heatherdale," she
said. And here I should explain that as there was
already a Martha in the house, my lady had expressed
her wish that I should be called "nurse," or "Heatherdale," from which came my name of "Heather,"
that I have always been called by. "Welcome to
Treluan, and don't go for to think that it's always as
dull as you see it just now, as like as not to-morrow
will be bright and sunny."

She was a homely-looking body with a very kind
face, not Cornish bred I found afterwards, though she
had lived there many years. Something about her
made me think of mother, and I felt the tears rise to
my eyes, though no one saw.

"Shall I show nurse the way upstairs, my lady?"
she said. For Mrs. Brent was like her looks, simple
and friendly like. She had never known Treluan in
its grand days of course, though she had known it
when things were a good deal easier than at present;

and that evening, when the children were asleep, she came up to sit with me a bit, and, though with perfect respect to her master and mistress and no love of gossip in her talk (for of that she was quite free), she explained to me a few things which already had puzzled me a little. No praise was too high for Sir Hulbert with her, and my lady was a really good, high-minded woman. "But she takes her troubles too heavy," said Mrs. Brent; "she's like to break her heart at having no son of her own, and that and other things make her not show her best self to poor little Master Francis, though, considering he's been here since he was four, 'tis a wonder he doesn't seem to her like a child of her own. And Sir Hulbert feels it; it's a real grief to him, for he loved Master Francis's father dearly through all the troubles he caused them, and anyway 'tis not fair to visit the father's sin on the innocent child."

Then she told me how Master Francis's father had made things worse by his extravagance, half-breaking his young wife's heart and leaving debts behind him, when he was killed by an accident; and that Sir Hulbert, for the honour of the family, had taken these debts upon himself.

"His wife was a pretty young creature, half a foreigner. Sir Hulbert had her brought here with the boy, and here she died, not long before Miss Lalage was born, and so, failing a son, Master Francis is the heir, and a sweet, good young gentleman he is, though nothing as to looks. 'Tis a pity he's so shy and timid in his way; it gives my lady the idea he's not straightforward, though that I'm very sure he is, and most affectionate at heart, though he hasn't the knack of showing it."

"Except to Miss Lally, I should say," I put in; "how those two do cling together, to be sure."

"He loves them all dearly, my lady too, though he's frightened of her. Miss Lally's the one he's most at home with, because she's so little, and none of Miss Bess's masterful ways about her. Poor dear Miss Lally, many's the trouble she's got into for Master Francis's sake."

All this was very interesting to me, and helped to clear my mind in some ways from the first, which was, I take it, a good thing. Mrs. Brent said little about Sharp, but I could see she had not approved of her; and she was so kind as to add some words about myself, and feeling sure I would make the children happy, especially the two whom it was easy to see were her own favourites, Miss Lally and her cousin. This made me feel the more earnest to do my very best in every way for the young creatures under my care.

CHAPTER IV.

WRITING down that talk with good Mrs. Brent
made me put aside the account of our arrival at
Treluan, clearly though I remember it. Even to
this day I never go up the great staircase — of
course it is not often that I pass that way — without
recalling the feelings with which I stepped up it for
the first time — Mrs. Brent in front, carrying a small
hand-lamp, the passages being so dark, though it was
still early in the evening; the children running on
before me, except Miss Baby, who was rather sleepy
and very cross, poor dear, so that half-way up I had
to lift her in my arms. All up the dark wainscoted
walls, dead and gone Penroses looked down upon us,
in every sort of ancient costume. They used to give
me a half eerie feeling till I got to know them better
and to take a certain pride in them, feeling myself,
as I came to do, almost like one of the family, though
in a humble way.

At the top of the great staircase we passed along
the gallery, which runs right across one side of the
hall below; then through a door on the right and
down a long passage ending in a small landing, from

which a back staircase ran down again to the ground
floor. The nurseries in those days were the two
large rooms beyond, now turned into a billiard-room,
my present lady thinking them scarcely warm enough
for the winter. It is handy too to have the billiard-
room near the tower, where the smoking-room now
is, and the spare rooms for gentlemen visitors. A
door close beside the nurseries opened on to the tower
stair; some little way up this stair another door leads
into the two or three big attics over the nurseries,
which the children used as playrooms in the wet
weather. Master Francis's room was the lowest door
on the tower staircase, half-way as it were, as to level,
between the nurseries and the attics. The ground-
floor rooms of the tower were entered from below, as
the separate staircase only began from the nursery
floor. All these particulars, of course, I learnt by
degrees, having but a very general idea of things
that first night; but plans of houses and buildings
have always had an interest for me, and as a girl I
think I had a quick eye for sizes and proportions. I
do remember the first time I saw the ground-floor
room of the tower, under Master Francis's, so to say,
wondering to myself how it came to be so low in the
ceiling, seeing that the floor of his room was several
feet higher than that of the nurseries. No doubt
others would have been struck by this also, had the
lowest room in the tower been one in regular use,
but as long as any one could remember it had only

been a sort of lumber-room. It was only by accident that I went into it one day, months after I had come to Treluan.

The nurseries were nice airy rooms; the school-room was underneath the day nursery, down on the ground floor; and Miss Bess's room was off the little landing I spoke of before you came to the nursery passage. But all seemed dim and dusky in the half light, that first evening. It was long before the days of gas, of course, except in towns, though that, I am told, is now thought nothing of compared to this new electric light, which Sir Bevil is thinking of estab-lishing here, to be made on the premises in some wonderful way. And even lamps at that time were very different from what they are now, when every time my lady goes up to town she brings back some beautiful new invention for turning night into day.

I was glad, I remember, June though it was, to see a bright fire in the nursery grate — Mrs. Brent was always thoughtful — and the tea laid out nice and tidy on the table. Miss Baby brightened up at sight of it, and the others gathered round to see what good things the housekeeper had provided for them by way of welcome home.

"I hope there's some clotted cream," said Miss Bess; "yes, that's right! Nurse has never seen it before, I'm sure. Fancy, Mrs. Brent, mamma says the silly people in London call it Devonshire cream, and I'm sure it's far more Cornish. And honey and some of your own little scones and saffron cakes, that is nice! Mayn't we have tea immediately?"

"I must wash my hands," said Master Francis, "they did get so black in the carriage."

"And mine too," said Miss Lally. "Oh, nurse, mayn't Francis wash his for once in the night nursery, to be quick?"

"Why didn't you both keep your gloves on, you dirty children?" said Miss Bess in her masterful way. "My hands are as clean as clean, and of course Francis mustn't begin muddling in the nursery. You'd never have asked Sharp that, Lally. It's just the sort of thing mamma doesn't like. I shall take my things off in my own room at once." And she marched to the door as she spoke, stopping for a moment on the way to say to me — "Heatherdale, you'll come into my room, won't you, as soon as ever you can, to talk about the new chair-covers?"

"I won't forget about them, Miss Bess," I said quietly; "but for a few days I am sure to be busy, unpacking and looking over the things that were left here."

The child said nothing more, but I saw by the lift of her head that she was not altogether pleased.

"Now Master Francis," I went on, "perhaps you had better run off to your own room to wash your hands. It's always best to keep to regular ways."

The boy obeyed at once. I had, to tell the truth, been on the point of letting him do as Miss Lally had wanted, but Miss Bess's speech had given me a hint, though I was not sorry for her not to have seen it. I should be showing Master Francis no true kindness to begin by any look of spoiling him, and I saw by a little smile on Mrs. Brent's face that she thought me wise, even though it was not till later in the evening that I had the long talk with her that I have already mentioned.

Our tea was bright and cheery, Miss Baby's spirits returned, and she kept us all laughing by her funny little speeches. My lady came in when we had nearly finished, just to see how all the children were —perhaps too, for she was full of kind thoughtfulness, to make me feel myself more at home. She sat down in the chair by the fire, with a little sigh, and I was sorry to see the anxious, harassed look on her beautiful face.

"You all look very comfortable," she said; "please give me a cup of tea, nurse. I found such a lot of things to do immediately, that I've not had time to think of tea yet, and poor Sir Hulbert is off in the rain to see about some broken fences. Oh dear! what a contrary world it seems," she added half laughingly.

"How did the fences get broken, mamma?" said Miss Bess; "and why didn't Garth get them mended at once without waiting to tease papa the moment he got home?"

"Some cattle got wild and broke them, and if they

are not put right at once, more damage may be done. But all these repairs are expensive. It only happened two days ago; poor Garth was obliged to tell papa before doing it. Dear me," she said again, "it really does seem sometimes as if money would put everything in life right."

"Oh! my lady," I exclaimed hastily, and then I got red with shame at my forwardness and stopped short. I felt very sorry for her; the one thought seemed never out of her mind, and bid fair to poison her happy home. I felt too that it was scarcely the sort of talk for the children to hear, Miss Bess being already in some ways so old for her years, and the two others scarce as light-hearted as they should have been.

My lady smiled at me.

"Say on, Heatherdale; I'd like to hear what you think about it."

I felt my face getting still redder, but I had brought it on myself.

"It was only, my lady," I began, "that it seems to me that there are so many troubles worse than want of money. There's my last lady's sister, for instance, Mrs. Vernon, — everything in the world has she that money can give, but she's lost all her babies, one after the other, and she's just heart-broken. Then there's young Lady Mildred Parry, whose parents own the finest place near my home, and she's their only child; but she had a fall from her horse two years ago and her back is injured for life; she often drives past our cottage, lying all stretched-out-like, in a carriage made on purpose."

My lady was silent. Suddenly, to my surprise, Master Francis looked up quickly.

"I don't think I'd mind that so very much," he said, "not if my back didn't hurt badly. I think it would be better than walking with your leg always aching, and I dare say everybody loves that girl dreadfully."

He stopped as suddenly as he had begun, giving a quick frightened glance round, and growing not red but still paler than usual, as was his way.

"Poor little Francie," said Miss Lally, stretching her little hand out to him and looking half ready to cry.

"Don't be silly, Lally; if Francis's leg hurts him he has only to say so, and it will be attended to as it has always been. If everybody loves that young Lady Mildred, no doubt it is because she is sweet and loving *to* everybody."

Then she grew silent again and seemed to be thinking.

"You are right, nurse," she said. "I am very grateful when I see my dear children all well and happy."

"And *good*," added Miss Bess with her little toss of the head.

"Well, yes, of course," said her mother smiling.

It was seldom, if ever, Miss Bess was pulled up for anything she took it into her head to say, whether called for or not.

"But," my lady went on in a lower voice, turning to me, as if she hardly wished the children to hear, "want of money isn't my only, nor indeed my worst trouble. — I must go," and she got up as she spoke; "there are twenty things waiting for me to attend to downstairs. Good-night, children dear; I'll come up and peep at you in bed if I possibly can, but I'm not sure if I shall be able. If not, nurse must do instead of me for to-night," and she turned towards the door, moving in the quick graceful way she always did.

"Franz!" said Miss Bess reprovingly; the poor boy was already getting off his chair, but he was too late to open the door. I doubt if his aunt noticed his moving at all.

"You're always so slow and clumsy," said his eldest cousin. The words sounded unkind, but it was greatly that Miss Bess wanted him to please her mamma, for the child had an excellent heart.

There was plenty to do after that first evening for all of us. I got sleepy Miss Baby to bed as soon as might be. The poor dear, she *was* sleepy! I remember how, when she knelt down in her little white nightgown to say her prayers, she could only just get out, " T'ank God for b'inging us safe home ; " as she had evidently been taught to say after a journey.

"Baby thinks that's enough, when she's been ter-a-velling," explained Miss Lally.

Then I set to work to unpack, and it was quite surprising how handy the two elder girls — and not they only, but Master Francis too — were in helping me, and explaining where their things were kept and all the nursery ways. Then I had to be shown Miss Bess's room, and nearly offended her little ladyship by saying I hadn't time just then to settle about the new covers. For I was determined to give some attention to Master Francis also.

His room was very plain, not to say bare; not that I hold with pampering boys, but he being delicate, it did seem to me he might have had a couch or easy-chair to rest his poor leg. He was very eager to make the best of things, telling me I had no idea what a beautiful view there was from his windows, of which there were three.

"I love the tower," he said. "I wouldn't change my room here for any other in the house."

And I must say I thought it was very nice of him to put things in that way, considering too the sharp tone in which I had heard his aunt speak to him that very evening.

When I woke the next morning I found that Mrs. Brent's words had come true, for the sun was pouring in at the window, and when I drew up the blind and looked out I would scarce have known the place to be the same. The outlook was bare, to be sure, compared with the well-wooded country about my home; but the grounds just around the house were carefully kept, though in a plain way, no bedding-out plants or rare foreign shrubs, such as I had been used to see at Mr. Wyngate's country place. But all about Treluan there was the charm which no money will buy — the charm of age, very difficult to put into words, though I felt it strongly.

A little voice just then came across the room.

"Nurse, dear." It was Miss Lalage. "It's a very fine day, isn't it? I have been watching the sun getting up ever so long. When I first wokened, it was nearly quite dark."

I looked at the child. She was sitting up in her cot; her face looked tired, and her large gray eyes had dark lines beneath them, as if she had not slept well. Miss Baby was still slumbering away in happy content — she was a child to sleep, to be sure! A round of the clock was nothing for her.

"My dear Miss Lally," I said, "you have never been awake since dawn, surely. Is your head aching, or is something the matter?"

She gave a little sigh.

"No, fank you, it's nothing but finking, I mean th-inking. Oh! I wish I could speak quite right, Bess says it's so babyish."

"Thinking! and what have you been thinking about, dearie? You should have none but happy thoughts. Isn't it nice to be at home again? and this beautiful summer weather! We can go such nice walks. You've got to show me all the pretty places about."

"Yes," said Miss Lally. "I'd like that, but we'll be having lessons next week, — not all day long, we can go beautiful walks in the afternoons."

"Was it about lessons you were troubling your little head?"

"No," she said, though not very heartily. "I don't like them much, at least not those *very* high up sums — up you know to the *very* top of the slate — that won't never come right. But I wasn't finking of them; it was about poor mamma, having such teroubles. Francie and I do fink such a lot about it. Bess does too, but she's so clever, she's sure she'll do something when she's big to get a lot of money for papa and mamma. But I'm not clever, and Francie has got his sore leg; we can't fink of anything we could do, unless we could find some fairies; but Francie's sure there aren't any, and he's past ten, so he must know."

" You can do a great deal, dear Miss Lally," I said. "Don't get it into your head you can't. Rich or poor, there's nothing helps papas and mammas so much as their children being good, and loving, and obedient; and who knows but what Master Francis may be a very clever man some day, whether his poor leg gets better or not."

The little girl seemed pleased. It needed but a kind word or two to cheer her up at any time.

" Oh! I am so glad Sharp has gone away and you comed," she said.

She was rather silent while I was dressing her, but when she had had her bath, and I was putting on her shoes and stockings, she began again.

" Nurse," she asked, " do stockings cost a lot of money to buy?"

"Pretty well," I said. " At my home, mother always taught us to knit our own. I could show you a pair I knitted before I was much bigger than you."

How the child's face did light up!

" I've seen a little girl knitting who's not much bigger than me. Couldn't you show me how to make some stockings, and then mamma wouldn't have to buy so many?"

"Certainly I could; I have plenty of needles with me, and I dare say we could get some wool," I replied. " I'll tell you what, Miss Lally; you might knit some for Master Francis; that would be pleasing him as well as your mamma. There's a village not far off, I suppose — you can generally buy wool at a village shop."

" There's our village across the park, and there's two shops. I'll ask Bess; she'll know if we could get wool. Oh! nurse, how pleased I am; I wonder if we could go to-day. I've got some pennies and a shilling. I do like to have nice things to think of. I wish Francie would be quick, I do so want to tell him, or do you think I should keep it a surprise for him ?"

And she danced about in her eager delight, which at last woke Miss Baby, who opened her eyes and stared about her, with a sleepy smile of content on her plump rosy face. She was a picture of a child, and so easy minded. It is wonderful, to be sure, how children brought up like little birds in one nest yet differ from each other. I began to feel very satisfied that I should never regret having come to Treluan.

CHAPTER V.

BEFORE many days had passed I felt quite settled down. The weather was most lovely for some time just then, and this I think always helps to make one feel more at home in a strange place. That first day, and for two or three following, we could not go long walks, as I had really so much to see to indoors, Miss Bess had to make up her mind to wait as patiently as she could, till other things were attended to, for the doing up of her room, and, what I was more sorry for, poor Miss Lally had also to wait about beginning the knitting she had so set her heart on.

I think it was the fourth day after our arrival that I began at last to feel pretty clear. All the nursery drawers and cupboards tidied up and neatly arranged; the children's clothes looked over and planned about for the rest of the summer. My lady went over them with me, and I could see that it was a comfort to her to feel assured that I understood the need for economy, and prided myself, thanks to my good old mother, on neat patches and darns quite as much as on skill on making new things. My poor lady — it went to my heart to see how often she would have liked to get fresh and pretty frocks and hats for the young ladies, for she had good taste and great love of order. But after all there is often a good deal of pleasure in contriving and making the best of what one has.

"You must take nurse a good walk to-day, children," said my lady as she left the room. "I shall be busy with your papa, but you might get as far as the sea, I think, if you took old Jacob and the little cart for Baby if she gets tired, and for Francis if his leg hurts him. How has it been, by the bye, for the last day or two, Francis?"

Her tone was rather cold, but still I could see a little flush of pleasure come over the boy's face.

"Oh! much better, thank you, auntie," he said eagerly. "It's only just after the day in the railway that it seems to hurt more."

"Then try to be bright and cheerful," she said. "Remember you are not the only one in the world that has troubles to bear."

The boy didn't answer, but I could see his thin little face grow pale again, and I just wished that my lady had stopped at her first kindly inquiry. A deal of mischief is done, it seems to me, by people not knowing when it is best to stop.

Jacob, the donkey, was old and no mistake. Larkins's "Peter" was young compared to him, and the cart was nothing but a cart such as light luggage might be carried in. It had no seats, but we took a couple of footstools with us, which served the purpose, and many a pleasant ramble we had with the shabby little old cart and poor Jacob.

"Which way shall we go?" said Miss Bess, as we started down the drive. "You know, nurse, there's ever so many ways to the sea here. It's all divided into separate little bays. You can't get from one to the other except at low tide, and with a lot of scrambling over the rocks, so we generally fix before we start which bay we'll go to."

"Oh! do let's go to Polwithan Bay!" said Miss Lally.

"It's not nearly so pretty as Trewan," said Miss Bess, "and there are the smugglers' caves at Trewan. We often call it the Smugglers' Bay because of that. We've got names of our own for the bays as well as the proper ones."

"There's one we call Picnic Bay," said Master Francis, "because there are such beautiful big flat stones for picnic tables. But I think the Smugglers' Bay is the most curious of all. I'm sure nurse would like to see it. Why do you want to go to Polwithan, Lally? It is rather a stupid little bay."

"Can we go to the Smugglers' Bay by the village?" asked Miss Lally, and then I understood her, though I did not know that tightly clutched in her hot little hand were the shilling and the three or four pennies she had taken out of her money box on the chance of buying the wool for her stockings.

"It would be ever such a round," said Miss Bess; but then she added politely — she was very particular about politeness, when she wasn't put out — "but of course if nurse wants to see the village that wouldn't matter. We've plenty of time. Would you like to see it, nurse?"

A glance at Miss Lally's anxious little face decided me.

"Well, I won't say but what it would interest me to see the village," I replied. "Of course it's just as well and might be handy for me to know my way about, so as to be able to find the post-office or fetch any little thing from the shop if it were wanted."

This was quite true, though I won't deny but that another reason was strongest and Miss Lally knew it, for she crept up to me and slid her little hand into mine gratefully.

"Very well, then," said Miss Bess, "we'll go round by the village. But remember if you're tired, Lally, you mustn't grumble, for it was you that first spoke of going that way."

"There's the cart if Miss Lally's tired," I said. "Three could easily get into it, and Jacob can't be knocked up if only Miss Baby goes in it all the way there."

"Nurse," said Miss Lally suddenly — I don't think she had heard what we were saying — "there's two shops in the village."

"Are there, my dear," I said; "and is one the post-office? And what do they sell?"

"Yes, one is the post-office, but they sell other things 'aside stamps," Miss Lally replied. "They are both *everything* shops."

"But the *not* the post-office one is much the nicest," said Master Francis. "It's kept by old Prideaux — he's an old sailor and — " Here the boy looked round, but there was no one in sight. Still he lowered his voice. "People do say that after he left off being a proper sailor he was a smuggler. It runs in the family, Mrs. Brent says," he went on in the old-fashioned way I noticed in all the children. "His father was a regular smuggler. Brent says she's seen some queer transactions when she was a girl in the kitchen behind the shop."

"I thought Mrs. Brent was a stranger in these parts by her birth and upbringing," I said.

"So she is," said Master Francis, "but she came here on a visit when she was a girl to her uncle at the High Meadows Farm, and that's how she came first to Treluan. Grandfather was alive then, and papa and Uncle Hulbert were boys. Even then Prideaux was an old man. Uncle Hulbert says he knows lots of queer stories — he does tell them sometimes, but not as if they had happened here, and you have to pretend to think he and his father had nothing to do with them themselves."

"It was he that told us first about the smugglers' caves, wasn't it?" said Miss Bess. "Fancy, nurse, some treasures were found in one of the caves, not so very long ago, hid away in a dark corner far in. There was lace and some beautiful fine silk stockings and some bottles of brandy —"

"And a lot of cigars and tobacco, but they had gone all bad, and some of the brandy hadn't any taste in it, though some was quite good. But grandpapa was a dreadfully honest man; he would send all the things up to London, just as they were found, for he said they belonged to the Queen."

"I wonder if the Queen wored the silk stockings her own self?" said Miss Lally.

"If *we* found some treasures," said Miss Bess, "do you think we'd have to send them to the Queen too? It would be very greedy of her to keep them, when she has such lots and lots of everything."

"That's just because she's queen; she can't help it. It's part of being a queen, and I dare say she gives away lots too. Besides, you wouldn't care for brandy or cigars, Bess?" said Master Francis.

"We could sell them," answered Miss Bess, "if they were good."

"P'raps the Queen would send us a nice present back," said Miss Lally. "Fancy, if she sent us a whole pound, what beautiful things we could buy."

"It would be great fun to find treasures, whatever they were," said Miss Bess. "If we see old Prideaux to-day, I'll ask him if he thinks possibly there's still some in the caves. Only it wouldn't do to go into his shop on purpose to ask him — he'd think it funny."

THEN THERE BURST UPON THE VIEW A WONDERFUL SURPRISE. — p. 63.

" And you'll have to be very careful how you ask him," said Master Francis. " Besides, I'm quite sure if there were any to be found, he'd have found them before this."

" Does he sell wool in his shop, do you think, Miss Bess?" I inquired, and I felt Miss Lally's hand squeeze mine. " Wool, or worsted for knitting stockings, I mean. I want to get some, and that would be a reason for speaking to him."

" I dare say he does; at least his daughter's always knitting, and she must get wool somewhere. Anyway we can ask," answered Miss Bess, quite pleased with the idea.

" Now, nurse," said Master Francis suddenly, " keep your eyes open. When we turn into the field at the end of this little lane — we've come by a short-cut to the village, for the cart can go through the field quite well — you'll have your first good view of the sea. We can see it from some of the windows at Treluan and from the end of the terrace, but nothing like as well."

I was glad he had prepared me, for we had been interested in our talking, and I hadn't paid much attention to the way we were going. Now I did keep my eyes open, and I was well rewarded. The field was a sloping one — sloping upwards, I mean, as we entered it — and till we got to the top of the rising ground we saw nothing but the clear sky above the grass, but then there burst upon the view a wonderful surprise. The coast-line lay before us for a considerable distance at each side. Just below us were the rocky bays or creeks the children had told me of. the sand gleaming yellow and white in the sunshine, for the tide was half-way out, though near enough still for us to see the glisten of the foam and the edge of the little waves, as they rippled in sleepily. And further out the deep purple-blue of the ocean, softening into a misty gray, there, where the sky and the water met or melted into each other. A little to the right rose the smoke of several houses —lazily, for it was a very still day. These houses lay nestled in together, on the way to the shore, and seemed scarcely enough to be called a village; but as we left the field again to rejoin the road, I saw that these few houses were only the centre of it, so to speak, as others straggled along the road in both directions for some way, the church being one of the buildings the nearest to Treluan house.

"It is a beautiful view," said I, after a moment's silence, as we all stood still at the top of the slope, . the children glancing at me, as if to see what I thought of it. "I've never seen anything approaching to it before, and yet it's a bare sort of country— many wouldn't believe it could be so beautiful with so few trees, but I suppose the sea makes up for a good deal."

"And it's such a lovely day," said Master Francis. "I should say the sun makes up for a good deal.

We've lots of days here when it's so gray and dull that the sea and the sky seem all muddled up together. I'm not so very fond of the sea myself. People say it's so beautiful in a storm, and I suppose it is, but I don't care for that kind of beauty, there's something so furious and wild about it. I don't think raging should be counted beautiful. Shouldn't we only call good things beautiful?"

He looked up with a puzzle in his eyes. Master Francis always had thoughts beyond his age and far beyond me to answer.

"I can't say, I'm sure," I replied. "It would take very clever people indeed to explain things like that, though there's verses in the Bible that do seem to bear upon it, especially in the Psalms."

"I know there are, but when it tells of Heaven, it says 'there shall be no more sea,'" said Master Francis very gravely. "And I think I like that best."

"Dear Francie," said Miss Lally, taking his hand, as she always did when she saw him looking extra grave, though of course she could not understand what he had been saying.

We were out of the field by this time, and Miss Bess caught hold of Jacob's reins, for up till now the old fellow had been droning along at his own pace.

"Come along, Jacob, waken up," she said, as she tugged at him, "or we'll not get to Polwithan Bay to-day, specially if we're going to gossip with old Prideaux on the way."

We passed the church in a moment, and close beside it the Vicarage.

" That's where Miss Kirstin lives," said Miss Bess. "Come along quick, I don't want her to see us."

"Don't you like her, my dear?" I said, a little surprised.

" Oh yes! we like her very well, but she makes us think of lessons, and while it is holidays we may as well forget them," and by the way in which Master Francis and Miss Lally joined her in hurrying past Mr. Kirstin's house, I could see they were of the same mind.

Miss Kirstin, when I came to know her, I found to be a good well-meaning young lady, but she hadn't the knack of making lessons very interesting. It wasn't perhaps altogether her fault; in those days books for young people, both for lessons and amusement, were very different from what they are now. School-books were certainly very dry and dull, and there was a sort of feeling that making lessons pleasant or taking to children would have been weak indulgence.

The church was a beautiful old building. I am not learned enough to describe it, and perhaps after all it was more beautiful from age than from anything remarkable in itself. I came to love it well; it was a real grief to me and to others besides me when it had to be partly pulled down a few years ago, and all the wonderful growth of ivy spoilt. Though I won't say but what our new vicar — the third from Mr. Kirstin our present one is — is well fitted for his work, both with rich and poor, and one whom it is impossible not to respect as well as love, though Mr. Kirstin was a worthy and kind old man in his way.

A bit farther along the road we passed the post-office, which the children pointed out to me. The mistress came to the door when she saw us, and curtsied to the little ladies, with a smile and a word of " Welcome home again, Miss Penrose!" She took a good look at me out of the corner of her eye, I could see. For having lived so much in small country places, I knew how even a fresh servant at the big house will set all the village talking.

Miss Lally glanced in at the shop window as we passed. There was indeed, as she had said, a mixture of "everything," from tin pails and mother-of-pearl buttons to red herrings and tallow-candles.

" Nurse," she whispered, " *in case* we can't get the wool at Prideaux', we might come back here, but I'm afraid Bess wouldn't like to turn back. Oh! I do hope " — with one of her little sighs — " they'll have it at the other shop."

And so they had, though when we got there a little difficulty arose. The two elder children both wanted to come in, having got their heads full of asking the old man about the smugglers' caves, and thinking it was for myself I wanted the wool. Never a word said poor Miss Lally, when her sister told her to stay outside with Miss Baby and the cart; but I was getting to know the look of her little face too well by this time not to understand the puckers about her eyes, and the droop at the corners of her mouth.

"We may as well all go in," I said, lifting Miss Baby out of the cart. "There's no one else in the shop, and I want Miss Lally's opinion about the wool."

"*Lally's!*" said Miss Bess rather scornfully; "she doesn't know anything about wool, or knitting stockings, nurse."

"Ah! well, but perhaps she's going to know something about it," I said. "It's a little secret we've got, Miss Bess; you shall hear about it all in good time."

"Oh, well, if it's a secret," said Miss Bess good-naturedly—she was a nice-minded child, as they all were — "Franz and I will keep out of the way while you and Lally get your wool. We'll talk to old Prideaux."

He was in the shop, as well as his daughter, who was knitting away as the children had described her, and the old wife came hurrying out of the kitchen, when she heard it was the little gentry from Treluan that were in the shop. They did make a fuss over the children, to be sure; it wasn't easy for Miss Lally and me to get our bit of business done. But Sally Prideaux found us just what we wanted — the same wool that she was knitting stockings of herself, only she had not much of it in stock, and might be some little time before she could get more. But I told Miss Lally there'd be enough for a short pair of socks for her cousin — boys didn't wear knickerbockers and long stockings in those days — adding that it was best not to undertake too big a piece of work for the first.

The wool cost one-and-sixpence. It was touching to see the little creature counting over the money she had been holding tightly in her hand all the way, and her look of distress when she found it only came up to one-and-fourpence-halfpenny.

"Don't you trouble, my dear," I said, "I have some coppers in my pocket."

She thanked me as if I had given her three pounds instead of three halfpence, saying in a whisper — "I'll pay you back, nursie, when I get my twopence next Saturday;" and then as happy as a little queen she clambered down off the high stool, her precious parcel in her hand.

"Won't Francie be pleased?" she said. "They must be ready for his birthday, nurse. And won't mamma be pleased when she finds I can knit stockings, and that she won't have to buy any more?"

CHAPTER VI.

THE others seemed to have been very well entertained while Miss Lally and I were busy. Mrs. Prideaux had set Miss Baby on the counter, where she was admiring her to her heart's content — Miss Baby smiling and chattering, apparently very well pleased. Miss Bess and Master Francis were talking eagerly with old Prideaux; they turned to us as we came near.

"Oh, nurse!" said Miss Bess, "Mr. Prideaux says that he shouldn't wonder if there were treasures hidden away in the smugglers' caves, though it wouldn't be safe for us to look for them. He says they'd be so very far in, where it's quite, quite dark."

"And one or two of the caves really go a tremendous way underground. Didn't you say there's one they've never got to the end of?" asked Master Francis.

"So they say," replied the old man, with his queer Cornish accent. It did sound strange to me then, their talk — though I've got so used to it now that I scarce notice it at all. "But I wouldn't advise you

MISS BESS AND MASTER FRANCIS WERE TALKING EAGERLY WITH OLD PRIDEAUX.—p. 70.

to begin searching for treasures, Master Francis. If there's any there, you'd have to dig to get at them. I remember when I was a boy a deal of talk about the caves, and some of us wasted our time seeking and digging. But the only one that could have told for sure where to look was gone. He met his death some distance from here, one terrible stormy winter, and took his secret with him. I have heard tell as he 'walks' in one of the caves, when the weather's quite beyond the common stormy. But it's not much use, for at such times folk are fain to stay at home, so there's not much chance of any one ever meeting him."

"Then how has he ever been seen?" asked Miss Bess in her quick way; "and who was he, Mr. Prideaux? do tell us."

But the old man didn't seem inclined to say much more. Perhaps indeed Miss Bess was too sharp for him, and he did not know how to answer her first question.

"Such things is best not said much about," he replied mysteriously; "and talking of treasures, by all accounts you'd have a better chance of finding some nearer home."

He smiled, as if he could have said more had he chosen to do so. The children opened their eyes in bewilderment.

"What do you mean?" exclaimed the two elder ones. Miss Lally's mind was running too much on her stockings for her to pay much attention. Prideaux did not seem at all embarrassed.

"Well, sir, it's no secret hereabouts," he said, addressing Master Francis in particular, "that the old, old Squire, Sir David, the last of that name — there were several David Penroses before him, but never one since — it's no secret, as I was saying, that a deal of money or property of some kind disappeared in his last years, and it stands to reason that, being as great a miser as was ever heard tell of, he couldn't have spent it. Why, more than half of the lands changed hands in his time, and what did he do with what he got for them?"

"That was our great, great grand-uncle," said Master Francis to me; "you remember I told you about him, but I never thought —" he stopped short. "It *is* very queer," he went on again, as if speaking to himself.

But just then, Miss Baby having had enough of Mrs. Prideaux' pettings, set up a shout.

"Nurse, nurse," she said, "Baby wants to go back to Jacob. Poor Jacob so tired waiting. Dood-bye, Mrs. Pideaux," and she began wriggling to get off the counter, so that I had to hurry forward to lift her down.

"We'd best be going on," I said, "or we'll be losing the finest part of the afternoon."

I didn't feel quite sure that Prideaux' talk was quite what my lady would approve of for the children.

They had a way of taking things up more seriously than is common with such young creatures, and certainly they had got in the way — and I couldn't but feel but what my lady was to blame for this — of thinking too much of the family troubles, especially the want of wealth, which seemed to them a greater misfortune than it need have done. Still, being quite a stranger, and them seeming at liberty to talk to the people about as they did, I didn't feel that it would have been my place to begin making new rules or putting a stop to things, as likely as not quite harmless. I resolved, however, to find out my lady's wishes in such matters at the first opportunity.

Another half hour brought us close to the shore; the road was a good one, being used for carting gravel and sea-weed in large quantities to the village and round about from the little bay — Treluan Bay, that is to say — it led directly to. But as we were bound for Polwithan Bay, where the smugglers' caves were, and had made a round for the sake of coming through the village, we had to cross several fields and follow a rough track instead of going straight down to the sands. Jacob didn't seem to mind, I must say, nor Miss Baby neither, though she must have been pretty well jolted, but it was worth the trouble.

"Isn't it lovely, nurse?" said Miss Bess, when at last we found ourselves in the bay on the smooth firm sand, the sea in front of us, and so encircled on

three sides by the rocks that even the path by which
we had come was hidden.

"This bay is so beautifully shut in," said Master
Francis. "You could really fancy that there was no
one in the world but us ourselves. I think it's such
a nice feeling."

"It's nice when we're all together," said Miss
Lally; "it would be rather frightening if anybody
was alone."

"Alone or not," said Miss Bess, "it wouldn't be at
all nice when tea-time came if we had nothing to eat.
And fancy, what *should* we do at night — we couldn't
sleep out on the sand?"

"We'd have to go into the caves," said Master
Francis. "It would be rather fun, with a good fire
and with lots of blankets."

"And where would you get blankets from, or wood
for a fire, you silly boy?" said Miss Bess.

"Can we see the caves?" I asked, for having heard
so much talk about them, I felt curious to see them.

"Of course," said Master Francis. "We always
explore them every time we come to this bay. Do
you see those two or three dark holes over there
among the rocks, nurse? Those are the caves; come
along and I'll show them to you."

I was a little disappointed. I had never seen a
cave in my life, but I had a confused remembrance
of pictures in an old book at home of some caves —
"The Mammoth Caves of Kentucky," I afterwards

found they were — which looked very large and wonderful, and somehow I suppose I had all the time been picturing to myself that these ones were something of the same kind. I didn't say anything to the children though, as they took great pride in showing me all the sights. And after all, when we got to the caves, they turned out much more curious and interesting than I expected from the outside. The largest one, though its entrance was so small, was really as big as a fair-sized church, and narrowing again far back into a dark mysterious-looking passage, from which Master Francis told me two or three smaller chambers opened out.

"And then," he said, "after that the passage goes on again — ever so far. In the old days the smugglers blocked it up with pieces of rock, and it isn't so very long ago that this was found out. It was somewhere down along that passage that they found the things I told you of."

We went a few yards along the passage, but it soon grew almost quite dark, and we turned back again.

"I can quite see it wouldn't be safe to try exploring down there," I said.

"Yes, I suppose so," said Master Francis, with a sigh. "I wish I could find some treasure, all the same. I wonder — " he went on, then stopped short. "Nurse," he began again, "did you hear what old Prideaux said of our great grand-uncle the miser?

Could it really be true, do you think, that he hid away money or treasures of some kind?" and he lowered his voice mysteriously.

"I shouldn't think it was likely," I replied. For I had a feeling that it would not be well for the children to get any such ideas into their heads. It sounded to me like a sort of fairy tale. I had never come across anything so romantic and strange in real life. Though for that matter, Treluan itself, and the kind of old-world feeling about the place, was quite unlike anything I had ever known before.

We were outside the cave again by this time; the sunshine seemed deliciously warm and bright after the chill and gloom inside. Miss Bess had been listening eagerly to what Master Francis was saying.

"I can't see but what old Sir David *might* have hidden treasures away, as he was a real miser," she said.

"And you know that misers are so suspicious, that even when they're dying they won't trust anybody. I know I've read a story like that," said the boy. "Oh! Bess, just fancy if we could find a lot of money or diamonds! Wouldn't uncle and aunt be pleased?"

His whole face lighted up at the very idea.

"I dare say he hid it all away in a stocking," put in Miss Lally, whose head was still full of her knitting. "I've heard a story of an old woman miser that did that."

"And where would the stocking be hid?" said Miss Bess. "Besides, if a stocking was ever so full, it couldn't hold enough money to be a real treasure."

"It might be stuffed with bank notes," said Master Francis. "There's bank notes worth ever so much; aren't there, nurse?"

"I remember once seeing one of a thousand pounds," I said. "That was at my last place. Mr. Wyngate had to do with business in the city, and he once brought one home to show the young ladies."

"Well, then, you see, Queen," said Miss Lally, "there might be a stocking with enough money to make papa and mamma as rich as rich."

"I'm quite sure Sir David's money wasn't put in a stocking," said Miss Bess decidedly. "You've got rather silly ideas, Lally, considering you're getting on for six."

Miss Lally began to look rather doleful. She had been so bright and cheerful all day that I didn't like to see her little face overcast. We had left Jacob outside the cave, of course; there was one satisfaction with him — he was not likely to run away.

"Miss Baby, dear," I said, "aren't you getting hungry? Where's the basket you were holding in the cart?"

"Nice cakes in basket," said the little girl. "Baby looked, but Baby didn't eaten them."

The basket was still in the cart, and I think they were all very pleased when they saw what I had brought for them. Some of Mrs. Brent's nice little saffron buns and a bottle of milk. I remember that I didn't like the taste of the saffron buns at first, and now I might be Cornish born and bred, I think it such an improvement to cakes!

"Another time," I said, "we might bring our tea with us. I dare say my lady wouldn't object."

"I'm sure she wouldn't mind," said Miss Bess. "We used to have picnic teas sometimes, when our *quite*, quite old nurse was with us — the one that's married over to St. Iwalds."

"Bess," said Master Francis, "you should say 'over at,' not 'over to.'"

"Thank you," said Miss Bess, "I don't want you to teach me grammar. *That* isn't parson's business."

Master Francis grew very red.

"Did you know, nurse," said Miss Lally, "Francie's going to be a clergy-gentleman?"

They couldn't help laughing at her, and the laugh brought back good humour.

"I want to be one," said Master Francis, "but I'm afraid it costs a great lot to go to college."

Poor children, through all their talk and plans the one trouble seemed always to keep coming up.

"I fancy that's according a good deal to how young gentlemen take it. There's some that spend a fortune at college, I've heard, but some that are very careful; and I expect you'd be that kind, Master Francis."

"Yes," he said, in his grave way. "I wouldn't want to cost Uncle Hulbert more than I can help. I wish one could be a clergyman without going to college though."

"You've got to go to school first," said Miss Bess. "You needn't bother about college for a long time yet."

Miss Lally sighed.

"I don't like Francie having to go to school," she said. "And the boys are so rough there; I hope they won't hurt your poor leg, Francie."

"It isn't *that* I mind," said Master Francie — the boy had a fine spirit of his own though he was so delicate — "what I mind is the going alone and being so far away from everybody."

"It's a pity," I said without thinking, "but what one of you young ladies had been a young gentleman, to have been a companion for Master Francis, and to have gone to school together, maybe."

"Oh!" said Miss Bess quickly, "you must never say that to mamma, nurse. You don't know what a trouble it is to her not to have a boy. She'd have liked Lally to be a boy most of all. She wanted her to be a boy; she always says so."

Here Master Francis gave a deep sigh in his turn.

"Oh! how I wish," he said, "that I could turn myself into a girl and Lally into a boy. I wouldn't *like* to be a girl at all, and I dare say Lally wouldn't like to be a boy. But to please Aunt Helen I'd do it."

"No," said Miss Lally, "I don't think I would — not even to please mamma. I couldn't bear to be a boy."

I was rather sorry I had led to this talk.

"Isn't it best," I said, "to take things as they are? Master Francis is just like your brother — the same name and everything."

"I'd like it that way," said Master Francis, with a pleased look in his eyes. But I heard Miss Bess, who was walking close beside me, say in a low voice, "Mamma will never think of it that way!"

This talk made some things clearer to me than before, and that evening, after the children were in bed, I went down to the housekeeper's room and eased my mind by telling her about it, I felt so afraid of having said anything uncalled for. But Mrs. Brent comforted me.

"It's best for you to know," she said, "that my lady does make a great trouble, too great a trouble, to my thinking, of not having a son. And no doubt it has to do with her coldness to Master Francis, though I doubt if she really knows this herself, for she's a lady that means to do right and justly to all about her; I will say that for her."

It was really something to be thankful for to have such a good and sensible woman to ask advice from, for a stranger, as I still was. The more I knew her, the more she reminded me of my good mother. Plain and homely in her ways, with no love of gossip about her, yet not afraid to speak out her mind when she saw it right to do so. Many things would have been harder at Treluan, the poor dear children would have had less pleasure in their lives, but for Mrs. Brent's kind thought for them. That very evening I had had a reason, so to say, for paying a special visit to the housekeeper's room; for when we had got in from our long walk, rather tired and certainly very hungry, a nice surprise was waiting for us in the nursery. The tea-table was already set out most carefully. There was a pile of Mrs. Brent's hot scones and a beautiful dish of strawberries.

"Oh, nurse!" cried Miss Bess, who had run on first, "quick, quick, look what a nice tea. I'm sure it's Mrs. Brent! Isn't it good of her?"

"It's like a birfday," said Miss Lally.

And Miss Baby, who had been grumbling a good deal and crying, "I want my tea," nearly jumped out of my arms — I had had to carry her upstairs — at the sight of it.

For I'm afraid there's no denying that in those days breakfast, dinner, and tea filled a large place in Miss Augusta's thoughts. I hope she'll forgive me for saying so, if she ever sees this.

CHAPTER VII

A RAINY DAY.

THAT lovely weather lasted on for about a fortnight without a break, and many a pleasant ramble we had, for though lessons began again, Miss Kirstin always left immediately after luncheon, which was the children's dinner, for the three elder ones always joined Sir Hulbert and my lady in the dining-room.

Two afternoons in the week, as I think I have said, Master Francis and Miss Bess had Latin lessons from Sir Hulbert. Miss Bess, by all accounts, did not take very kindly to the Latin grammar, and but for Master Francis helping her — many a time indeed sitting up after his own lessons were done to set hers right — she would often have got into trouble with her papa. For indulgent as he was, Sir Hulbert could be strict when strictness was called for.

Miss Bess was a curious mixture; to see her and hear her talk you'd have thought her twice as clever as Miss Lally, and so in some ways she was. But when it came to book learning, it was a different story. Teaching Miss Lally — and I had something to do with her in this way, for I used to hear over the lessons she was getting ready for Miss Kirstin — was really like running along a smooth road, the child was so eager and attentive, never losing a word of what was said to her. Miss Bess used to say that her sister had a splendid memory by nature. But in my long life I've watched and thought about some things a great deal, and it seems to me that a good memory has to do with our own trying, more than some people would say, — above all, with the habit of really giving attention to whatever you're doing. And this habit Miss Bess had not been taught to train herself to; and being a lively impulsive child, no doubt it came a little harder to her.

A dear child she was, all the same. Looking back upon those days, I would find it hard to say which of them all seemed nearest my heart.

The days of the Latin lessons we generally had a short walk in the morning, as well as one after tea, so as to suit Sir Hulbert's time in the afternoon; and those afternoons were Miss Lally's great time for her knitting, which she was determined to keep a secret till she had made some progress in it and finished her first pair of socks. How she did work at it, poor dear! Her little face all puckered up with earnestness, her little hot hands grasping the needles, as if she would never let them go. And she mastered it really wonderfully, considering she was not yet six years old!

She had more time for it after a bit, for the beautiful hot summer weather changed, as it often does, about the middle of July, and we had two or three weeks of almost constant rain. Thanks to her knitting, Miss Lally took this quite cheerfully, and if poor Master Francis had been left in peace, we should have had no grumbling from him either. A book and a quiet corner was all he asked, and though he said nothing about it, I think he was glad now and then of a rest from the long walks which my lady thought the right thing, whenever the weather was at all fit for going out. But dear, dear! how Miss Bess did tease and worry sometimes! She was a strong child, and needed plenty of exercise to keep her content.

I remember one day, when things really came to a point with her, and, strangely enough, — it is curious on looking back to see the thread, like a road winding along a hill, sometimes lost to view and sometimes clear again, unbroken through all, leading from little things to big, in a way one could never have pictured, — strangely enough, as I was saying, the trifling events of that very afternoon were the beginning of much that changed the whole life at Treluan.

It was raining that afternoon, not so very heavily, but in a steady hopeless way, rather depressing to the spirits, I must allow. It was not a Latin day — I think some of us wished it had been!

"Now, Bess!" said Master Francis, when the

three children came up from their dinner, "before
we do anything else" — there had been a talk of
a game of "hide-and-seek," or "I spy," to cheer them
up a bit — "before we do anything else, let's get our
Latin done, or part of it, anyway, as long as we
remember what uncle corrected yesterday, and then
we'll feel comfortable for the afternoon."

"Very well," said Miss Bess, though her voice
was not very encouraging.

She was standing by the window, staring out at
the close-falling rain, and as she spoke she moved
slowly towards the table, where Master Francis was
already spreading out the books.

"I don't think it's a good plan to begin lessons
the very moment we've finished our dinner," she
added.

"It isn't the very minute after," put in Miss Lally,
not very wisely. "You forget, Queen, we went into
the 'servatory with mamma, while she cut some
flowers, for ever so long."

Being put in the wrong didn't sweeten Miss
Bess's temper.

"'Servatory — you baby!" said she. "Nurse, can't
you teach Lally to spell 'Constantinople'?"

Miss Lally's face puckered up, and she came close
to me.

"Nursie," she whispered, "may I go into the other
room with my knitting; I'm sure Queen is going to
tease me."

I nodded my head. I used to give her leave sometimes to go into the night nursery by herself, when she was likely to be disturbed at her work, and that generally by Miss Bess. For though Master Francis couldn't have but seen she had some secret from him, he was far too kind and sensible to seem to notice it. Whereas Miss Bess, who had been taken into her confidence, never got into a contrary humour without teasing the poor child by hints about stockings, or wool, or something. And the contrary humour was on her this afternoon, I saw well.

"Now, Bess, begin, do!" said Master Francis. "These are the words we have to copy out and learn. I'll read them over, and then we can write them out and hear each other."

He did as he said, but it was precious little attention he got from his cousin, though it was some time before he found it out. Looking up, he saw that she had dressed up one hand in her handkerchief, like an old man in a nightcap, and at every word poor Master Francis said, made him gravely bow. It was all I could do to keep from laughing, though I pretended not to see.

"O Bess!" said the boy reproachfully, "I don't believe you've been listening a bit."

"Well, never mind if I haven't. I'd forget it all by to-morrow morning anyway. Show me the words, and I'll write them out."

She leant across him to get the book, and in so doing upset the ink. The bottle was not very full, so not much damage would have been done if Master Francis's exercise-book had not been lying open just in the way.

"Oh! Bess," he cried in great distress. "Just look. It was such a long exercise and I had copied it out so neatly, and you know uncle hates blots and untidiness."

Miss Bess looked very sorry.

"I'll tell papa it was my fault," she said. But Master Francis shook his head.

"I must copy it out again," I heard him say in a low voice, with a sigh, as he pushed it away and gave his attention to his cousin and the words she had to learn.

She was quieter after that, for a while, and in half an hour or so Master Francis let her go. He set to work at his unlucky exercise again, and seeing this, should really have sobered Miss Bess. But she was in a queer humour that afternoon, it only seemed to make her more fidgety.

"You really needn't do it," she said to Master Francis crossly. "I told you I'd explain it to papa." But the boy shook his head. He'd have taken any amount of trouble rather than risk vexing his uncle.

"It was partly my own fault for leaving it about," he said gently, which only seemed to provoke Miss Bess more.

"You do so like to make yourself a martyr. It's quite true what mamma says," she added in a lower voice, which I did think unkind.

But in some humours children are best left alone for the time, so I took no notice.

Miss Bess returned to her former place in the window. Miss Baby was contentedly setting out her doll's tea-things on the rug in front of the fire, — at Treluan even in the summer one needs a little fire when there comes a spell of rainy weather. Miss Bess glanced at her, but didn't seem to think she'd find any amusement there. Miss Baby was too young to be fair game for teasing.

"What's Lally doing?" she said suddenly, turning to me. "Has she hidden herself as usual? I hate secrets. They make people so tiresome. I'll just go and tell her she'd better come in here."

She turned, as she spoke, to the night nursery.

"Now, Miss Bess, my dear," I couldn't help saying, "do not tease the poor child. I'll tell you what you might do. Get one of your pretty books and read aloud a nice story to Miss Lally in the other room, till Master Francis is ready for a game."

"I've read all our books hundreds of times. I'll tell her a story instead!" she replied.

"That would be very nice," I could not but say, though something in her way of speaking made me feel a little doubtful, as Miss Bess opened the night nursery door and closed it behind her carefully.

For a few minutes we were at peace. No sound to be heard, except the scratching of Master Francis's busy pen and Miss Augusta's pressing invitations to the dollies to have — "thome more tea" — or — "a bit of this bootiful cake," and I began to hope that in her quiet way Miss Lally had smoothed down her elder sister, when suddenly — dear, dear! my heart did leap into my mouth — there came from the next room the most terrible screams and roars that ever I have heard all the long years I have been in the nursery!

"Goodness gracious!" I cried, "what can be the matter. There's no fire in there!" and I rushed towards the door.

To my surprise Master Francis and Miss Baby remained quite composed.

"It's only Lally," said the boy. "She does scream like that sometimes, though she hasn't done it for a good while now. I dare say it's only Bess pulling her hair a little."

It was not even that. When I opened the door, Miss Bess, who was standing by her sister — Miss Lally still roaring, though not quite so loudly — looked up quietly.

"I've been telling her stories, nurse," she said. "But she doesn't like them at all."

Miss Lally ran to me sobbing. I couldn't but feel sorry for her, as she clung to me, and yet I was provoked, thinking it really too bad to have had such a fright for nothing at all.

"Queen has been telling me such *howid* things," she said among her tears, as she calmed down a little. "She said it was going to be such a pretty story and it was all about a little girl, who wasn't a little girl, weally. They tied her sleeves with green ribbons, afore she was christened, and so the naughty fairies stealed her away and left a howid squealing pertence little girl instead. And it was just, *just* like me, and, Queen says, they *did* tie me in green ribbons. She knows they did, she can 'amember;" and here her cries began again. "And Queen says p'raps I'll never come right again, and I can't bear to be a pertence little girl. Queen told it me once before, but I'd forgot, and now it's all come back."

She buried her face on my shoulder. I had sat down and taken her on my knees, and I could feel her all shaking and quivering, though through it all she still clutched her knitting and the four needles.

"Miss Bess," I said, in a voice I don't think I had yet used since I had been with them, "I *am* surprised at you! Come away with me, my dear," I said to Miss Lally. "Come into the other room. Miss Bess will stay here till such time as she can promise to behave better, both to you and Master Francis."

Miss Bess had turned away when I began to speak, and I think she had felt ashamed. But my word about Master Francis had been a mistake.

"You needn't scold me about spilling the ink on

Francis's book!" she said angrily. "You know that was an accident."

"There's accidents and accidents," I replied, which I know wasn't wise; but the child had tried my temper too, I won't deny.

I took Miss Lally into a corner of the day nursery and talked to her in a low voice, not to disturb Master Francis, who was still busy writing.

"My dear," I said, "so far as I can put a stop to it, I won't have Miss Bess teasing you, but all the same I can't have you screaming in that terrible way for really nothing at all. Your own sense might tell you that there's no such things as fairies changing babies in that way. Miss Bess only said it to tease."

She was still sobbing, but all the same she had not forgotten to wrap up her precious knitting in her little apron, so that her cousin shouldn't catch sight of it, and her heart was already softening to her sister.

"Queen didn't mean to make me cry," she said. "But I can't bear that story; nobody would love me if I was only a pertence little girl."

"But you're not that, my dear; you're a very real little girl," I said. "You're your papa's and mamma's dear little daughter and God's own child. That's what your christening meant."

Miss Lally's sobs stopped.

"I forgot about that," she said very gravely, seeming to find great comfort in the thought. "If I had been a pertence little girl, I couldn't have been took to church like Baby was. Could I? And I know I was, for I have got godfather and godmother and a silver mug wif my name on."

"And better things than that, thank God, as you'll soon begin to understand, my dear Miss Lally," I answered, as she held up her little face to be kissed.

"May I go back to Queen now?" she asked, but I don't think she was altogether sorry when I shook my head.

"Not just yet, my dear, I think," I replied.

"Only where am I to do my knitting?" she whispered. "I can't do it here; Francie would be sure to see," and the corners of her mouth began to go down again. "Oh! I know," she went on in another moment, brightening up. "I could work so nicely in the attic, there's a little seat in the corner, by the window, where Francie and I used to go sometimes when Sharp told us to get out of the way."

"Wouldn't you be cold, my dear," I said doubtfully. But I was anxious to please her, so I fetched a little shawl for her and we went up together to the attic.

It did not feel chilly, and the corner by the window — the kind they call a "storm window," with a sort of little separate roof of its own — was very cosy. You have a peep of the sea from that window too.

"Isn't it a good plan?" said Miss Lally joyfully. "I can knit here *so* nicely, and I have been getting on so well this afternoon. There's no stitches dropped, not one, nursie. Mightn't I come here every day?"

"We'll see, my dear," I said, thinking to myself that it might really be good for her — being a nervous child, and excitable too, for all she seemed so quiet — to be at peace and undisturbed now and then by herself. "We'll see, only you must come downstairs at once if you feel cold or chilly."

I looked round me as I was leaving the attic. There was a big cupboard, or closet rather, at the end near the door. Miss Lally's window was at this end too. The closet door stood half open, but it seemed empty.

"That's where we wait when we're playing 'I spy' up here," said Miss Lally. "Mouses live in that cupboard. We've seen them running out of their holes; but I like mouses, they've such dear bright eyes and long tails."

I can't say that I agreed with Miss Lally's tastes. Mice are creatures I've never been able to take to, still they'd do her no harm, that was certain, so seeing her quite happy at her work I went down to the nursery again.

CHAPTER VIII

THE OLD LATIN GRAMMAR.

MASTER FRANCIS was still writing busily when I went back to the nursery. He looked pale and tired, and once or twice I heard him sigh. I knew it was not good for him to be stooping so long over his lessons, especially as the children had not been out all that day.

"Really," I said, half to myself, but his ears were quick and he heard me, "Miss Bess has done nothing but mischief this afternoon. I feel sometimes as if I couldn't manage her."

The boy looked up quickly.

"O nurse!" he said, "please don't speak like that. I mean I wouldn't for anything have uncle or auntie think I had put her out, or that there had been any trouble. It just comes over her sometimes like that, and she's very sorry afterwards. I suppose Lally and I haven't spirits enough for her, she is so clever and bright, and it must be dull for her, now and then."

"I'm sure, Master Francis, my dear," I said, "no one could be kinder and nicer with Miss Bess than you; and as for cleverness, she may be quick and bright, but I'd like to know where she'd be for her lessons but for you helping her many a time."

I was still feeling a bit provoked with Miss Bess, I must allow.

"I'm nearly three years older, you know," replied Master Francis, though all the same I could see a pleased look on his face. It wasn't that he cared for praise — boy or man, I have never in my life known any human being so out and out humble as Mr. Francis; it's that that gives him his wonderful power over others, I've often thought, — but he did love to think he was of the least use to any of those he was so devoted to.

"I'm so glad to help her," he said softly. "Nurse," he added after a little silence, "I do feel so sad about things sometimes. If I had been big and strong, I might have looked forward to doing all sorts of things for them all, but now I often feel I can never be anything but a trouble, and such an expense to uncle and aunt. You really don't know what my leg costs," he added in a way that made me inclined both to laugh and cry at once.

"Dear Master Francis," I said, "you shouldn't take it so." I should have liked to say more, but I felt I could scarcely do so without hinting at blame where I had no right to do so.

He didn't seem to notice me.

"If it had to be," he went on in the same voice, "why couldn't I have been a girl, or why couldn't one of them have been a boy? That would have stopped it being quite so bad for poor auntie."

"Whys and wherefores are not for us to answer, my dear, though things often clear themselves up when least expected," I said. "And now I must see what Miss Bess is after, that's to say if you've got your writing finished."

"It's just about done," he said, "and I'm sure Bess won't tease any more. Do fetch her in, nurse. Why, Baby! what is it, my pet?" he added, for there was Miss Augusta standing beside him, having deserted her toys on the hearthrug. For, though without understanding anything we had been saying, she had noticed the melancholy tone of her cousin's voice.

"Poor F'ancie," she said pitifully. "So tired, Baby wants to kiss thoo."

The boy picked her up in his arms, and I saw the fair shaggy head and fat dimpled cheeks clasped close and near to his thin white face, and if there were tears in Master Francis's eyes I am sure it wasn't anything to be ashamed of. Never was a braver spirit, and no one that knows him now could think him less a hero could they look back over the whole of his life.

I found Miss Bess sitting quietly with the pincushion on her lap, by the window, making patterns with the pins, apparently quite content. She had not been crying, indeed it took a great deal to get a tear from that child, she had such a spirit of her

"Poor F'ancie," she said pitifully. "So tired, Baby wants to kiss thoo." — p. 96.

own. Still she was sorry for what she had done, and she bore no malice, that I could see by the clear look in her pretty eyes as she glanced up at me.

"Nurse," she said, though more with the air of a little queen granting a favour than a tiresome child asking to be forgiven, "I'm not going to tease any more. It's gone now, and I'm going to be good. I'm very sorry for making Lally cry, though she is a little silly — of course I wouldn't care to do it if she wasn't, — and I'm *dreadfully* sorry for poor old Franz's exercise. Look what I have been doing to make me remember," and I saw that she had marked the words "Bess sorry" with the pins. "If you leave it there for a few days, and just say 'pincushion' if you see me beginning again, it'll remind me."

It wasn't very easy for me to keep as grave as I wished, but I answered quietly —

"Very well, Miss Bess, I hope you'll keep to what you say," and we went back, quite friendly again, to the other room.

Master Francis and she began settling what games they would play, and I took the opportunity of slipping upstairs to the attic to call Miss Lally down. She came running out, as bright as could be, and gave me her knitting to hide away for her.

"Nursie," she said, "I really think there's good fairies in the attic. I've got on so well. Four whole rows all round and none stitches dropped."

So that rainy day ended more cheerfully than it had begun.

Unluckily, however, the worst of the mischief caused by Miss Bess's heedlessness didn't show for some little time to come. The next Latin lesson passed off by all accounts very well, especially for Miss Bess. For, thanks to her new resolutions, she was in a most biddable mood, and quite ready to take her cousin's advice as to learning her list of words again, giving up half an hour of her playtime on purpose.

She came dancing upstairs in the highest spirits.

" Nursie," she said, — and when she called me so I knew I was in high favour, — " I'm getting so good, I'm quite frightened at myself. Papa said I had never known my lessons so well."

" I am very glad, I am sure, my love; and I hope," I couldn't help adding, " that Master Francis got some of the praise of it."

For Master Francis was following her into the room, looking not quite so joyful. Miss Bess seemed a little taken aback.

" Do you know," she said, " I never thought of it. I was so pleased at being praised." And as the child was honesty itself, I was certain it was just as she said.

" I'll run down now," she went on, " and tell papa that it was Franz who helped me."

" No, please don't," said the boy, catching hold

of her. "I am as pleased as I can be, Bess, that you got praised, and it's harder for you than for me, or even for Lally, to try hard at lessons, for you've always got such a lot of other things' taking you up; and I wouldn't like," he added slowly, "for uncle to think I wanted to be praised. You see I'm older than you."

"I'm sure you don't get too much praise ever, poor Franz!" said Miss Bess. "Your exercise was as neat as neat, and yet papa wasn't pleased with it."

Then I understood better why Master Francis looked a little sad.

"It was the one I had to copy over," he said.

All the same he wouldn't let Miss Bess go down to her papa. Sir Hulbert was busy, he knew; he had several letters to write, he had heard him say, so Miss Bess had to give in.

"I'll tell you what it is," she said. "People who are generally rather naughty, like me," — Miss Bess was in a humble mood! — "get made a great fuss about when they're good. But people who are always good, like Franz, never get any praise for it, and if ever they do the least bit wrong, they are far worse scolded."

This made Master Francis laugh. It was something, as Miss Bess said, among the children themselves. Miss Lally, who was always loving and gentle to her cousin, he just counted upon in a quiet steady sort of way. But a word of approval from flighty Miss Bess would set him up as if she'd been the Queen herself.

That was a Friday. The next Latin day was Tuesday. Of course I don't know much about such things myself, but the lessons were taken in turns. One day they'd words and writing exercises out of a book on purpose, and another day they'd have regular Latin grammar, out of a thick old book, which had been Sir Hulbert's own when he was a boy, and which he thought a great deal of. Lesson-books were still expensive too, and even in small things money was considered at Treluan. It was on that Tuesday then that, to my distress, I saw that Master Francis had been crying when he came back to the nursery. It was the first time I had seen his eyes red, and he had been trying to make them right again, I'm sure, for he hadn't come straight up from the library. Miss Bess was not with him; it was a fine day and she had gone out driving with her mamma, having been dressed all ready and her lessons shortened for once on purpose.

I didn't seem to notice Master Francis, sorry though I felt, but Miss Lally burst out at once.

"Francie, darling," she said, running up to him and throwing her arms round him. "What's the matter? It isn't your leg, is it?"

"I wouldn't mind that, you know, Lally," he said.

"But sometimes, when the pain's been dreadful bad, it squeezes the tears out, and you can't help it," she said.

"No," he answered, "it isn't my leg. I think I'd better not tell you, Lally, for you might tell it to Bess, and I just won't have her know.' Everything's been so nice with her lately, and it just would seem as if I'd got her into trouble."

"Was papa vexed with you for something?" the child went on. "You'd better tell me, Francie, I really won't tell Bess if you don't want me, and I'm sure nursie won't. I'm becustomed to keeping secrets now. Sometimes secrets are quite right, nursie says."

I could scarcely help smiling at her funny little air.

"It wasn't anything *very* much, after all," said Master Francis. "It was only that uncle said —" and here his voice quivered and he stopped short.

"Tell it from the beginning," said Miss Lally in her motherly way, "and then when you get up to the bad part it won't seem so hard to tell."

It was a relief to him to have her sympathy, I could see, and I think he cared a little for mine too.

"Well," he began, "it's all about that Latin grammar — no, not the lesson," seeing that Miss Lally was going to interrupt him, "but the book. Uncle's fat old Latin grammar, you know, Lally. We didn't use it last Friday, it wasn't the day, and we hadn't needed to look at it ourselves since last Wednesday — that was the ink-spilling day. So it was not found out till to-day; and — and uncle was — so — so vexed when he saw how spoilt it was, and the worst of it was I began something about it having been Bess, and that she hadn't told me, and that made uncle much worse — " Here Master Francis stopped, he seemed on the point of crying again, and he was a boy to feel very ashamed of tears, as I have said.

"I don't think Miss Bess could have known the book had got inked," I said. " And I scarce see how it happened, unless the ink got spilt on the table, and it may have been lying open — I've seen Miss Bess fling her books down open on their faces, so to speak, many a time, — and it may have dried in and been shut up when all the books were cleared away, and no one noticed."

" Yes," said Master Francis eagerly, " that's how it must have been. I never meant that Bess had done it and hidden it. I said it in a hurry because I was so sorry for uncle to think I hadn't taken care of his book, and I was very sorry about the book too. But I made it far worse. Uncle said it was mean of me to try to put my carelessness upon another, a younger child, and a girl; O Lally! you never heard him speak like that; it was *dreadful*."

" Was it worse than that time when big Jem put the blame on little Pat about the dogs not being fed?" asked Miss Lally very solemnly.

Master Francis flushed all over.

" You needn't have said that, Lally," he said turning away. " I'm not so bad as that, anyway."

It was very seldom he spoke in that voice to Miss Lally, and she hadn't meant to vex him, poor child, though her speech had been a mistake.

"Come, come, Master Francis," I said, "you're taking the whole thing too much to heart, I think. Perhaps Sir Hulbert was worried this morning."

"No, no," said Master Francis, "he spoke quite quietly. A sort of cold, kind way, that's much worse than scolding. He said whatever Bess's faults were, she was quite, quite open and honest, and of course I know she is; but he said that this sort of thing made him a little afraid that my being delicate and not — not like other boys, was spoiling me, and that I must never try to make up for not being strong and manly by getting into mean and cunning ways to defend myself."

Young as she was, Miss Lally quite understood; she quite forgot all about his having been vexed with her a moment before.

"O Francie!" she cried, running to him and flinging her arms round him, in a way she sometimes did, as if he needed her protection; "how could papa say so to you? Nobody could think you mean or cunning. It's only that you're too good. I'll tell Bess as soon as she comes in, and she'll tell papa all about it, then he'll see."

"No, dear," said Master Francis, "that's just what you mustn't do. Don't you remember you promised?"

Miss Lally's face fell.

"Don't you see," Master Francis went on, "that *would* look mean? As if I had made Bess tell on herself to put the blame off me. And I do want everything to be happy with Bess and me ourselves as long as I am here. It won't be for so very long," he added. "Uncle says it will be a very good thing indeed for me to go to school."

This was too much for Miss Lally, she burst out crying, and hugged Master Francis tighter than before. I had got to understand more of her ways by now, and I knew that once she was started on a regular sobbing fit, it soon got beyond her own power to stop. So I whispered to Master Francis that he must help to cheer her up, and between us we managed to calm her down. That was just one of the things so nice about the dear boy, he was always ready to forget about himself if there was anything to do for another.

Miss Bess came back from her drive brimming over with spirits, and though it would have been wrong to bear her any grudge, it vexed me rather to see the other two so pale and extra quiet, though Master Francis did his best, I will say, to seem as cheerful as usual.

Miss Bess's quick eyes soon saw there had been something amiss. But I passed it off by saying Miss Lally had been troubled about something, but we weren't going to think about it any more.

Think about it I did, however, so far as it concerned Master Francis, especially. Till now I had been always pleased to see that his uncle was really much attached to the boy, and ready to do him justice. But this notion, which seemed to have begun in Sir Hulbert's mind, that just because the poor child was delicate and in a sense infirm, he must be mean spirited and unmanly in mind, seemed to me a very sad one, and likely to bring much unhappiness. Nor could I feel sure that my lady was not to blame for it. She was frank and generous herself, but inclined to take up prejudices, and not always careful enough in her way of speaking of those she had any feeling against.

I did what I could, whenever I had any opportunity, to stand up for the boy in a quiet way, and with all respect to those who were his natural guardians. But, on the whole, much as I knew we should miss him in the nursery, I was scarcely sorry to hear not many weeks after the little events I have been telling about, that Master Francis's going to school was decided upon. It was to be immediately after the Christmas holidays, and we were now in the month of October.

CHAPTER IX.

But, as everybody knows, things in this world seldom turn out as they are planned.

There was a great deal of writing and considering about Master Francis's school, and I could see that both Sir Hulbert and my lady had it much on their minds. They would never have thought of sending him anywhere but of the best, but in those days schools, even for little boys, cost, I fancy, quite as much or more than now. And I can't say but what I think that the worry and the difficulty about it rather added to his aunt's prejudice against the boy.

However, before long, all was settled, the school was chosen and the very day fixed, and in our different ways we began to get accustomed to the idea. Master Francis, I could see, had two quite opposite ways of looking at it: he was bitterly sorry to go, to leave the home and those in it whom he loved so dearly, more dearly, I think, than any one understood. And he took much to heart also the fresh expenses for his uncle. But, on the other hand, he was eager to get on with his learning; he liked it for its own sake, and, as he used to say to me sometimes when we were talking alone —

"It's only by my mind, you know, nurse, that I can hope to be good for anything. If I had been strong and my leg all right, I'd have been a soldier like papa, I suppose."

"There's soldiers and soldiers, you must remember, Master Francis," I would reply. "There's victories to be won far greater than those on the battlefield. And many a one who's done the best work in this world has been but feeble and weakly in health."

His eyes used to brighten up when I spoke like that. Sometimes, too, I would try to cheer him by reminding him there was no saying but what he might turn out a fairly strong man yet. Many a delicate boy got improved at school, I had heard.

But alas! — or "alas" at least it seemed at the time — everything was changed by what happened that winter.

It was cold, colder than is usual in this part of the world, and I think Master Francis had got it in his head to try and harden himself by way of preparing for school life. My lady used to say little things sometimes, with a good motive, I dare say, about not minding the cold and plucking up a spirit, and what her brothers used to do when they were young, all of which Master Francis took to heart in a way she would not have then believed if she had been told it. Dear me! it is strange to think of it, when I remember how perfectly in later years those two came to understand each other, and how nobody — after she lost her good husband — was such a staff and support to her, such a counsellor and comfort, as the nephew she had so little known — her " more than son," as I had often heard her call him.

But I am wandering away from my story. I was just getting to Master Francis's illness. How it came about no one could really tell. It is not often one can trace back illnesses to their cause. Most often I fancy there are more than one. But just after Christmas Master Francis began with rheumatic fever. We couldn't at first believe it was going to be anything so bad. For my lady's sake, and indeed for everybody's, I tried to cheer up and be hopeful, in spite of the doctor's gloomy looks. It was a real disappointment to myself and took down my pride a bit, for I had done my best by the child, hoping to start him for school as strong and well as was possible for him. And any one less just and fair than my lady might have had back thoughts, such as damp feet, or sheets not aired enough, or chills of some kind, that a little care might have avoided.

It was my belief that he had been feeling worse than usual for some time, but never a complaint had he made, perhaps he wouldn't own it to himself.

It wasn't till two nights after Christmas that, sitting by the nursery fire, just after Miss Augusta had been put to bed, he said to me —

• "Nurse, I can't help it, my leg is so dreadfully bad, and not my leg only, the pain of it seems all over. I'm *all* bad legs to-night," and he tried to smile. "May I go to bed now, and perhaps it will be all right in the morning?"

I *was* frightened! Sir Hulbert and my lady were dining out that evening, which but seldom happened, and when I got over my start a little I wasn't sorry for it, hoping that a good night might show it was nothing serious.

We got him to bed as fast as we could. There was no going down to dessert that evening, so Miss Bess and Miss Lalage set to work to help me, like the womanly little ladies they were; one of them running downstairs to see about plenty of hot water for a good bath and hot bottles, and the other fetching the under housemaid to see to a fire in his room. I doubt if he had ever had one before. Bedroom fires were not in my lady's rule, and I don't hold with them myself, except in illness or extra cold weather.

He cheered up a little, and even laughed at the fuss we made. And before his uncle and aunt returned he was sound asleep, looking quiet and comfortable, so that I didn't think it needful to say anything to them that night. But long before morning, for I crept upstairs to his room every hour or two, I saw that it was not going off as I had hoped. He started and moaned in his sleep, and once or twice when I found him awake, he seemed almost lightheaded, and as if he hardly knew me. Once I heard him whisper: "Oh! it hurts so," as if he could scarcely bear it.

About five o'clock I dressed myself and took up my watch beside him. My lady was an early riser; by eight o'clock, in answer to a message from me, she was with us herself in her dressing-gown. Master Francis was awake.

"O my lady!" I said, "I'd no thought of bringing you up so early, and you were late last night too." For they had had a long drive. "It was only that I dursn't take upon me to send for the doctor without asking."

"No, no, of course not," she said. And indeed that was a liberty my lady would not have been pleased with any one's taking. "Do you really think it necessary?"

The poor child was looking a little better just then, the pain was not so bad. He seemed quiet and dreamy-like, though his face was flushed and his eyes very bright.

"Auntie!" he said, smiling a very little; "how pretty you look!"

And so she did in her long white dressing-gown, with her lovely fair hair hanging about, for all the world like Miss Lally's.

I think myself the fever was on his brain a little already, else he would scarce have dared speak so to his aunt.

"AUNTIE!" HE SAID, SMILING A VERY LITTLE ; "HOW PRETTY YOU
LOOK!"—p. 110.

She took no notice, but drew me out of the room.

"What in the world's the matter with him?" she said, anxious and yet irritated at the same time. "Has he been doing anything foolish that can have made him ill?"

I shook my head.

"It's seldom one can tell how illness comes, but I feel sure the doctor should see him," I replied.

So he was sent for, and before the day was many hours older, there was little doubt left — though, as I said before, I tried for a bit to hope it was only a bad cold — that Master Francis was in for something very serious.

Almost from the first the doctor spoke of rheumatic fever. There was a sort of comfort in this, bad as it was — the comfort of knowing there was no infection to fear. It was a great comfort to Master Francis himself, whenever he felt the least bit easier, now and then to see his cousins for a minute or two at a time, without any risk to them. For one of his first questions to the doctor was whether his illness was anything the others could catch.

After that for a few days he was so bad that he could really think of nothing but how to bear the pain patiently. Then when he grew a shade better, he began about going to school.

"What was the day of the month? Would he be well, *quite* well, by the 20th, or whatever day school began? Uncle would be *so* disappointed if it had to be put off " — and so on, over and over again, till at last I had to speak, not only to the doctor, but to Sir Hulbert himself, about the way the boy was worrying in his mind.

The doctor tried to put him off by saying he was getting on famously, and such-like speeches. A few quiet words from Sir Hulbert had far more effect.

" My dear boy," he said gravely, " what you have to do is to try to get well and not fret yourself. If it is God's will that your going to school should be put off, you must not take it to heart. You're not in such a hurry to leave us as all that, are you? "

The last few words were spoken very kindly and he smiled as he said them. I was glad of it, for I had not thought his uncle quite as tender of the boy as he had used to be. They pleased Master Francis, I could see, and another thought came into his mind which helped to quiet him.

" Anyway, nurse," he said to me one day, " there'll be a good deal of expense saved if I don't go to school till Easter."

It never struck him that there are few things more expensive than illness, and as I had no idea till my lady told me that the term had to be paid for, whether he went to school or not, I was able to agree with him.

I was deeply sorry for my lady in those days. Some might be hard upon her, for not forgetting all else in thankfulness that the child's life was spared, and I know she tried to do so, but it was difficult. And when she spoke out to me one day, and told me about the schooling having to be paid all the same, I really did feel for her ; knowing through Mrs. Brent, as I have mentioned, all the past history of the troubles brought about by poor Master Francis's father.

"I hope he'll live to be a comfort to you yet, if I may say so, my lady, and I've a strong feeling that he will," I said (she reminded me of those words long after), "and in the meantime you may trust to Mrs. Brent and me to keep all expense down as much as possible, while seeing that Master Francis has all he needs. I'm sure we can manage without a sick-nurse now."

For there had been some talk of having one sent for from London, though in those days it was less done than seems the case now.

And after a while things began to mend. It was not a *very* bad attack, less so than we had feared at first. In about ten days' time Mrs. Brent and Susan the housemaid and I, who had taken it in turns to sit up all night, were able to go to bed as usual, only seeing to it that the fire was made up once in the night, so as to last on till morning, and the day's work grew steadily lighter.

Once they had finished their lessons, the little girls were always eager to keep their cousin company. He was only allowed to have them one at a time. Miss Bess used to take the first turn, but it was hard work for her, poor child, to keep still, though it grew easier for her when it got the length of his being able for reading aloud. But Miss Lally from the first was a perfect model of a little sick-nurse. Mouse was no word for her, so still and noiseless and yet so watchful was she, and if ever she was left in charge of giving him his medicine at a certain time, I could feel as sure as sure that it wouldn't be forgotten. When he was inclined to talk a little, she knew just how to manage him — how to amuse him without exciting him at all, and always to cheer him up.

The weather was unusually bad just then, though we did our best to prevent Master Francis feeling it, by keeping his room always at an even heat, but there were many days on which the young ladies couldn't get out. Altogether it was a trying time, and for no one more than for my lady.

I couldn't help thinking sometimes how different it would have been if Master Francis had been her own child, when the joy of his recovering would have made all other troubles seem nothing. I felt it both for her and for him, though I don't think he noticed it himself; and after all, now that I can look back on things having come so perfectly right, perhaps it is foolish to recall those shadows. Only it makes the pictures of their lives more true.

Through it all I could see my lady was trying her best to have none but kind and nice feelings.

"The doctor says that though Francis will really be almost as well as usual in three or four weeks from now, there can be no question of his going to school for ever so long — perhaps not at all this year."

"Dear, dear," I said. "But you won't have to go on paying for it all the same, my lady?"

She smiled at this.

"No, no, not quite so bad as that, only this one term, which is paid already. Sir Hulbert might have got off paying it if he had really explained how difficult it was. But that's just the sort of thing it would really be lowering for him to do," and she sighed. "The doctor says too," she went on again, "that by rights the boy should have a course of German baths, that might do him good for all his life; but how we *could* manage that I can't see, though Sir Hulbert is actually thinking of it. I doubt if he would think of it as much if it were for one of our own children," she added rather bitterly.

"He feels Master Francis a sort of charge, I suppose," I said, meaning to show my sympathy.

"He is a charge indeed," said his aunt. "And to think that all this time he might have been really improving at school."

I could say nothing more, but I did grieve that she couldn't take things in a different spirit.

"It's an ill wind that blows nobody any good."
Miss Lally had a fine time for her knitting just then,
with Master Francis out of the way. Of course if he
had been at school there would have been no difficulty, and she had planned to have his socks ready
to send him on his birthday, the end of March. Now
she had got on so fast — one sock finished and the
heel of the other turned, though not without many
sighs and even a few tears — that she hoped to have
them as a surprise the first day he came down to the
nursery.

"I'll have to begin working in the attic again,
after that," she said to me, "for I'm going to make
a pair for baby."

"That's to say if the weather gets warmer," I said
to her. "You certainly couldn't have sat up in the
attic these last few weeks, Miss Lally."

CHAPTER X.

THE NEW BABY.

THE weather did improve. The winter having
been so unusually severe was made up for, as I think
often happens, by a bright and early spring. By the
beginning of April Master Francis was able to be out
again, though of course only for a little in the middle
of the day, and we had to be very careful lest he
should catch the least cold. I was exceedingly glad,
really more glad than I can say, that his getting
well went through without any backcasts. For
himself he was really better than the doctor had
dared to hope, but as he began to move about more
freely I was grieved to see that the stiffness of his
leg seemed worse than before his illness. I don't think
it pained him much, at least he didn't complain.

In the meantime I thought it would be best to
say nothing about it, half hoping that he didn't
notice it himself, but I heard no talk of his going to
school.

I shall never forget one morning in April — it was
towards the end of the month, a most lovely sunny
morning it was, as I went up the winding staircase
leading to Master Francis's room in the tower. The

sunshine came pouring in through the narrow windows as brilliant as if it had been midsummer, and the songs of the birds outside seemed to tell how they were enjoying it, yet it was only half-past six! The little ladies below were all sleeping soundly, but Master Francis, I knew, always woke very early, and somehow I had a feeling that he must be the first to hear the good news.

As I knocked at the door I heard him moving inside. He had got up to open the window; the room seemed flooded with light as I went in. Master Francis was sitting up in bed reading, or learning some of his lessons more likely, for he was well enough now to have gone back to regular ways. He looked up very brightly.

"Isn't it a most beautiful morning, nurse?" he said. "The sunshine woke me even earlier than usual, so I'm looking over my Latin. Auntie doesn't mind my reading in bed in the morning. It isn't like at night with candles."

"No, of course not," I said. "But, Master Francis, I want you to leave off thinking about your lessons for a minute. I rather fancy you'll have a holiday to-day. I've got a piece of news for you! I wonder if you can guess what has happened?"

He opened his eyes wide in surprise.

"It must be something good," he said, "or you wouldn't look so pleased. What *can* it be? It can't be that Uncle Hulbert's got a lot of money."

"There are some things better than money," I said. "What would you think if a dear little baby boy had come in the night?"

His whole face flushed pink with pleasure.

"Nurse!" he said. "Is it really true? Oh! how pleased I am. Just the very thing auntie has wanted so — a little boy of her own. I may count him like a brother, mayn't I? Won't Bess and Lally be pleased! Do they know? Mayn't I get up at once, and when do you think I may see him?"

"Some time to-day, I hope," I answered. "No, the young ladies don't know yet. They're fast asleep. But I thought you'd like to know."

"How good of you!" he said. "I'm just *so* pleased that I don't know what to do."

What a morning of excitement it was, to be sure! The children were all half off their heads with delight. All, that is to say, except Miss Baby, who burst out crying in the middle of her breakfast, sobbing that she "wouldn't have no — something —" We couldn't make out what for ever so long, till we found it was her name she was crying about, as of course we were all talking of the new little brother as "the baby." We comforted her by saying that anyway he would not be "Miss Baby"; and perhaps from that it came about that her old name clung to her till she was quite a big girl, and almost from the first Master Bevil got his real name.

He was a great darling — so strong and hearty too

— and so handsome even as an infant. Everything seemed to go right with him from the very beginning.

"Surely," I often said to myself, " he will bring a blessing with him. And now that my lady's great wish has been granted, I do hope she will feel more trustful and less anxious."

I hoped too that she would now have happier feelings to poor Master Francis, especially when she saw his devotion to the baby boy. For of all the children I must say he was the one who loved the little creature the most.

And for a while all seemed tending in the right way, but when the baby was a few weeks old, I began to fear that something of the old trouble was in the air again. Fresh money difficulties happened about that time, though of course I didn't know exactly what they were. But it was easy to see that my lady was fretted, she was not one to hide anything she was feeling.

One day, it was in June, as far as I remember, my lady was in the nursery with Miss Lally and Miss Baby and the real baby. The two elder children were downstairs at their lessons with Sir Hulbert. Master Bevil was looking beautiful that afternoon. We had laid him down on a rug on the floor, and he was kicking and crowing as if he had been six months old, his little sisters chattering and laughing to him, while my lady sat by in the rocking-chair, looking for once as if she had thrown all her cares aside.

"He really is getting on beautifully," she said to me. "Doesn't he look a great big boy?"

I was rather glad of the remark, for it gave me a chance to say something that had been on my mind.

"We'll have to be thinking of short-coating him, before we know where we are, my lady," I said with a smile. "And there's another thing I've been thinking of. He's such a heavy boy to carry already, and as time gets on it would be a pity for our walks to be shortened in the fine weather. We had a beautiful basket for the donkey at Mrs. Wingate's, it was made so that even a little baby could lie quite comfortably in it."

"That would be very nice," my lady answered. "I'll speak to Sir Hulbert about it. Only —" and again a rather worried look came into her face. I could see that she had got back to the old thought, "everything costs money." "We must do something about it before long," she added.

Just then Miss Bess ran into the room, followed more slowly by her cousin.

"What are you talking about?" she said.

"About how dear fat baby is to go walks with us when he gets still fatter and heavier," said Miss Lally. "Poor nurse couldn't carry him so very far, you know, and mamma says perhaps —"

"Oh! nonsense," interrupted Miss Bess; "we'd carry him in turns, the darling."

My lady looked up quickly at this.

"Don't talk so foolishly, child," she said sharply. For, fond as she was of Miss Bess, she could put her down sometimes, and just now the little girl scarcely deserved it, it seemed to me. "I won't allow anything of that kind," she went on. "You are far too young, all of you — Francis especially, must never attempt to carry baby. Do you hear, children? Nurse, you must be strict about this."

"Certainly, my lady," I replied. "Master Francis and the young ladies have never done more than just hold Master Bevil in their arms for a moment, me standing close by."

Then they went on to talk about getting a basket for the donkey, which they were very much taken up about. I didn't notice at the time that Master Francis had only looked in for an instant and gone off again; but that evening at tea time, when Miss Bess and Miss Lally said something about old Jacob, Master Francis asked what they meant, which I remembered afterwards as showing that he had not heard his aunt's strict orders.

It was a week or two after that, that one lovely afternoon we all set out on a walk together. We had planned to go rather farther than we had yet been with the baby, resting here and there on the way, it was so warm and sunny and he was not *yet* so very heavy, of course.

All went well, and we found ourselves close to home again in nice time. For of course I knew that if we stayed out too long it would be only natural for my lady to be anxious.

"It's rather too soon to go in and it's such a beautiful afternoon," said Miss Bess as we were coming up the drive. "Do let us go into the little wood, for half an hour or so, nurse, and you might tell us a story."

The little wood skirts the drive at one side. It is a sweet place, in the early summer especially, so many wild flowers and ferns, and lots of squirrels overhead among the branches, and little rabbits scudding about down below.

We found a cosy nook, where we settled ourselves. The little brother was fast asleep, the three elder ones sat round me, while Miss Baby toddled off a little way, busy about some of her own funny little plays by herself, though well within sight.

I was in the middle of a long story of having been lost in the fir-woods at home as a child, when a loud scream made us all start, and looking up I saw to my alarm that Miss Baby was no longer to be seen.

"Dear, dear," I cried, jumping up in a fright. "She must have hurt herself. Here, Master Francis, hold the baby for a moment, don't get up;" and I put his little cousin down safely in his arms.

I meant him not to stir till I came back, but he didn't understand this. Miss Bess was already off after her little sister, and after a minute or two we found her, not hurt at all, but crying loudly at having fallen down and dirtied her frock in running away from what *she* called a "bear," coming out of the wood — most likely only a branch of a tree swaying about.

It took a little time to quiet her and to set her to rights again, and when we got back to the other children I was surprised to see that the baby was now in Miss Lally's arms, Master Francis kneeling beside them wiping something with his handkerchief.

"There's nothing wrong, I hope," I said, rather startled again.

"Oh no!" said Miss Lally. "It's only that little brother cried and Francie walked him up and down and somefing caught Francie's foot and he felled, but baby didn't fall. Francie held him tight, only a twig scratched baby's nose a tiny little bit. But he doesn't mind, he's laughing."

So he was, though sure enough there was a thin red line right across his plump little nose, and the least little mark of blood on the handkerchief with which his cousin had been tenderly dabbing it. Master Francis himself was so pale that I hadn't the heart to say more to him than just a word.

"I had meant you to sit still with him, my dear."

"But he cried so," said the boy.

However, there was no harm done, though I thought to myself I'd be more careful than ever, but unluckily just as we were within a few steps of the house whom should we see but my lady coming to meet us. I'm never one for hiding things, but I did wish she had not happened to come just then.

She noticed the scratch in a moment, as she stooped to kiss the baby, though really there was nothing to mind, seeing the dear child so rosy and happy looking.

"What's the matter with his nose?" she said quickly. "You haven't any pins about you, nurse, surely?"

Pins were not in my way, certainly, but I could have found it in my heart to wish I could own to one just then, for Master Francis started forward.

"Oh no! Aunt Helen," he said, "it was my fault. I was walking him about for a minute or two, while nurse went after Baby, and my foot slipt, but I only came down on my knees and *he* didn't fall. It was only a twig scratched his nose, a tiny bit."

My lady grew first red then white.

"He might have been killed," she said; and she caught the baby from me and kissed him over and over again. Then she turned to Master Francis, and I could see that she was doing her best to keep in her anger.

"Francis, how dared you, after what I said the other day so very strongly about your *never* carrying the baby? Your own sense might have told you you are not able to carry him, but besides that, what

I said makes it distinct disobedience. Nurse, did you *know* of it?"

"It was I myself gave Master Bevil to Master Francis to hold," I said, flurried like at my lady's displeasure. "I hadn't meant him to walk about with him."

"Of course not," said my lady. "There now, you see, Francis, double disobedience! I must speak to your uncle. Take back baby, nurse, he must have some *pomade divine* on his nose when he gets in;" and before any of us had time to speak again she had turned and hurried back to the house. My lady had always a quick way with her, pleased or displeased.

"She's gone to tell papa," said the young ladies, looking very distressed.

Master Francis was quite white and shaking like.

"Nurse," he said at last, when he had got voice enough to speak, "I really don't know what auntie meant about something she said the other day."

"O Franz! you can't have forgotten," said Miss Bess, who often spoke sharply when she was really very sorry. "Mamma did say most plainly that none of us were to carry baby about."

But the boy still looked quite puzzled, and when we talked it over, we were all satisfied that he hadn't been in the room at the time.

"I must try to put it right with my lady," I said, feeling that if any one had been to blame in the matter it was certainly me much more than Master Francis, for not having kept my eye better on Miss Baby in the wood.

But we were a very silent and rather sad party as we made our way back slowly to the house.

I couldn't see my lady till late that evening, and then, though I did my best, I didn't altogether succeed. She had already spoken to Sir Hulbert, and nothing would convince her that Master Francis had not heard at least some part of what she said.

Sir Hulbert was always calm and just; he sent for the boy the next morning, and had a long talk with him. Master Francis came back to the nursery looking pale and grave, but more thoughtful than unhappy.

"Uncle has been very good and kind," was all he said. "And I will try never to vex him and auntie again."

Later that evening, when he happened to be alone with me, after the young ladies had gone to bed, he said a little more. I was sitting by the fire with Master Bevil on my knee. Master Francis knelt down beside me and kissed the little creature tenderly. Then he stroked his tiny nose — the mark of the scratch had almost gone already.

"You darling!" he said. "Oh! how glad I am you weren't really hurt. Nurse," he went on, "I'd do anything for this baby, I do *love* him so. I only wish I could say it to auntie the way I can to you.

If only I were big and strong, or very clever, and could work for him, to get him everything he should have, and then it would make up a little for all the trouble I've been always to them."

He spoke quite simply. There wasn't a thought of himself — as if he had anything to complain of, or put up with, I mean — in what he said. But all the more it touched me very much, and I felt the tears come into my eye, but I wouldn't have Master Francis see it, and I began laughing and playing with the baby.

"See his dear little feet," I said. "They're almost the prettiest part of him. He kicks so, he wears out his little boots in no time. It would be nice if Miss Lally could knit some for him."

Master Francis looked surprised.

"Why," he said, "do you call those little white things boots? And are they made the same way as my socks? I've got them on now; aren't they splendid? I really think it was very clever of Lally."

CHAPTER XI.

IN DISGRACE AGAIN.

He held out one foot to be admired.

"Yes," I said, "they are very nice indeed, and Miss Lally was so patient about them. I'll have to think of some other knitting for her."

"O nurse!" said Master Francis quickly, then he stopped. "I must ask Lally first," he went on; and I heard him say, as if speaking to himself—"it would be nice to please auntie."

For a day or two after that I saw there was some mystery going on. Master Francis and Miss Lally were whispering together and looking very important, and one fine afternoon the secret was confided to me.

Miss Bess was out with her mamma, and Master Francis had disappeared when we came in from our walk, a rather short one that day. Suddenly, just as we were sitting down to tea, and I was wondering what had become of him, he hurried in, and threw a small soft white packet on to Miss Lally's lap.

"O Francie!" she said, "have you really got it?"

Then she undid the parcel and showed it to me; it was white wool.

"Francie has bought it with his own money," she said, "for me to knit a pair of boots for baby, and oh! nursie, will you show me how? They're to be a present from Francie and me; me the knitting and Francie the wool, and we want it to be quite a secret till they're ready. It's so warm now I can knit up in the attic. Won't mamma be pleased?"

"Certainly, my dear," I said. "I'll do my best to teach you. They'll be rather difficult, for we'll have to put in some fancy stitches, but I think you can manage it now."

Master Francis stood by, looking as interested and pleased as Miss Lally herself.

"That was all the wool Prideaux' daughter had," he said. "Do you think there'll be enough, nurse? She'll have some more in a few days."

"I doubt if there'll be enough," I said, "but I can tell better when we've got them begun."

Begun they were, that very evening. Miss Lally and Master Francis set to work to wind the wool, having first spent some time at an extra washing of their hands, for fear of soiling it in the very least.

"It's so beautifully white," said Miss Lally, "like it says in the Bible, isn't it, nursie? It would be a pity to dirty it."

Dear me! how happy those two were over their innocent secret, and how little I thought what would come of Master Bevil's white wool bootikins!

The knitting got on nicely, though there were

some difficulties in the way. The weather was getting warmer, and it is not easy for even little ladies to keep their hands quite spotlessly clean. The ball of wool had to be tied up in a little bag, as it would keep falling on the floor, and besides this, Miss Lally spread out a clean towel in the corner where she sat to work in the attic.

I gave Miss Bess a hint that there was a new secret and got her to promise not to tease the children, and she was really good about it, as was her way if she felt she was trusted. Altogether, for some little time things seemed to be going smoothly. Master Francis was most particular to do nothing that could in the least annoy his uncle and aunt, or could seem like disobedience to them.

After the long spell of fine weather, July set in with heavy rain. I had now been a whole year with the dear children. I remember saying so to them one morning when we were all at breakfast.

It was about a week since the baby's boots had been in hand. One was already finished, in great part by Miss Lally herself, though I had had to do a little to it in the evenings after they were all in bed, setting it right for her to go on with the next day.

With the wet weather there was less walking out, of course, and all the more time for the knitting. On the day I am speaking of the children came down from the attic in the afternoon with rather doleful faces.

"Nursie," said Miss Lally, "I have been getting on so nicely," and indeed I had not required to do more than glance at her work for two or three days. "I thought I would have had it ready for you to begin the lace part round the top, only, just fancy, the wool's done!"

"They'll have more at the shop by now," said Master Francis. "If only it would clear up I could go to the village for it."

"It may be finer to-morrow," I said, "but there's no chance of you going out to-day; even if it left off raining, the ground's far too wet for you with your rheumatism. Now, Miss Lally, my dear, don't you begin looking so doleful about it; you've got on far quicker than you could have expected."

She did look rather doleful all the same, and the worst of it was that though Master Francis would have given up anything for himself, he never could bear Miss Lally to be disappointed.

"I'm so much better now, nurse," he said. "I don't believe even going out in the rain would hurt me."

"It's *possible* it mightn't hurt you, but—" I was beginning, when I heard Master Bevil crying out in the other room. Miss Lally had now a little room of her own on the other side of the nursery, and we had saved enough of Miss Bess's chintz to smarten it up. This had been done some months ago. I hadn't too much time now, and the young girl who helped me was no hand at sewing at all. Off I hurried to the baby without finishing what I was saying to Master Francis, and indeed I never gave another thought to what he'd said about fetching the wool till tea-time came, and he didn't answer when we called him, thinking he was in his own room.

Just then, unluckily, my lady came up to the nursery to say good-bye to the children, or good-night rather, for she and Sir Hulbert were going to dine at Carris Court, which is a long drive from Treluan, and the roads were just then very heavy with the rain. She came in looking quite bright and cheery. I can see her now in her black lace dress — it was far from new — it was seldom my lady spent anything on herself — but it suited her beautifully, showing off her lovely hair and fair complexion. One little diamond star was her only ornament. I forget if I mentioned that as well as the strange disappearance of money at the death of old Sir David, a great many valuable family jewels, worth thousands of pounds, were also missing, so it was but little that Sir Hulbert had been able to give his wife, and what money she had of her own she wouldn't have spent in such ways, knowing from the first how things were with him.

She came in, as I said, looking so beautiful and bright that I felt grieved when almost in a moment her look changed.

"Where is Francis?" she asked quickly.

"He must be somewhere downstairs, my lady," I

said. "He's not in his room, but no doubt he'll be coming directly."

Esther, the nursery-maid, was just then coming in with some tea-cakes Mrs. Brent had sent us up.

"Go and look for Master Francis, and tell him to come at once," said my lady. "Surely he can't have gone out anywhere," she added to me; "it's pouring, besides he isn't allowed to go out without leave."

"He'd never think of such a thing," I said quickly, "after being so ill too." But even as I spoke the words, there came into my mind what the boy had said that afternoon, and I began to feel a little anxious, though of course I didn't let my lady see it, and I did my best to smooth things when Esther came back to say that he was nowhere to be found. It was little use, however, my lady began to be thoroughly put out.

She hurried off to Sir Hulbert, feeling both anxious and angry, and a good half-hour was spent in looking for the boy before Sir Hulbert could persuade her to start. He was vexed too, and no wonder, just when my lady had been looking so happy.

"Really," I thought to myself, "Master Francis is tiresome after all." And I was thankful when they at last drove off, there being no real cause for anxiety.

No sooner had the sound of the carriage-wheels died away than the nursery door opened and Master Francis burst in, looking for once like a regular pickle of a boy. His eyes bright and his cheeks rosy, though he was covered with mud from head to foot, his boots really not to be thought of as fit to come up a tidy staircase.

"Hurrah!" he cried, shaking a little parcel over his head. "I've got it, Lally. And I'm not a bit wet after all, nurse!"

"Oh no!" said Miss Bess, who did love to put in her word, "not at all. Quite nice and dry and tidy and fit to sit down to tea, after worrying mamma out of her wits and nearly stopping papa and her going to Carris."

Master Francis's face fell at once. I was sorry for him and yet that provoked I couldn't but join in with Miss Bess.

"Go upstairs to your room at once, Master Francis, and undress and get straight into your bed. I'll come up in a few minutes with some hot tea for you. How you could do such a thing close upon getting better of rheumatic fever, and the trouble and worry it gave, passes me! And considering, too, what I said to you this very afternoon."

"You didn't actually say I wasn't to go," he said quickly. "You know quite well why I went, and I'm not a *bit* wet really. I'm all muffled up in things to keep me dry. I'm nearly suffocating."

"All the worse," I said. "If you're overheated all the more certain you'll get a chill. Don't stand talking, go at once."

He went off, and I was beginning to pour out the tea, which had been kept back all this time, when, as I lifted the teapot in my hand I almost dropped it, nearly scalding Miss Baby who was sitting close by me, so startled was I by a sudden terrible scream from Miss Lally; and, as I have said before, anything like Miss Lally's screams I never did hear in any nursery. Besides which, once she was started, there was never any saying when she'd leave off.

"Now, whatever's the matter with you, my dear?" I said, but it was little use talking quietly to her. She only sobbed something about "poor Francie and nursie scolding him," and then went on with her screaming till I was obliged to put her in the other room by herself to get quiet.

Of all the party Miss Bess and Miss Baby were the only ones who did justice to Mrs. Brent's tea-cakes that evening. They did take Miss Lally's screaming fits quietly, I must say, which was a good thing, and even Master Bevil had strong nerves, I suppose, for he slept on sweetly through it all, poor dear. For myself, I was out and out upset for once, provoked and yet sorry too.

I went up to Master Francis and did the best I could for him to prevent his taking cold. He was as sorry as could be by this time, and he had really not meant to be disobedient, but though I was ready to believe him, I felt much afraid that this new scrape wouldn't be passed over very lightly by his uncle and aunt. After a while Miss Lally quieted down, partly, I think, because I promised her she might go up to her cousin if she would leave off crying, and the two passed the evening together very soberly and sadly, winding the fresh skein of white wool 'which had been the cause of all the trouble.

After all Master Francis did not take cold. He came down to breakfast the next morning looking pretty much as usual, though I could see he was uneasy in his mind. Miss Lally too was feeling rather ashamed of her screaming fit the night before, for she was growing a big girl now, old enough to understand that she should have more self-command. Altogether it was rather a silent nursery that morning, for Miss Bess was concerned for her cousin too.

I had quite meant to try to see my lady before anything was said to Master Francis. But she was tired and later of getting up than usual, and I didn't like to disturb her. Sir Hulbert, I found, had gone out early and would not be in till luncheon-time, so I hoped I would still have my chance.

I hardly saw the elder children till their dinner time. It was an extra long morning of lessons with Miss Kirstin, for it was still raining, and on wet days she sometimes helped them with what they had to learn by themselves.

The three hurried up together to make themselves tidy before going down to the dining-room, and I just saw them for a moment. Master Bevil was rather fractious, and I was feeling a little worried about him, so that what had happened the night before was not quite so fresh in my mind as it had been; but I did ask Miss Lally, who came to me to have her hair brushed, if she had seen her mamma, and if my lady was feeling rested.

"She's getting up for luncheon," was the child's answer, "but I haven't seen her. Mrs. Brent told us she was very tired last night. Mrs. Brent waited up to tell mamma Francie had come in."

After luncheon the two young ladies came up together. I looked past them anxiously for Master Francis.

"No," said Miss Lally, understanding my look, "he's not coming. He's gone to papa's room, and papa and mamma are both there."

My heart sank at the words.

"Mamma's coming up to see baby in a little while," said Miss Bess. "She was so tired, poor little mamma, she only woke in time to dress for luncheon, and papa said he was very glad."

Miss Lally came round and whispered to me.

"Nurse," she said, "may I go up to the attic? I want to knit a great lot to-day, and if I stayed down here mamma would see."

"Very well, my dear," I said. "Only be sure to come downstairs if you feel chilly."

There was really no reason, now that she had a

room of her own, for her ever to sit in the attic, but she had taken a fancy to it, I suppose, and off she went.

Miss Bess stood looking out of the window, in a rather idle way she had.

"Oh dear!" she said impatiently; "is it *never* going to leave off raining? I am so tired of not getting out."

"Get something to do, my dear," I said. "Then the time will pass more quickly. It won't stop raining for you watching it, you know. Weren't you saying something about the schoolroom books needing arranging, and that you hadn't had time to do them?"

Miss Bess was in a very giving-in mood.

"Very well," she said, moving off slowly. "I suppose I may as well do them. But I need somebody to help me; where's Lally?"

"Don't disturb her yet awhile, poor dear," I said. "She does so want to get on with the work I've told you about."

Miss Bess stood looking uncertain. Suddenly an idea struck her.

"May I have Baby then?" she asked. "She could hold up the books to me, and that's about all the help I need, really."

I saw no objection, and Miss Baby trotted off very proud, Miss Bess leading her by the hand.

The nursery seemed very quiet the next half-hour

or so, or maybe longer. I was beginning to wonder when my lady would be coming, and feeling glad that Master Bevil, who had just wakened up from a nice sleep, was looking quite like himself again before she saw him, when suddenly the door burst open and Master Francis looked in. He was not crying, but his face had the strained white look I could not bear to see on it.

"Is there no one here?" he said.

Somehow I didn't like to question him, grieved though I felt at things going wrong again.

"No," I replied. "Miss Bess is in the schoolroom with—" then it suddenly struck me that my lady might be coming in at any moment, and that it might be better for Master Francis not to be there. "Miss Lally," I went on quickly, "is at her knitting in the attic, if you like to go to her there."

He turned and went. Afterwards he told me that he caught sight of my lady coming along the passage as he left the room, and that he hurried upstairs to avoid her. He didn't find Miss Lally in the attic as he expected, but her knitting was there lying on the floor, thrown down hurriedly, and though she had not forgotten to spread out the clean towel as usual, in her haste she hadn't noticed that the newly-wound ball of white wool had rolled some distance away from the half-finished boot and the pins.

Afterwards I will tell what happened to Master Francis, up there by himself in the attic.

To make all clear, I may here explain why he had not found Miss Lally in her nook. The book-tidying in the schoolroom had gone on pretty well, but after a bit, though Miss Baby did her best, Miss Bess found the want of some one who could read the titles, and she ran upstairs to beg Miss Lally to come for a few minutes. The few minutes turned into an hour or more, for the young ladies, just like children as they were, came across some old favourites in their tidying, and began reading out bits here and there to each other. And then to please Miss Baby they made houses and castles of the books on the floor, which she thought a beautiful new game, so that Miss Lally forgot about her knitting, while feeling, so to say, at the back of her mind quite easy about it, thinking she had left it safely lying on the clean cloth.

They were both so much taken up with what they were about, that it never struck them to wonder what Master Francis was doing with himself all the afternoon.

My lady and I meanwhile were having a long talk in the nursery. It had been as I feared, Sir Hulbert having spoken most severely to the boy, and my lady having said some bitter things, which already she was repenting, more especially when I was able to explain that Master Francis had really not been so distinctly disobedient as had seemed the case.

" We must try and put it right again, I suppose,"

she said rather sadly, as she was leaving the room. " I wish I didn't take up things so hotly at the time, but I was really frightened as well as angry. Still Sir Hulbert would not have spoken so strongly if it hadn't been for me."

This was a great deal for my lady to say, and I felt honoured by her confidence. I began to be more hopeful again, and tried to set out the tea rather nicer than usual to cheer them up a little.

CHAPTER XII.

THE three young ladies came in together, Miss
Baby looking very important, but calling out for her
tea.

"It's quite ready, my dear," I said. "But where's
Master Francis?"

"*I* don't know," said Miss Bess. "I haven't seen
him all the afternoon."

I turned to Miss Lally.

"He went up to sit with you, my dear, in the
attic," I said.

"I didn't see him," said Miss Lally, and then she
explained how Miss Bess had fetched her down ever
so long ago. "I dare say Francie's in his own room,"
she went on. "I'll run up and see, and I'll look in
the attic too, for I left my work lying about."

She ran off.

"Nurse," said Miss Bess, "do you think Francis
got a very bad scolding? You saw him, didn't you?
Did he seem very unhappy?"

"I'm afraid so, my dear, but I think it will come
all right again. I've seen your mamma since, and

she quite sees now that he didn't really mean to be disobedient."

"I wish you had told mamma that before they spoke to Francis," said Miss Bess, who I must say was rather a Job's comforter sometimes.

We waited anxiously till we heard Miss Lally's footsteps returning. She ran in alone, looking rather troubled.

"He's not there, not in his own room, or the attic, or nowhere, but he must have been in the attic, for my work's gone."

A great fear came over me. Could the poor boy have run away in his misery at having again angered his uncle and aunt? for the look on his face had been strange, when he glanced in at the nursery door, asking for Miss Lally. Was he meaning perhaps to bid her good-bye before setting off in some wild way? And what she said of the knitting having gone made me still more uneasy. Had he perhaps taken it with him as a remembrance? for of all the queer mixtures of old-fashionedness and childishness that ever I came across, Master Francis was the strangest, though, as I have said, there was a good deal of this in all the children.

I got up at Miss Lally's words. Master Bevil was asleep, luckily.

"You go on with your tea, my dears, there's good children," I said. "I must see about Master Francis, he must be somewhere about the house. He'd never have thought of going out again in such weather," for it was pouring in torrents.

I went downstairs, asking everybody I met if they had seen him, but they all shook their heads, and at last, after searching through the library and the big drawing-rooms, and even more unlikely places, I got so frightened that I made bold to knock at Sir Hulbert's study door, where he was busy writing, my lady working beside him.

They had been talking of Master Francis just before I went in, and they were far more distressed than annoyed at my news, my lady growing quite pale.

"O Hulbert!" she exclaimed, "if he has run away it is my fault."

"Nonsense, Helen," he said, meaning to cheer her. "The boy has got sense and good feeling, he'd never risk making himself ill again. And where would he run away to? He couldn't go to sea. But certainly the sooner we find him the better."

He went off to speak to some of the men, while my lady and I, Mrs. Brent and some of the others, started again to search through the house. We did search, looking in really impossible corners, where he couldn't have squeezed himself in. Then the baby awoke, and I had to go to him, and Miss Bess and Miss Lally took their turn at this melancholy game of hide-and-seek, but it was all no use. The dull gray afternoon darkened into night, the rain still pouring down, and nothing was heard of the missing boy. Sir Hulbert at last left off pretending not to be anxious. He had his strongest horse put into the dog-cart, and drove away to the town to give notice to the police, stopping on the way at every place where it was the least likely the boy could have been seen.

He didn't get back till eleven o'clock. My lady and Mrs. Brent and me were waiting up for him, for Master Bevil was sleeping sweetly, and I had put the nursery-maid to watch beside him. The young ladies, poor dears, were in bed too, and, as is happily the way with children, had fallen asleep in spite of their tears and sad distress.

We knew the moment we saw Sir Hulbert that he had no good tidings to give us. His sunburnt face looked almost white, as he came into the hall soaking wet and shook his head.

"I have done everything, Nelly," he said, "everything that can be done, and now we must try to be patient till some news comes. It is impossible, everybody says, that a boy like him, so well known in the neighbourhood too, could disappear without some one seeing him, or that he could remain in hiding for long. It is perfectly extraordinary that we have not found him already, and somehow I can scarcely believe he is doing it on purpose. He has such good feeling, and must know how anxious we should be."

Sir Hulbert was standing by the fire, which my lady had had lighted in the hall, as he spoke. He seemed almost thinking aloud. My lady crept up to him with a look on her face I could not bear to see.

"Hulbert," she said in a low voice, "I said things to him enough to make him doubt our caring at all." And then she broke down into bitter though silent weeping.

We got her to bed with difficulty. There was really no use whatever in sitting up, and who knew what need for strength the next day might bring? Then there were the other poor children to think of. So by midnight the house was all quiet as usual. I was thankful that the wind had fallen, for all through the evening there had been sounds of wailing and sobbing, such as stormy weather always brings at Treluan, enough to make you miserable if there was nothing the matter — the rain pattering against the window like cold tiny hands, tapping and praying to be let in.

Sad as I was, and though I could scarcely have believed it of myself, I had scarcely laid my head down before I too, like the children, fell fast asleep. I was dreaming, a strange confused dream, which I never was able to remember clearly; but it was something about searching in the smugglers' caves for Master Francis, followed by an old man, who I somehow fancied was the miser baronet, Sir David. His hair was snow white, and there was a confusion

in my mind of thinking it like Miss Lally's wool.
Anyhow, I had got the idea of whiteness in my head,
so that, when something woke me — afterwards I
knew it was the sound of my own name — and I
opened my eyes to see by the glimmer of the night-
light what seemed at first a shining figure by my
bed-side, I did not feel surprised. And the first
words I said were "white as wool."

"No, no," said Miss Lally, for it was she, in her
little night-dress, her fair hair all tumbling over her
shoulders, "it isn't about my wool, nurse, please wake
up quite. It's something so strange — such a queer
noise. Please get up and come to my room to see
what it is."

Miss Lally's room was a tiny place at the side of
the nursery nearest the tower, though not opening
on to the tower stair.

I got up at once and crossed the day nursery with
her, lighting a candle on the way. But when we got
into her room all was perfectly silent.

"What was it you heard, my dear?" I asked.

"A sort of knocking," she said, "and a queer kind
of little cry, like a rabbit caught in a trap when you
hear it a long way off."

"It must have been the wind and rain again," I
was beginning to say, but she stopped me.

"Hush, listen!" she said, holding up her little
hand, "there it is again."

It was just as she had said, and it seemed to come
from the direction of the tower.

"Isn't it like as if it was from Francie's room?" said Miss Lally, shivering a little; "and yet we know he's not there, nursie."

But something was there, or close by, and something *living*, I seemed to feel.

"Put on your dressing-gown," I said to the little girl, "and your slippers, and we'll go up and see. You're not frightened, dear?"

"Oh no!" she said. "If only it was Francie!"

But she clung to my hand as we went up the stair, leaving the nursery door wide open, so as to hear Master Bevil if he woke up.

Master Francis's room was all dark, of course, and it struck very chill as we went in, the candle flickering as we pushed the door open. It seemed so strange to see the empty bed, and everything unused about the room, just as if he was really quite away. We stood perfectly still. All was silent. We were just about leaving the room to go to the attic when the faintest breath of a sound seemed to come again, I couldn't tell from where. It was more like a sigh in the air.

"Stop," said Miss Lally, squeezing my hand, and then again we heard the muffled taps, much more clearly than downstairs. Miss Lally's ears were very sharp.

"I hear talking," she whispered, and before I knew what she was about she had laid herself down on the floor and put her ear to the ground, at a part where there was no carpet. "Nursie," she went on, looking up with a very white face and shining eyes, "it is Francie. He must have felled through the floor. I can hear him saying, ' O Lally! O Bess! Oh, somebody come.' "

I stooped down as she had done. It was silent again; but after a moment began the knocking and a sort of sobbing cry; my ears weren't sharp enough to make it into words, but I seized the first thing that came to hand, I think it was the candlestick, and thumped it on the floor as hard as ever I could, calling out, close down through the boarding, "Master Francie, we hear you."

But there was nothing we could do by ourselves, and we were losing precious time.

"Miss Lally," I said, "you won't be frightened to stay here alone; I'll leave you the candle. Go on knocking and calling to him, to keep up his heart, in case he can hear, while I go for your papa."

In less time than it takes to tell it, I had roused Sir Hulbert and brought him back with me, my lady following after. Nothing would have kept her behind. We were met by eager words from Miss Lally.

"Papa, nursie," she cried, "I've made him hear, and I can make out that he says something about the window."

Without speaking Sir Hulbert strode across the room and flung it open. Oh, how thankful we were that the wind had fallen and all was still.

"Francis, my boy," we heard Sir Hulbert shout — he was leaning out as far as ever he could — "Francis, my boy, can you hear me?"

Something answered, but we inside the room couldn't distinguish what it said, but in another moment Sir Hulbert turned towards us.

"He says something about the cupboard in the attic," he said. "What can he mean? But come at once."

He caught up my lady's little hand-lamp and led the way, we three following. When we reached the attic he went straight to the big cupboard I have spoken of. The doors were standing wide open. Sir Hulbert went in, but came out again, looking rather blank.

"I can see nothing," he said. "I fancied he said the word 'mouse,' but his voice had got so faint."

"If you knock on the floor," I began, but Miss Lally stopped me by darting into the closet.

"Papa," she said, "hold the light here. I know where the mouse-hole is."

What they had thought a mouse-hole was really a hole with jagged edges cut out in one of the boards, which you could thrust your hand into. Sir Hulbert did so, beginning to see what it was meant for, and pulled. A trap-door, cleverly made, for all that it looked so roughly done, gave way, and by the light of the lamp we saw a kind of ladder leading downwards into the dark. Sir Hulbert stooped down and leaned over the edge.

"Francis," he called, and a very faint voice — we couldn't have heard it till the door was opened — answered —

"Yes, I'm here.   Take care, the ladder's broken."

Luckily there was another ladder in the attic. Sir Hulbert and I dragged it out, and managed to slip it down the hole, in the same direction as the other.   We were so afraid it would be too short, but it wasn't.   My lady and I held it steady at the top, while Sir Hulbert went down with the lamp, Miss Lally holding a candle beside us.

Sir Hulbert went down very slowly, not knowing how or in what state Master Francis might be lying at the foot.   Our hearts were beating like hammers, for all we were so quiet.

First we heard an exclamation of surprise.   I rather think it was "by Jove!" though Sir Hulbert was a most particular gentleman in his way of speaking — then came a hearty shout —

"All right, he's here, no bones broken."

"Shall I come down?" cried my lady.

"I think you may," Sir Hulbert answered, "if you're very careful.   I'll bring the light to the foot of the ladder again."

When my lady got down, Miss Lally and I strained our ears to hear.   I knew the child was quivering to go down herself, and it was like her to be so patient.

Strange were the words that first reached us.

"Auntie, auntie!" we heard Master Francis say, in

Sir Hulbert, holding Master Francis with one Arm and the Side of the Ladder with the other, followed. — p. 153.

his poor weak voice. "It's Old Sir David's treasure! You won't be poor any more. Oh! I'm so glad now I fell down the hole, but I thought I'd die before I could tell any one."

Miss Lally and I stared at each other. Could it be true? or was Master Francis off his head? We had not long to wait.

They managed to get him up — after all it was not so very far to climb, — my lady coming first with the lamp, and Sir Hulbert, holding Master Francis with one arm and the side of the ladder with the other, followed, for the boy had revived wonderfully, once he knew he was safe.

My lady was crying, I saw it the moment the light fell on her face, and as soon as Master Francis was up beside us, she threw her arms round him and kissed him as never before.

"Oh! my poor dear boy," she said, "I am so thankful, but do tell us how it all happened."

She must have heard, and indeed seen something of the strange discovery that had been made, but for the moment I don't think there was a thought in her heart except thankfulness that he was safe.

Before Master Francis could answer, Sir Hulbert interrupted.

"Better not ask him anything for a minute or two," he said. "Nurse, you will find my brandy-flask downstairs in the study. He'd better have a little mixed with water; and ring the bell as you pass to waken Crooks, and some one must light the fire in Francis's room."

I was back in five minutes with what was wanted; and then I found Miss Lally having her turn at petting her cousin. As soon as he had had a little brandy and water we took him down to the nursery, where the fire was still smouldering, Sir Hulbert carefully closing the trap-door as it had been before, and then following us downstairs.

Once in the nursery, anxious though we were to get him to bed, it was impossible not to let him tell something of what had happened. It began by a cry from Miss Lally.

" Why, Francie, you've got my knitting sticking out of your pocket. But two of the needles has dropped out," she went on rather dolefully.

" They'll be lying down in that room," said Master Francis. " I was carrying it in my hand when I went down the ladder after the ball of wool, and when I fell I dropped it, and I found it afterwards. It was the ball of wool that did it all," and then he went on to explain.

He had not found Miss Lally in the attic, for Miss Bess had already called her down, but seeing her knitting lying on the floor, he had sat down to wait for her, thinking she'd be sure to come back. Then he noticed that the ball of wool must have rolled away as she threw her work down, and disappeared into the cupboard. The door was wide open, and he traced it by the thread in his hand to the " mouse-hole " in the corner, down which it had dropped, and putting his hand through to see if he could feel it, to his surprise the board yielded. Pulling a little more, the trap-door opened, and he saw the steps leading downwards.

It was not dark in the secret room in the daytime, for it had two narrow slits of windows hardly to be noticed from the outside, so, with a boy's natural curiosity, he determined to go down. He hadn't strength to lift the trap-door fully back, but he managed to stick it open enough to let him pass through; he had not got down many steps, however, before he heard it bang to above him. The shock may have jarred the ladder, which was a roughly-made rotten old thing. Anyway, the next moment Master Francis felt it give way, and he fell several feet on to the floor below. He was bruised, and a little stunned for a few minutes, but he soon came quite to himself, and, still full of curiosity, began to look about him. The place where he was was only a sort of entrance to a larger room, which was really under his own bedroom, and lighted, as I have said, by narrow deep windows, without glass. And though there was no door between the two, the large room was on a much lower level, and another ladder led down to it. This time he was very careful, and got to the bottom without any accident.

Looking about him, he saw standing along one side of the room a collection of the queerest-shaped objects of all sizes that could be imagined, all wrapped up in some kind of linen or canvas, grown gray with age and dust.

CHAPTER XIII.

"OLD SIR DAVID'S" SECRET.

AT first he thought the queer-looking things he saw must be odd-shaped pieces of stone, or petrifactions, such as you see in old-fashioned rockeries in gardens sometimes. But when he went close up to them and touched one, he found that the covering was soft, though whatever was inside it was hard. He pulled the cloth off it, and saw to his surprise that it was a heavy silver tea-urn, though so black and discoloured that it looked more like copper or iron. He examined two or three other things, standing by near it; they also proved to be large pieces of plate — great heavy dinner-table centres, candelabra, and such things, — and, child though he was, Master Francis could see they must be of considerable value. But this was not what struck him the most. Like a flash of lightning it darted into his mind that there must be still more valuable things in this queer storeroom.

"I do believe," he said to himself, " that this is old Sir David's treasure ! "

He was right. It would take too long to describe how he went on examining into all these strange objects. Several, that looked like well-stuffed sacks, were tied up so tightly that he couldn't undo the cord. He made a little hole in one of them with his pocket-knife, and out rolled, to his delight, ever so many gold pieces!

"Then," said Master Francis to us, "I really felt as if I could have jumped with joy; but I thought I'd better fetch Uncle Hulbert before I poked about any more, and I went up the short ladder again, meaning to go back the way I'd come. I had never thought till that minute that I couldn't manage it, but the long ladder was broken away so high above my head that I couldn't possibly reach up to it, and the bits of it that had fallen on to the floor were quite rotten. And the trap-door seemed so close shut, that I was afraid no one would hear me however I shouted."

He did shout though, poor boy; it was the only thing he could do. The short ladder was a fixture and he couldn't move it from its place, even if it had been long enough to be of any use. After a while he got so tired of calling out, that he seemed to have no voice left, and I think he must have fallen into a sort of doze, for the next thing he remembered was waking up to find that it was quite dark. Then he began to feel terribly frightened, and to think that perhaps he would be left there to die of hunger.

"And the worst of it was," he said in his simple way, "that nobody would ever have known of the treasure."

He called out again from time to time, and then a new idea struck him. He felt about for a bit of wood on the floor and set to work, knocking as hard as he could. Most likely he fell asleep by fits and starts, waking up every now and then to knock and call out again, and when the house was all shut up and silent for the night, of course the sound he made seemed much louder, only unluckily we were all asleep and might never have heard it except for dear little Miss Lally.

It was not till after Master Francis caught the sound of our knocking back in reply that it came into his head to make his way close up to the windows —luckily it was not a very dark night—and call through them, for there was no glass in them, as I have said. If he had done that before it is just possible we might have heard him sooner, as in our searching we had been in and out of his room, above where he was, several times.

There is not much more for me to tell. Master Francis was ill enough to have to stay in bed for a day or two, and at first we were a little afraid that the cold and the terror, and the strange excitement altogether, might bring on another illness. But it was not so. I think he was really too happy to fall ill again!

In a day or two Sir Hulbert was able to tell him all about the discovery. It was kept quite secret till the family lawyer could be sent for, and then he and my lady and Sir Hulbert all went down through the trap-door again with Mr. Crooks, the butler, to help them, and everything was opened out and examined. It was a real miser's hoard.

Besides the plate, which was really the least valuable, for it was so clumsy and heavy that a good deal of it was only fit to be melted down, there were five or six sacks filled with gold and some with silver coin. Of course something was lost upon it with its being so old, but taking it all in all, a very large sum was realised, for a great many of the Penrose diamonds had been hidden away also, *some* of which — the most valuable, though not the most beautiful — were sold.

Altogether, though it didn't make Sir Hulbert into a millionaire, it made him a rich man, as rich, I think, as he cared to be. And, strangely enough, as the old proverb has it, "it never rains but it pours," only two or three years after, money came to my lady which she had never expected. So that to any one visiting Treluan, as it now is, and seeing all that has been done by the family, not only for themselves, but for those about them, — the church, the schools, the cottages on the estate being perfect models of their kind — it would be difficult to believe there had ever been want of money to be wisely and generously spent.

Dear, dear, how many years ago it all is now! There's not many living, if any, to remember the ins and outs as I do, which is indeed my excuse for having put it down in my own way.

Miss Bess, — Miss Penrose, as I should say, — Miss Lalage, and even Miss Augusta have been married this many a day; and Lady Helen, Miss Bess's eldest daughter, is sixteen past, and it is she that has promised to look over my writing and correct it.

Master Bevil, Sir Bevil now, for Sir Hulbert did not live to be an old man, has two fine boys of his own, whom I took care of from their babyhood, as I did their father, and I'm feeling quite lost since Master Ramsey has gone to school.

And of dear Master Francis. What words can I say that would be enough? He is the only one of the flock that has not married, and yet who could be happier than he is? He never thinks of himself, his whole life has been given to the noblest work. His writings, I am told, though they're too learned for my old head, have made him a name far and wide. And all this he has done in spite of delicate health and frequent suffering. He seems older than his years, and Sir Bevil is in hopes that before long he may persuade his cousin to give up his hard London parish and make his regular home where he is so longed for, in Treluan itself, as our vicar, and indeed I pray that it may be so while I am still here to see it.

Above all, for my dear lady's sake. I scarcely like to own to myself that she is beginning to fail, for though I speak of myself as an old woman and feel it is true, yet I can't bear to think that her years are running near to the appointed threescore and ten, for she is nine years older than I. She has certainly never been the same, and no wonder, since Sir Hulbert's death, but she has had many comforts, and almost the greatest of them has been, as I think I have said before, Master Francis.

*   *   *   *   *   *   *

Mother and my aunts want me to add on a few words of my own to dear old nurse's story. She gave it me to read and correct here and there, more than a year ago, and I meant to have done so at once. But for some months past I hardly felt as if I had the heart to undertake it, especially as I didn't like bringing back the remembrance of their old childish days to mother and my aunts, or to Uncle Bevil and Uncle Francis, as we always call him, just in the first freshness of their grief at dear grandmamma's death. And I needed to ask them a few things to make the narrative quite clear for any who may ever care to read it.

But now that the spring has come back again, making us all feel bright and hopeful (we have all been at Treluan together for Uncle Bevil's birthday), I have enjoyed doing it, and they all tell me that they have enjoyed hearing about the story and answering my questions.

Dear grandmamma loved the spring so! She was so gentle and sweet, though she never lost her quick eager way either. And though she died last year, just before the daffodils and primroses were coming out, somehow this spring the sight of them again has not made us feel sad about her, but *happy* in the best way of all.

Perhaps I should have said before that I am "Nelly," "Miss Bess's" eldest daughter. Aunt Lalage has only one daughter, who is named after mother, and *I* think very like what mother must have been at her age.

There are five of *us*, and Aunt Augusta has two boys, like Uncle Bevil.

What used to be "the secret room," where our miser ancestor kept the hoard so strangely discovered, has been joined, by taking down the ceiling, to what in the old days was Uncle Francis's room, and enters from a door lower down the tower stair, and Uncle Bevil's boys have made it into what they call their "Museum." We are all very fond of showing it to visitors, and explaining how it used to be, and telling the whole story. Uncle Francis always maintains that Aunt Lally saved his life, and though she gets very red when he says so, I do think it is true. She really was very brave for such a little girl. If I heard knockings in the night, I am afraid I should hide my head under the clothes, and put my fingers in my ears.

Uncle Francis and Aunt Lally always do seem almost more brother and sister to each other than any of the rest; and her husband, Uncle Geoffrey, whom next to Uncle Francis I think I like best of all my uncles, was one of *his* — I mean Uncle Francis's; what a confusion I'm getting into — best friends at college.

When I began this, after correcting nurse's manuscript, I thought nothing would be easier than to write a story in the most beautiful language, but I find it so much harder than I expected that I am not sorry to think that there is really nothing more of importance to tell. And I must say my admiration for the way in which nurse has performed *her* task has increased exceedingly!

THE END.

" 'What is the matter, little girls?' said the lady."

LITTLE MISS
PEGGY:
ONLY A NURSERY STORY
BY
MRS: MOLESWORTH
WITH PICTURES BY
WALTER CRANE
LONDON:
MACMILLAN & CO.
1893

First Edition printed (Crown 8vo) 1887.
Reprinted (Globe 8vo) 1888, 1891.

𝔗𝔬 𝔱𝔥𝔢 𝔐𝔢𝔪𝔬𝔯𝔶 𝔬𝔣

E. L.

THE DEAR YOUNG FRIEND

WHO SUGGESTED ITS NAME TO THIS LITTLE STORY

AND FROM WHOSE LATE HOME

SO INTIMATELY ASSOCIATED WITH HER

THIS DEDICATION IS MADE

BINDON, August, 1887

" Would I could paint the serious brow,
  The eyes that look the world in face,
Half-questioning, doubting, wondering how
  This happens thus, or that finds place."

— My Opposite Neighbour.

" - Baby, who required a great deal of room to himself at table, baby though he was. He had so many things to do during a meal,

you see, which grown-up children think quite unnecessary. He had to drum with a spoon first in one fat hand and then in the other; he had to dip his crust first in nurse's cup of tea and next in Hal's jug of milk to see which tasted best, and there would have been no fun in doing either if he hadn't had to stretch a long way across; and besides all this he felt really obliged now and then to put his feet up on the table for a change, one at a time, of course."

PEGGY: A NURSERY STORY.

CHAPTER I.

A BREAKFAST PARTY.

"No," said Peggy to herself, with a little sigh, "the naughty clouds has covered it up to-day. I can't see it."

"Miss Peggy," came nurse's voice from the other side of the room, "your breakfast's waiting. Come to the table, my dear, and stand quiet while Master Thor says the grace."

Nurse spoke kindly, but she meant what she said. Peggy turned slowly from the window and took her place among her brothers. She, and Thorold and Terence, the two oldest boys, sat opposite nurse, and beside nurse was Baby, who required a great deal of room to himself at table, baby though he was. He had so many things to do during the meal, you see, which grown-up children think quite unnecessary. He had to drum with a spoon, first in one fat hand and then in the other; he had to dip his crust first in nurse's cup of tea and next in Hal's jug of milk to see which tasted best, and there would have been no fun in doing either if he hadn't had to stretch a long way across; and besides all this he felt really obliged now and then to put his feet upon the table for a change, one at a time, of course. For even he, clever as he was, could not have got both together out of the bars of his chair without toppling over. Nurse had for some time past been speaking about beginning "to break Master Baby in," but so far it had not got beyond speaking, and she contented herself with seating him beside her and giving him a good quarter of the table to himself, the only objection to which was that it gave things in general a rather lopsided appearance.

At the two ends sat Baldwin and Hal. Hal's real name, of course, was Henry, though he was never called by it. Baldwin, on the contrary, had no short name, partly perhaps because mamma thought " Baldie " sounded so ugly, and partly because there was something about Baldwin himself which made one not inclined to shorten his name. It suited him so well, for he was broad and comfortable and slow. He was never in a hurry, and he gave you the feeling that you needn't be in a hurry either. There was plenty of time for everything, for saying the whole of his name as well as for everything else.

That made a lot of brothers, didn't it? Five,

counting baby, and to match them, or rather not to match them — for five and one are not a match at all — only one little girl! She wondered about it a good deal, when she had nothing else more interesting to wonder about. It seemed so very badly managed that she should have five brothers, and that the five brothers should only have one sister each. It wasn't always so, she knew. The children at the back had plenty of both brothers and sisters; she had found that out already. But I must not begin just yet about the children at the back; you will hear about them in good time.

There was a nice bowl of bread-and-milk at each child's place, and as bread-and-milk is much better hot than cold, it was generally eaten up quickly. But this morning, even after the grace was said, and the four brothers who weren't baby had got on very well with theirs, Peggy sat, spoon in hand, gazing before her and not eating at all.

"What's the matter, Miss Peggy?" said nurse, when she had at last made Baby understand that he really *wasn't* to try to put his toes into her tea-cup, which had struck him suddenly as a very beautiful thing to do; "you've not begun to eat. Are you waiting for the sugar or the salt, or can't you fix which you want this morning?"

For there was a very nice and interesting rule in that nursery that every morning each child might choose whether he or she would have salt or sugar in the bread-and-milk. The only thing was that they had to be quick about choosing, and that was not always very easy.

Peggy looked up when nurse spoke to her.

"Peggy wasn't 'toosing," she said. Then she grew a little red. "*I* wasn't 'toosing," she went on. For Peggy was five — five a good while ago — and she wanted to leave off baby ways of talking. "I was wondering."

"Well, eat your breakfast, and when you've got half-way down the bowl you can tell us what you were wondering about," said nurse.

Peggy's spoon, already laden, continued its journey to her mouth. But when it got there, and its contents were safely deposited between her two red lips, she gave a little cry.

"Oh!" she said, "it doesn't taste good. There's no salt or sugar."

"'Cos you didn't put any in, you silly girl," said Thor. "I saw, but I thought it'd be a good lesson. People shouldn't wonder when they're eating."

"Peggy wasn't eating; she was only going to eat," said Terry. "Never mind, Peg-top. Thor shan't tease you. Which'll you have? Say quick," and he pulled forward the sugar-basin and the salt-cellar in front of his sister.

"Sugar, pelease," said Peggy. "It's so told this morning."

At this Thor burst out laughing.

"What a Peggy-speech," he said. "Sugar's no warmer than salt."

"Yes," said Baldwin, solemnly, from the other end of the table. "'Tis. There's sugar in toffee and in jam, and they're hot, leastwise they're hot to be made. And there's salt in ices, for mamma said they're made with salt."

"What rubbish!" said Thor. "Nurse, isn't it rubbish? And when did you ever see ices, I'd like to know, Baldwin?"

"I did," Baldwin maintained. "Onst. But I'll not tell you when, if you say rubbish."

"It is rubbish all the same, and I'll prove it," said Thor. "You know that nice smooth white sugar on the top of bridescake?—well, they ice that to put it on—I know they do. Don't they, nurse?"

"They call it icing, to be sure," nurse replied. "But that's no proof that ices themselves mayn't be made with salt, Master Thor, for when you come to think of it, ices have sugar in them."

"To be sure they have," Thor cried, triumphantly. "Nurse has proved it—that sugar's no warmer than salt," which was not what nurse had intended to say at all.

But now Peggy, who all this time had been steadily eating, looked up again.

"Peggy was wondering," she said, "what's clouds. Is clouds alive?"

Thor was all ready with his "you silly girl" again, but this time Terry was before him.

"They can't be alive," he said. "They've got no hands, or feet, or mouths, and noses, and eyes, and—"

"They *has* noses," said Peggy, eagerly. "Peggy's seen them, and they has wings — the little ones has wings, they fly so fast. And p'raps they has got proper faces on their other sides, to look at the sun with. I've seen shiny bits of the other sides turned over."

"Yes," said Baldwin, solemnly again, as if that settled it, "so has I."

"But they're not alive, Peggy, they're really not. They fly because the wind blows them," said Terence.

"Oh!" said Peggy, with a deep-drawn breath, "I see. Then if we all blowed very hard at the window, if we all blowed together, couldn't we blow them away? I do so want to blow them away when they come over my hills."

But when she had said this she grew very red, just as if she had told something she had not meant to tell, and if any one had looked at her quite close they would have seen that there were tears in her eyes. Fortunately, however, no one had noticed her last words, for Thorold and Terence too had burst out laughing at the beginning of her speech.

"Fancy us all blowing out of the window together," they said. And they began puffing out their cheeks and pretending to blow very hard, which made them look so funny that Peggy herself burst out laughing too.

"I'll tell you what," said Thor, when they were tired of laughing, "that reminds me of soap-bubbles, we haven't had any for such a time. Nurse, will you remember to let us have them the first wet half-holiday? Mamma'll let us if you will."

"And the pipes?" said nurse. "There was six new got the last time, and they were to last, certain sure till the next time, and then —"

"Oh I know," said Thor, "we took them to school and never brought them back. Never mind — we'll get some more from old Mother Whelan. She always keeps lots. We'll keep our halfpennies for two Saturdays — that'll do. But we must be going, Terry and Baldwin. *I'm* all ready."

And he jumped up as he spoke, and pulled his satchel of books from under his chair, where he had put them to be all ready. Baldwin slowly got down from his place, for he was not only broad, but his legs were very short, and came up to nurse to be helped on with his little overcoat, while Terence began rushing about the room in a fuss, looking for one of his books, which as usual couldn't be found at the last minute.

"I had it just before breakfast, I'm *sure* I had," he went on repeating. "I haven't finished learning it, and I meant to look it over. Oh dear, what shall I do?"

The nursery party was too accustomed to Terry's misfortunes to be much upset by them. Peggy sat still for a moment or two considering. Then she spoke.

"Terry," she said, "look in Baby's cot."

Off flew Terence, returning in triumph, grammar in hand.

"I'll learn it on the way to school. How did you know it was there, Peggy?"

"I sawed you reaching over to kiss Baby when you comed in to ask nurse for a new shoe-lace this morning," said Peggy, with great pride.

"Good girl," said Terence, as he slammed the door and rushed downstairs to overtake his two brothers.

The nursery seemed very quiet when the three big boys had gone. Quiet but not idle; there was always a great deal to do first thing of a morning, and Peggy had her own share of the doing to see to. She took off her own breakfast pinafore and put on a quite clean one — one that looked quite clean anyway, just as if it had never been on, even though it had really been used two or three times. Peggy called it her "prayers pinafore," and it always lasted a whole week, as it was only worn to go down to the dining-room for five or ten minutes. Then she washed her hands and stood still for nurse to give a tidying touch to her soft fair hair, though it really didn't need it, — Peggy's hair never looked messy, —

and then she took off Hal's over pinafore which he wore on the top of his blouse at meal times, and helped him to wash his hands, by which time nurse and baby were also ready, and the little procession set off on their journey. If the prayers bell had not sounded yet, or did not sound as they made their way down, nurse would stop at mamma's door and tap, and the answer was sure to be "Come in." Then nurse would go on downstairs with Baby, and Peggy and Hal would trot in to see mamma, and wait a moment or two till she was ready. She was almost always nearly ready, unless she was very, very tired; and in that case she would tell them to go downstairs and come up and see her again after prayers, as she was going to have breakfast in bed. They rather liked these days, though of course they were sorry for mamma to be so tired, but it was very interesting to watch her having her breakfast, and generally one or two dainty bits of toast and marmalade would find their way to the two little mouths.

It was only since last winter that mamma had been so often tired and not able to get up early. Before then she used always to come up to the nursery to see her six children at breakfast, and prayers were early enough for the three boys to stay for them, instead of having them at school. For mamma was not at all a "lazy" mother, as you might think if I did not explain. But last winter she had been very ill indeed, so ill that papa looked dreadfully unhappy, and the boys had to take off their boots downstairs so as not to make any noise when they passed her door, and the days seemed very long to Peggy and Hal, worst to Peggy of course, for Hal was still so little that almost all his life belonged to the nursery. It was during that time that Peggy first found out the white spot on the hill, which I am going to tell you about, for she used to climb up on the window-sill and sit there looking out at whatever there was to see for hours at a time.

This morning mamma was evidently not tired, for just as the children got to the landing on to which her door opened, out she came.

"Well, darlings," she said, "there you are! Have the boys got off to school all rightly, nurse?"

"Oh yes, ma'am," nurse was beginning, but Peggy interrupted her.

"Terry loosed his book, mamma dear, and Peg — *I* founded it; I knewed where it was 'cos I used my eyes like you said."

"That was a very good thing," said mamma. She had talked to Peggy about using her eyes a good deal, for Peggy had rather a trick of going to sleep with her eyes open, like many children, and it becomes a very tiresome trick if it isn't cured, and makes one miss a great many chances of being useful to others, and of enjoying pleasant things one's self. "Poor Terry — I wish he wasn't so careless. Where was his book this time?"

"In such a funny place, mamma dear," said Peggy. "In Baby's cot," and at the sound of his name Baby crowed, which made both Peggy and Hal burst out laughing, so that mamma had to hold their hands firmly to prevent their tumbling down stairs.

After prayers were over nurse took Baby and Hal away, but papa said Peggy might stay for a few minutes.

"I've scarcely seen you the last day or two, old woman," he said; "you were fast asleep when I came home. What have you been about?"

"About," Peggy repeated, looking puzzled.

"Well — what have you been doing with yourself?" he said again.

"I've been doing nothing with *myself*," Peggy replied, gravely. "I've done my lessons and my sewing, and I've used my eyes."

"Well, and isn't all that yourself?" asked papa, who was rather a tease. "You've done your sewing with your fingers and your lessons with your mind, and you've used your eyes for both — mind, fingers, eyes — those are all parts of yourself."

Peggy spread out her two hands on the table and looked at the ten pink fingers.

"Them's my fingers," she said, "but I don't know where that other thing is — that what thinks. I'd like to know where it is. Papa, can't you tell me?"

There came a puzzled look into her soft gray

eyes — mamma knew that look; when it stayed long it was rather apt to turn into tears.

"Arthur," she said to Peggy's papa, "you're too fond of teasing. Peggy dear, nobody can see that part of you; there are many things we can't ever see, or hear, or touch, which are real things all the same."

Peggy's face lightened up again. She nodded her head softly, as if to say that she understood. Then she got down from her chair and went up to her father to kiss him and say good-bye.

"Going already, Peg!" he said. "Don't you like papa teasing you?"

"I don't mind," said Peggy, graciously; "you're only a big boy, papa. I'm going 'cos nurse wants me to keep Baby quiet while she makes the beds."

But when she got round to the other side of the table to her mother, she lingered a moment.

"Mamma," she whispered, "*it's* not there this morning — Peggy's fairy house. It's all hided up. Mamma — "

"Well, darling?"

"Are you *sure* it'll come back again?"

"Quite sure, dear. It's only hidden by the clouds, as I've told you before. You know you've often been afraid it was gone, and it's always come again."

"Yes, to be sure," said Peggy. "What a silly little girl I am, mamma dear."

And she laughed her own little gentle laugh. I

can't tell how it was that Peggy's little laugh used sometimes to bring tears to her mother's eyes.

When she got up to the nursery again she found she was very much wanted. Nurse was in the night nursery which opened into the day one, and looked out to the back of the house just as the other looked to the front. And Baby was sitting on the hearth-rug, with Hal beside him, both seeming far from happy.

" Baby's defful c'oss, Peggy," said poor Hal.

And Baby, though he couldn't speak, pouted out his lips and looked very savage at Hal, which of course was very unreasonable and ungrateful of him, as Hal had been doing everything he could to amuse him, and had only objected to Baby pulling him across the floor by his curls.

"Oh Baby," said Peggy, "that isn't good. Poor Hal's hair — see how you've tugged it."

For Baby was still grasping some golden threads in his plump fists.

" Him sinks zem's feaders," said Hal, apologeti-cally. He was so fond of Baby that he couldn't bear any one to say anything against him except himself.

" But Baby must learn hairs isn't feathers," said Peggy, solemnly. " And it isn't good to let him pull the feathers out of his parrot either, Hal," she con-tinued, " for some day he might have a *live* parrot, and then it would be cooel, and the parrot would *bite* him — yes it would, Baby."

This was too much for Baby. He drew the corner of his mouth down, then he opened it wide, very wide, and was just going to roar when Peggy threw her arms round him and kissed him vigorously.

"He's sorry, Hal—dear Baby—he's so very sorry. Kiss him, Hal. Let's all kiss together," and the three soft faces all met in a bunch, which Baby found so amusing that instead of continuing his preparations for a good cry, he thought better of it, and went off into a laugh.

"That's right," said Peggy. "Now if you'll both be very good boys I'll tell you a story. Just wait a minute till I've tooked off my prayers pinafore."

She jumped up to do so. While she was unfastening it her eyes moved to the window; she gave a little cry and ran forward. The day was clearing up, the sun was beginning faintly to shine, and the clouds were breaking.

"Mamma was right," exclaimed Peggy, joyfully; "I can see it—I can see it! I can see my white house again, my dear little fairy house."

She would have stayed there gazing out contentedly half the morning if her little brothers had not called her back.

"Peggy," said Hal, plaintively, "do tum. Baby's pulling Hal's 'air adain."

"Peggy's coming, dear," said the motherly little voice.

And in another moment they were settled on the

"And in another moment they were settled on the hearth-rug— Baby on Peggy's lap— on, and off it too, for it was much too small to accomodate the whole of him; Hal on the floor beside her, his curly head leaning on his sisters shoulder in blissful and trustful content "

p. 14

CHAPTER II.

THE WHITE SPOT ON THE HILL.

> "O reader! had you in your mind
> Such stores as silent thought can bring,
> O gentle reader! you would find
> A tale in everything.
> What more I have to say is short,
> And you must kindly take it:
> It is no tale; but, should you think,
> Perhaps a tale you'll make it."
>
> W. WORDSWORTH.

"TELLING stories," when the teller is only five and some months old, and the hearers one and a quarter and three, is rather a curious performance. But Peggy was well used to it, and when in good spirits quite able to battle with the difficulties of amusing Hal and Baby at the same time. And these difficulties were not small, for, compared with Baby, Hal was really "grown-up."

It is all very well for people who don't know much about tiny children to speak of them all together, up to — six or seven, let us say — as "babies," but we who think we *do* know something about them, can assure the rest of the world that this is an immense mistake. One year in nursery arithmetic counts for ten or even more in *real* "grown-up" life. There was a great difference between Peggy and Hal for instance, but a still greater between Hal and Baby, and had there been a new baby below him again, of course it would have been the greatest of all. Peggy could not have explained this in words, but she knew it thoroughly all the same, and she had learnt to take it into account in her treatment of the two, especially in her stories telling. In reality the story itself was all for Hal, but there was a sort of running accompaniment for Baby which he enjoyed very much, and which, to tell the truth, I rather think Hal found amusing too, though he pretended it was for Baby's sake.

This morning her glance out of the window had made Peggy feel so happy that the story promised to be a great success. She sat still for a minute or two, her arms clasped round Baby's waist, gently rocking herself and him to and fro, while her gray eyes stared before her, as if reading stories in the carpet or on the wall.

" Peggy," said Hal at last, giving her a hug — he had been waiting what he thought a very long time — " Peggy, do on — no, I mean begin, p'ease."

" Yes, Hal, d'reckly," said Peggy. " It's coming, Hal, yes, now I think it's comed. Should we do piggies first, to please Baby before we begin?"

" Piggies is *so* silly," said Hal, disdainfully.

" Well, we'll kiss him instead — another kiss all together, he does so like that;" and when the kissing was over — "now, Baby dear, listen, and p'raps you'll understand *some*, and if you're good we'll have piggies soon."

Baby gave a kind of grunt; perhaps he was thinking of the pigs, but most likely it was just his way of saying he would be very good.

"There was onst," Peggy began, "a little girl who lived in a big house all by herself."

"Hadn't she no mamma, or nurse, or — or — brudders?" Hal interrupted.

"No, not none," Peggy went on. "She lived quite alone, and she didn't like it. The house was as big as a — as a church, and she hadn't no bed, and no chairs or tables, and there was very, *very* high stairs."

"Is there stairs in churches?" asked Hal.

Peggy looked rather puzzled.

"Yes, I think there is," she said. "There's people high up in churches, so there must be stairs. But I didn't say it *were* a church, Hal; I only said as big as a church. And the stairs was for Baby — you'll hear — p'raps there wasn't *reelly* stairs. Now, Baby, one day a little piggy-wiggy came up the stairs — one, two, three," and Peggy's hand came creeping up Baby's foot and leg and across his pinafore and up his bare arm again, by way of illustrating piggy's progress, "and when he got to the top he said 'grumph,' and poked his nose into the little girl's neck" — here Peggy's own nose made a dive among

Baby's double chins, to his exceeding delight, setting him off chuckling to himself for some time, which left Peggy free to go on with the serious part of the story for Hal's benefit — "and there was a window in the big house, and the little girl used to sit there always looking out."

"Always?" asked Hal again. "All night too? Didn't her ever go to bed?"

"She hadn't no bed, I told you. No, she didn't sit there all night, 'cos she couldn't have see'd in the dark. Never mind about the night. She sat there all day, always looking out, 'cos there was something she liked to see. If I tell you you won't tell nobody what it was, will you, Hal?"

Hal looked very mystified, but replied obediently,

"No, won't tell nobody," he said.

"Well, then, I'll tell you what it was. It was a —" But at this moment Baby, having had enough of his own meditations, began to put in a claim to some special attention. The piggy had to be summoned and made to run up and down stairs two or three times before he would be satisfied and allow Peggy to proceed.

"Well, Peggy?" said Hal eagerly.

"It was a —" Oh dear, interrupted again! But this time the interruption was a blessing in disguise. It was nurse come to fetch Baby for his morning sleep.

"And thank you, Miss Peggy, my dear, for keeping him so nice and good. I heard you come up, and I knew they'd be all right with you," she said, as she walked away with Baby, who was by no means sure that he wanted to go.

"Now," said Hal, edging closer to Peggy, "we'll be comfable. Go on, Peggy — what she sawed."

"It was a hill — far, far away, neely as far as the sky," said Peggy, in a mysterious tone. "When the sun comed she could see it plain — the hill and what was there, but when the sun goed she couldn't. There was a white spot on the hill, Hal, and that white spot was a lovely white cottage. She knowed it, though she'd never see'd it."

"How did she know it?"

"Her mam — no, that's wrong, she hadn't no mamma — well, never mind, *somebody*'d told her."

"Were it *God?*" asked Hal, in an awestruck whisper.

"I don't know. No, I don't think so. I think it's a little naughty to say that, Hal. No, dear, don't cry," for signs of disturbance were visible in Hal's round face. "You didn't mean, and it isn't never naughty when we don't mean, you know. We'll go on about the little girl. She knowed it was a lovely cottage, and she wanted *very* much, as much as could be, to go there, for the big house wasn't pretty, and it was dark, nearly black, and the cottage was all white."

"Her house wasn't as nice as *zit*, were it? Zit house isn't b'ack," said Hal.

" No," said Peggy, doubtfully. "*It* wasn't as nice as this, but the white house was much prettier than this."

" How?" asked Hal.

" Oh!" said Peggy, letting her eyes and her fancy rove about together, " I think it was beautiful all over. It was all shiny white; the walls was white, and the carpets was white, and the tables and the chairs was white — all shiny and soft like — like — "

" Baby's best sash," suggested Hal.

" Well, p'raps — that'll do. And there was a cow and chickens and sheep, and a kitchen where you could make cakes, and a garden with lots of flowers and strawberries — "

" All white?" asked Hal.

" No, of course not. Strawberries couldn't be white, and flowers is all colours. 'Twas the *droind-room* that was all white."

" And the milk and the eggs. Zem *is* white," said Hal, triumphantly.

" Very well. I didn't say they wasn't. But the story goes on that the little girl didn't know how to get there; it was so far and so high up. So she sat and cried all alone at the window."

" All alone, *poor* little girl," said Hal, with deep feeling. " Kick, Peggy, kick, I'm doing to cry; make it come right *kick*. The crying's just coming."

" Make it wait a minute. I can't make it come right all so quick," said Peggy. " It's going to come,

so make the crying wait. One day she was crying
d'edful, worst than never, 'cos the sun had goned,
and she couldn't see the white cottage no more, and
just then she heard something saying, ' mew, mew,'
and it was a kitten outside the window, and it was
just going to fall down and be killed."

"That's not coming right. I *must* cry," said Hal.

"But she opened the window — there now, you
see — and she pulled the kitten in, so it didn't fall
down, and it was so pleased it kissed her, and when
it kissed her it turned into a fairy, and it touched
her neck and made wings come, and then it opened
the window again and flewed away with the little
girl till they came to the white cottage, and then the
little girl was quite happy for always."

"Did the fairy stay with her always?" asked Hal.

"No; fairies never does like that. They go back
to fairyland. But the little girl had nice milk and
eggs and cakes, and she made nosegays with the
flowers, and the sun was *always* shining, so she was
quite, *quite* happy."

"Her couldn't be happy all alone," said Hal. "I
don't like zat story, Peggy. You haven't made it
nice at all. It's a nonsense story."

Hal wriggled about and seemed very cross. Poor
Peggy was not so much indignant as distressed at
failing in her efforts to amuse him. What was the
matter? It couldn't be that he was getting sleepy —
it was far too early for his morning sleep.

'And above the tops of all the houses, clear though faint, was now to be seen the outline of a range of hills, so softly gray-blue in the distance that but for the irreg: ular line never changing in its form, one could easily have fancied it was only the edge of a quickly pass- ing ridge of clouds. Peggy, however, knew better.

"See, Hal." she said, "over there, far, far a: way, *nearly* in the sky, does you see that bluey hill?"'

"It isn't a nonsense story," she said, and she glanced towards the window as she spoke. Yes, the sun was shining brightly, the morning clouds had quite melted away; it was going to be a fine day after all. And clear and white gleamed out the spot on the distant hill which Peggy loved to gaze at! "Come here, Hal," she said, getting on to her feet and helping Hal on to his, "come with me to the window and you'll see if it's a nonsense story. Only you've never to tell nobody. It's Peggy's own secret."

Hal forgot his crossness in a minute, he felt so proud and honoured. Peggy led him to the window. It was not a very pretty prospect; they looked out on to a commonplace street, houses on both sides, though just opposite there was a little variety in the shape of an old-fashioned, smoke-dried garden. Beyond that again, more houses, more streets, stretching away out into suburbs, and somewhere beyond all that again the mysterious, beautiful, enchanting region which the children spoke of and believed in as "the country," not really so far off after all, though to them it seemed so.

And above the tops of all the houses, clear though faint, was now to be seen the outline of a range of hills, so softly gray-blue in the distance that but for the irregular line never changing in its form, one could easily have fancied it was only the edge of a quickly passing ridge of clouds. Peggy, however, knew better.

"See, Hal," she said, "over there, far, far away, *neely* in the sky, does you see that bluey hill?"

Of course he saw, agreeing so readily that Peggy was sure he did not distinguish rightly, which was soon proved to be the case by his announcing that "The 'ill were sailing away."

"No, no, it isn't," Peggy cried. "You've mustooked a cloud, Hal. See now," and by bringing her own eyes exactly on a level with a certain spot on the glass she was able to place his correctly, "just over that little bubble in the window you can see it. Its top goes up above the bubble and then down and then up again, and it never moves like the clouds — does you see now, Hallie dear?"

"Zes, zes," said Hal, "but it's a *wenny* little 'ill, Peggy."

"No, dear," his sister explained. "It only looks little 'cos it's so far away. *You* is too little to understand, dear, but it's true that it's a big hill, neely a mountain, Hal. Mamma told me."

"Oh," said Hal, profoundly impressed and quite convinced.

"Mountings is *old* hills, or big hills," Peggy continued, herself slightly confused. "I don't know if they is the papas and mammas of the little ones, but I think it's something like that, for onst in church I heard the clergymunt read that the little hills jumped for joy, so they must be the children. I'll ask mamma, and then I'll tell you. I'm not quite sure if

he meaned the same kind, for these hills never jumps
—that's how mamma told me to know they wasn't
clouds."

"Zes," said Hal, "but go on about the secret,
Peggy. Hal doesn't care about the 'ills."

"But the secret's *on* the hills," replied Peggy.
"Look more, Hal—does you see a teeny, *teeny*
white spot on the bluey hill? Higher up than the
bubble, but not at the top quite?"

Hal's eyes were good and his faith great.

"Zes, zes," he cried. "I does see it—kite plain,
Peggy."

"Well, Hallie," Peggy continued, "*that's* my
secret."

"Is it the fairy cottage, and is the little girl zere
now?" Hal asked, breathlessly.

Peggy hesitated.

"It is a white cottage," she said. "Mamma told
me. She looked at it through a seeing pipe."

"What's a seeing pipe?" Hal interrupted.

"I can't tell you just now. Ask mamma to show
you hers some day. It's too difficult to understand,
but it makes you see things plain. And mamma
found out it was reely a cottage, a white cottage,
all alone up on the hill—isn't it sweet of it to be
there all alone, Hallie? And she said I might think
it was a fairy cottage and keep it for my own secret,
only I've telled you, Hal, and you mustn't tell
nobody."

"And is it all like Baby's best sash, and are there cakes and f'owers and cows?" asked Hal.

"I don't know. I made up the story, you know, Hal, to please you. I've made lots — mamma said I might. But I've never see'd the cottage, you know. I *dare say* it's beautiful, white and gold like the story, that's why I said it. It does so shine when the sun's on it — look, look, Hal!"

For as she spoke the sunshine had broken out again more brilliantly; and the bright, thin sparkle which often dazzles one between the showers in unsettled weather, lighted up that quarter of the sky where the children were gazing, and, to their fancy at least, the white spot caught and reflected the rays.

"Oh zes, I see," Hal repeated. "But, Peggy, I'd like to *go* zere and to see it. Can't we go, Peggy? It would be so nice, nicer than making up stories. And do you think — oh do you think, Peggy, that p'raps there's *pigs* zere, real pigs?"

He clasped his hands entreatingly as he spoke. Peggy must say there were pigs. Poor Peggy — it was rather a comedown after her fairy visions. But she was too kind to say anything to vex Hal.

"I thought you said pigs was silly," she objected, gently.

"Playing pigs to make Baby laugh is silly," said Hal, "and pigs going to market and stayin' at 'ome and roast beeffin', is *d'edful* silly. But not real pigs."

"Oh well, then, *you* may think pigs if you like," said Peggy. "I don't think I will, but that doesn't matter. You may have them in the cottage if you like, only you mustn't tell Thor and Terry and Baldwin about it."

"I won't tell, on'y you *might* have them too," said Hal discontentedly. "You're not kind, Peggy."

"Don't let's talk about the cottage any more, then," said Peggy, though her own eyes were fixed on the far-off white spot as she spoke. "I think p'raps, Hallie, you're *rather* too little to care about it."

"I'm not," said Hal, "and I do care. But I do like pigs, real pigs. I sawed zem in the country."

"You can't remember," said Peggy. "It's two whole years since we was in the real country, Hallie, and you're only three and a half. I know it's two years. I heard mamma say so to papa, so you wasn't two then."

"But I did see zem and I do 'amember, 'cos of pictures," said Hal.

"Oh yes, dear, there is pictures of pigs in your scrap-book, I know," Peggy agreed. "You get it now and we'll look for them."

Off trotted Hal, returning in a minute with his book, and for a quarter of an hour or so his patient little sister managed to keep him happy and amused. At the end of that time, however, he began to be cross and discontented again. Peggy did not know what to make of him this morning, he was not often so difficult to please. She was very glad when nurse came in to say it was now *his* time for his morning sleep, and though Hal grumbled and scolded and said he was not sleepy she carried him off, and Peggy was left in peace.

She was not at a loss to employ herself. At half-past eleven she usually went down to mamma for an hour's lessons, and it must be nearly that time now. She got her books together and sat looking over the one verse she had to learn, her thoughts roving nevertheless in the direction they loved best — away over the chimneys and the smoke; away, away, up, up to the fairy cottage on the distant hill.

CHAPTER III.

"THE CHILDREN AT THE BACK."

"It seems to me if I'd money enough,
My heart would be made of different stuff;
I would think about those whose lot is rough."
MRS. HAWTREY.

THESE children's home was not in a very pretty place. In front, as I have told you, it looked out on to a rather ugly street, and there were streets and streets beyond that again — streets of straight, stiff, grim-looking houses, some large and some small, but all commonplace and dull. And in and out between these bigger streets were narrower and still uglier ones, scarcely indeed to be called streets, so dark and poky were they, so dark and poky were the poor houses they contained.

The street immediately behind the children's house, that on to which its back windows looked out, was one of these poorer ones, though not by any means one of the most miserable. And ugly though it was, Peggy was very fond of gazing out of the night nursery window on to this street, especially on days when it was "no use," as she called it to herself, looking out at the front; that meant, as I dare say you can guess, days on which it was too

dull and cloudy to see the distant hills, and above
all the white spot, which had taken such hold on her
fancy. For she had found out some very interesting
things in that dingy street. Straight across from the
night nursery window was a very queer miserable
sort of a shop, kept by an old Irishwoman whose
name was Mrs. Whelan. It is rather absurd to call
it a shop, though it was a place where things were
bought and sold, for the room in which these buyings
and sellings went on was Mrs. Whelan's kitchen,
and bedroom, and sitting-room, and wash-house, as
well as her shop! It was on the first floor, and you
got up to it by a rickety staircase — more like a
ladder indeed than a staircase, and underneath it on
the ground-floor lived a cobbler, with whom Mrs.
Whelan used to quarrel at least once a day, though
as he was a patient, much enduring man, the quarrels
never went farther than the old Irishwoman's opening her window and shouting down all manner of
scoldings to the poor fellow, of which he took no
notice.

On Sundays the cobbler used to tidy himself up
and go off to church "like a gentleman," the boys
said. But Mrs. Whelan, alas, never tidied herself
up, and never went to church, and though she made
a great show of putting a shutter across that part of
the window which showed "the shop," nurse had
more than once shaken her head when the children
were dressing for church, and told them not to look

"She was rather a ter-rible-looking old woman; she always wore a short bed-gown, that is a loose kind of jacket roughly drawn in at the waist, of washed out cotton, which never looked clean, and yet somehow never seemed to get much dirtier, a black stuff petticoat, and a cap with flapping frills which quite hid her face unless you were very near her, and she was generally to be seen with a pipe in her mouth. Her voice was both loud and shrill, and when she was in a temper you could almost hear what she said, though the nursery window was shut."

over the way, she was sadly afraid the shutting or
shuttering up was all a pretence, and that Mrs.
Whelan made a good penny by her Sunday sales of
tobacco and pipes to the men, or maybe of sugar,
candles, or matches to careless housekeepers who
had let their stock run out too late on Saturday
night.

She was rather a terrible-looking old woman; she
always wore a short bed-gown, that is, a loose kind
of jacket roughly drawn in at the waist, of washed-
out cotton, which never looked clean, and yet somehow never seemed to get much dirtier, a black stuff
petticoat, and a cap with flapping frills which quite
hid her face unless you were very near her, and she
was generally to be seen with a pipe in her mouth.
Her voice was both loud and shrill, and when she
was in a temper you could almost hear what she
said, though the nursery window was shut. All the
neighbours were afraid of her, and in consequence
treated her with great respect. But like most people
in this world, she had some good about her, as you
will hear.

Good or bad, the children, Peggy especially, found
Mrs. Whelan very interesting. Peggy had never
seen her nearer than from the window, and though
she had a queer sort of wish to visit the shop and
make closer acquaintance with the old crone, she
was far too frightened of her to think of doing so
really. The boys, however, had been several times

inside Mrs. Whelan's dwelling, and used to tell wonderful stories of the muddle of things it contained, and of the old woman herself. They always bought their soap-bubble pipes there, "three a penny," and would gladly have bought some of the toffee-balls and barley-sugar which were also to be had, if this had not been strictly forbidden by mamma, in spite of their grumbling.

"It isn't so *very* dirty, mamma," they said, "and you get a lot more for a penny than in a proper shop."

But mamma would not give in. She knew what Mrs. Whelan was like, as she used sometimes to go over herself to talk to the poor old woman, but that, of course, was a different matter.

"I don't much like your going there at all," she would say, "but it pleases her for us to buy some trifles now and then."

But in her heart she wished very much that they were not obliged to live in this dreary and ugly town, where their poor neighbours were rarely the sort of people she could let her children know anything of. Mamma, in *her* childhood, had lived in that fairyland she called "the country," and so had papa, and they still looked forward to being there again, though for the present they were obliged to make the best of their home in a dingy street.

It seemed much less dull and dingy to the children than to them, however. Indeed I don't think the children ever thought about it at all. The boys were busy at school, and found plenty of both work and play to make the time pass quickly, and Peggy, who might perhaps have been a little dull and lonely in her rather shut-up life, had her fancies and her wonders — her interesting things to look at both at the front and the back of the house, and mamma to tell all about them to! And this reminds me that I have not yet told you what it was she was *most* fond of watching from the night nursery window. It was not Mrs. Whelan or the cobbler; it was the tenants of the third or top story of the rickety old house — the family she always spoke of to herself as "the children at the back."

Such a lot of them there were. It was long before Peggy was able to distinguish them "all from each other," as she said, and it took her longer still to make names by which she could keep a clear list in her head. The eldest looked to her quite grown-up, though in reality she was about thirteen; she was a big red-cheeked girl, though she lived in a town; her arms were red too, poor thing, especially in winter, for they were seldom or never covered, and she seemed to be always at work, scrubbing or washing, or running out to fetch two or three of the little ones in from playing in the gutter. Peggy called her "Reddy," and though it was the girl's red cheeks and arms which made her first choose the name, in a while she came to think of it as meaning "ready" also, for Peggy did not know much about spelling as yet, and the thought in her mind of the look of the two words was the same. For a good while Peggy fancied that Reddy was the nurse or servant of the family, but one day when she said something of the kind to her own nurse she was quickly put right.

"Their servant, my dear! Bless you, no. How could they afford to keep · a servant; they've hard enough work to keep themselves, striving folk though they seem. There's such a many of them, you see, and mostly so little — save that big girl and the sister three below her, there's none really to help the mother. And the cripple must be a great charge."

"What's the cripple, nursey?" Peggy asked.

"Why, Miss Peggy, haven't you noticed the white-faced girl on crutches? You must have seen her dragging up and down in front of the house of a fine day."

"Oh yes," said Peggy, "but I didn't know that was called cripple. And she's quite little; she's as little as me, nurse!"

"She's older than she looks, poor thing," said nurse — "maybe oldest of them all."

This, however, Peggy could not believe. She fixed in her own mind that "Crippley" came after the two boys who were evidently next to Reddy — she did not give the boys names, for they did not interest her as much as the girls. Having so many brothers of her own and no sister, it seemed to her as if a sister must be the very nicest thing in the world, and of all the children at the back, the two that she liked most to watch were a pair of little girls about three years older than herself, whom she named " The Smileys," " Brown Smiley " and " Light Smiley " when she thought of them separately, for though they were very like each other, the colour of their hair was different. They were very jolly little girls, poorly clad and poorly fed though they were, taking life easily, it seemed — too easily in the opin- ion of their eldest sister Reddy, and the sister next above them — between them and Crippley, accord- ing to Peggy's list. This sister was the only one whose real name Peggy knew, by hearing it so fre- quently shouted after her by the mother and Reddy. For this child, " Mary-Hann," was rather deaf, though it was not till long afterwards that Peggy found this out.

" Mary-Hann " was a patient stupid sort of girl, a kind of second in command to Reddy, and she was like Reddy in appearance, except that she was several sizes smaller and thinner, so that even supposing that her arms were as red as her sister's they did not strike one in the same way.

Below the Smileys came another boy, who was generally to be seen in their company, and who, according to Peggy, rejoiced in the name of " Tip."

And below Tip were a few babies, in reality I believe never more than three, during the years through which their little over-the-way neighbour watched them. But even she was obliged to give up hopes of classifying the babies, for there always seemed to be *a* baby about the same age, and one or two others just struggling into standing or rather tumbling alone, and for ever being picked up by Reddy or her attendant sprite Mary-Hann.

Such were Peggy's " children at the back." And many a dull day when it was too rainy to go a walk, and too cloudy to be " any use " to gaze out at the front of the house, did these poor children, little as they guessed it, help to make pass more quickly and pleasantly for the sisterless maiden. Many a morning when Hal and Baby were asleep and nurse was glad to have an hour or so for a bit of ironing, or some work of the kind down in the kitchen — for my Peggy's papa and mamma were not rich and could not keep many servants, so that nurse, though she was plain and homely in her ways, was of far more use than a smarter young woman to them — many a morning did the little girl, left in the night nursery in charge of her sleeping brothers, take up her stand at the window which overlooked Mrs. Whelan's and the cobbler and the Smileys with all their brothers and sisters. There was always something new to see or to ask nurse to explain afterwards. For ever so long it took up Peggy's thoughts, and gave much conversation in the nursery to "plan" how the ten or eleven children, not to speak of the papa and mamma, *could* all find place in two rooms. It kept Peggy awake at night, especially if the weather happened to be at all hot or close, to think how *very* uncomfortable poor Reddy and Crippley and Mary-Hann and the Smileys must be, all sleeping in one bed as nurse said was too probably the case. And it was the greatest relief to her mind, and to nurse's too, I do believe, to discover by means of some cautious inquiries of the cobbler when nurse took him over some of the boys' boots to mend, that the family was not so short of space as they had feared.

"They've two other rooms, Miss Peggy, as doesn't show to the front," said nurse, " two attics with sloping windows in the roof to their back again. And they're striving folk, he says, as indeed any one may see for theirselves."

"Then how shall we plan it now, I wonder," said Peggy, looking across to the Smileys' mansion with new respect. But nurse had already left the room, and perhaps, now she was satisfied their neighbours were not quite so much to be pitied, would scarcely have had patience to listen to Peggy's "wonderings" about them. So the little girl went on to herself —

"I should think the downstairs room is the papa's and mamma's and the teeniest baby's, and perhaps

Crippley sleeps there, as she's ill, like me when I had the hooping-cough and I couldn't sleep and mamma kept jumping up to me. And then the big boys and Tip has one room — 'ticks,' nurse calls the rooms with windows in the roof. I think I'd like to sleep in a 'tick' room; you must see the stars so plain without getting up; and — and — let me see, Reddy and Mary-Hann and the Smileys and the old babies — no, that's too many — and I don't know how many old babies there is. We'll say *one* — if there's another it must be a boy and go in the boys' tick — and that makes Reddy and Mary — ''

" Miss Peggy, your mamma's ready for your lessons," came the housemaid's voice at the door, and Peggy hurried off. But she was rather in a brown study at her lessons that morning. Mamma could not make her out at all, till at last she shut up the books for a minute and made Peggy tell her where her thoughts were wool-gathering.

" Not so very far away, mamma dear," said Peggy, laughing. She never could help laughing when mamma said "funny things like that." " Not so very far away. I was only wondering about the children at the back."

She called them always " the children at the back " when she spoke of them — for even to mamma she would have felt shy of telling her own names for them. And then she went on to repeat what nurse had heard from the cobbler. Mamma agreed that it was very interesting, and she too was pleased to think "the children at the back's house," as Peggy called it, was more commodious than might have been expected. But still, even such interesting things as that must not be allowed to interfere with lessons, Peggy must put it all out of her head till they were done with, and then mamma would talk about it with her.

"Only, mamma," said Peggy, "I don't know what com — commo — that long word you said, means."

"I should not have used it, perhaps," said mamma. "And yet I don't know. If we only used the words you understand already, you would never learn new ones — eh, Peggy! Commodious just means large, and not narrow and squeezed up."

Peggy nodded her head, which meant that she quite understood, and then the lessons went on smoothly again.

When they were over, mamma talked about poor people, especially about poor children, to Peggy, and explained to her more than she had ever done before about what being poor really means. It made Peggy feel and look rather sad, and once or twice mamma was afraid she was going to cry, which, of course, she did not wish her to do. But Peggy choked down the crying feeling, because she knew it would make her mother sorry and would not do the poor people any good.

"Mamma," she said, "it *neely* makes me cry, but I won't. But when I'm big can't I do something for the children at the back?"

"They won't be children then, Peggy dear. You may be able to do something for them without waiting for that. I'll think about it. I don't fancy they are so *very* poor. As I have been telling you, there are many far poorer. But I dare say they have very few pleasures in their lives. We might try to think of a little sunshine for them now and then."

"The Smile — " began Peggy, but she stopped suddenly, growing red — " the littler ones do play a good deal in the gutter, mamma dear," she said, anxious to state things quite fairly; "but I don't think that's *very* nice play, and the sun very seldom shines there. And Red — the big ones, mamma dear, and the one that goes on — I can't remember the name of those sticks." '

" Crutches," said mamma.

" Yes, crutches — *her* never has no plays at all, I don't think. She'd have more sunshine at the 'nother side of our house, mamma dear."

Mamma smiled. Peggy did not understand that mamma did not mean "sunshine" exactly as she took it; she forgot, too, that of actual sunshine more fell on the back street than she thought of. For it was only on dull or rainy days that she looked out much on the children at the back. On fine days her eyes were busy in another direction.

"I'll think about it," said mamma. So Peggy for the present was satisfied.

This talk about the Smileys and the rest of them had been a day or two before the morning on which we first saw Peggy — the morning that Thor tried so to make fun of her about choosing sugar in her bread and milk, because it was cold. Mamma had not said any more about the children at the back, and this particular morning Peggy herself was not thinking · very much about them. Her head was running a good deal on the white cottage and all her fancies about it, and she was feeling rather disappointed that she had not succeeded better in amusing Hal by her stories.

"It must be, I suppose," she said to herself, "that he's rather too little for that kind of fancy stories. I wonder if Baldwin would like them; it would be nice to have somebody to make fancies with me."

But somehow Baldwin and the fairy cottage did not seem to match. And Thor and Terry were both much too big — Thor would laugh at her, and Terry would think it waste of time ; he had so many other things to amuse himself about. No, Peggy could not think of any one who would "understand," she decided, with a sigh !

CHAPTER IV.

"REAL" FANCIES.

"Mine be a cot beside the hill."
SAMUEL ROGERS.

JUST then came the usual summons to her lessons. Mamma was waiting for her little girl in the corner of the drawing-room, where she always sat when she was teaching Peggy. It was a very nice corner, near the fire, for though it was not winter it was rather chilly, and mamma often felt cold. Thor used to tell her that she should take a good run or have a game of cricket to warm her; it would be much better than sitting near the fire. Peggy thought it was rather unkind of Thor to say so, but mamma only laughed at him, so perhaps it was just his boy way of speaking.

Peggy said her lessons quite well, but she looked rather grave; no smiles lighted up her face, and when lessons were over she sat still without speaking, and seemed as if she scarcely knew what she wanted to do with herself.

"Is there anything the matter, dear?" mamma asked.

"I'm rather tired, I think, mamma," Peggy replied.

"Tired!" mamma repeated, in some surprise. It wasn't often that Peggy talked of being tired. "What is that with? You've not been worrying yourself about the children who live over Mrs. Whelan's, I hope? You mustn't do that, you know, dear; it would do you harm and them no good."

For mamma knew that Peggy sometimes did "worry" about things — "Once she takes a thing in her head she'll work herself up so, for all she seems so quiet," nurse would say.

"No, mamma dear," Peggy replied; "I'm not tired because of that. I like thinking about the children at the back. I wish — "

"What?" said mamma.

"I wish I'd sisters like them. I'm rather lonely, mamma. I do think God might have gaved *one* sister to Peggy, and not such a great lot to the children at the back."

"But you have your brothers, my dear little girl. You might have been an only child."

"The big ones is always neely at school, and Hal's too little to understand. It's Hal that's tired me, mamma dear. He was so d'edfully cross afore nurse put him to bed."

"Cross, was he?" said mamma. "I'm afraid he must be getting those last teeth. He may be cross for some time; if so, it would not do to leave him."

She seemed to be speaking to herself, but when she caught sight of Peggy's puzzled face she stopped. "Tell me about Hal, dear," she went on. "What was it that tired you so?"

"I was trying to amuse him and tell him stories about my white cottage up on the hill, and he was so cross. He couldn't understand, and he said they was 'nonsense' stories."

"He is too little, perhaps, to care for fancies," said her mother, consolingly. "You must wait till he is a little older, Peggy dear."

"But when he's older he'll be a *boy*, mamma," said Peggy; "he'll be like Thor and Terry, who don't care for things like that, or Baldwin, who thinks stories stupid. Oh, mamma, I wish I had a sister. *That's* what I want," she added, with conviction.

Mamma smiled.

"Poor Peggy," she said. "I'm afraid it can't be helped. You can never have a sister near your own age, and I'm afraid a baby sister, even if you had one, would be no good."

"Oh no, we've had enough babies," said Peggy, decidedly. "But, mamma, mightn't there be some little girl who'd play with me like a sister? If there *is* a fairy living in that cottage, mamma, how I do wish she would find a little girl for me!"

Mamma looked a very little bit troubled.

"Peggy dear," she said, "you mustn't let your

"Mama dear," she began, "will
you tell me what the little
white house is reely like, then?
If you will, I'll promise not
to think there's fairies there
— only — "

"Only what, dear?"

"If you don't mind, said
Peggy, very anxious not to
hurt her mother's feelings,
"I'd rather not have pigs. I
don't think I like pigs
very much."

fancies run away with you too far. I told you they would do you no harm if you kept plain in your head that they *were* fancies, but you mustn't forget that. You know there couldn't really be a fairy living in that little white cottage."

" No," Peggy agreed, " I know that, mamma, because fairies *really* live in fairyland."

She looked up gravely into her mother's face as she said so. Mamma could not help laughing.

" Fairies *really*," she said, " live in Peggy's funny little head, and in many other funny little heads, I have no doubt. But nowhere — "

" Mamma, mamma," Peggy interrupted, putting her fingers in her ears as she spoke, " I *won't* listen. You mustn't, mustn't say that. I must have my fairies, mamma. I've no sisters."

" Well, keep them in fairyland then, or at least only let them out for visits now and then. But don't mix them up with real things too much, or you will get quite a confusion, and never be sure if you're awake or dreaming."

Peggy seemed to consider this over very seriously. After a minute or two she lifted her face again, and looked straight into her mother's with her earnest gray eyes.

" Mamma dear," she began, " will you tell me what the little white house is *reely* like, then? If you will, I'll promise not to think there's fairies there — only — "

"Only what, dear?"

"If you don't mind," said Peggy, very anxious not to hurt her mother's feelings, "I'd *rather* not have pigs. I don't think I like pigs very much."

"Well, we needn't have pigs then. But remember I can only 'fancy' it. I've never seen that particular cottage, you see, Peggy. But I have seen other cottages in Brackenshire, and so I can fancy what it *most likely* is. You see there are different kinds of fancying — there's fancying that is all fancy, like fairy stories, and there's fancying that might be true and real, and that very likely is true and real. Do you understand?"

"Yes," said Peggy, drawing a deep breath. "Well, mamma, go on real-fancying, please. What's that place you've been at — Brat — what is it?"

"Brackenshire," mamma replied. "That's the name of that part of the country that we see far off, from the windows upstairs."

"And is all the cottages white there, and is they *very* pretty?" asked Peggy, with deep interest. "Oh, mamma, do tell me, quick."

"I don't know if they're all white, but I think they are mostly. And there are some pretty and some ugly. Of course it depends a good deal upon the people that live in them. If they're nice, clean, busy people, who like their house to be neat and pretty, and work hard to keep it so, of course it's much more likely to be so than if they were careless and lazy."

"Oh," said Peggy, clasping her hands. "I do so hope my cottage has nice people living in it. I *think* it has, don't you, mamma? It looks *so* white."

"My dear Peggy," said mamma, smiling, "we can't tell, when it's so far away. But we may hope so."

"Yes," said Peggy, "we'll hope so, and we'll think so." But then a rather puzzled look came over her face again, though she smiled too. "Mamma," she went on, "there's such a funny thing come into my head, only I don't know quite how to say it. I think that the far-away helps to make it pretty — why is far-away so pretty, mamma?"

Mamma smiled again.

"I'm afraid I can't tell you why. Wouldn't it spoil some things if we knew the why of them, little Peggy?"

Peggy did not answer. This was another new thought for her, and rather a difficult one. She put it away in her mind, in one of the rather far back cupboards there, and locked it up, to think about it afterwards.

"Mamma," she said, coaxingly, "I want you to tell me a real fancy about the cottage. It will be so nice when I look at it to think it's most likely *reely* like that."

"Well, then, let us see," mamma began.

"Wait just one minute, mamma dear, till I've shut my eyes. First I must get the bluey hills and the white spot into them, and then I'll shut them and see what you tell.   Yes — that's all right now."

So mamma went on.

"I fancy a cottage on the side of a hill.   The cottage is white, of course, and the hill is green.   Not very green — a kind of brown-green, for the grass is short and close, nibbled by the sheep and cows that find their living on the hill most of the year.   The cottage is very white, for last summer it had a nice wash all over, and that lasts clean a good while in the country.   There is a little low wall round it shutting it in from the hillside, and this wall is not very white, though it once was so, for it is covered with creeping plants, so that you can scarcely see what its own colour is.   At the front of the house there is a little garden, quite a tiny one — there are potatoes and gooseberry bushes and cabbages at one side, but in front of them are some nice old-fashioned flowers, and at the other side there are strawberry plants, and behind them some rose-bushes.   In summer I am sure there will be some pretty roses."

"Oh how nice," said Peggy; "go on, go on, please."

"There is a funny little wooden shed behind the house, leaning against the wall, which has a door big enough for a child to go in by, or a big person if they stooped down very much, and besides this it has a *very* little door in the wall, leading on to the hillside. Can you guess what the shed is for, Peggy, and what the tiny door is for?"

Peggy thought and thought, but her country knowledge was but scanty.

"I can't think," she said. "It couldn't be for pigs, 'cos there isn't any in the cottage. Nor it couldn't be for cows, 'cos cows is so big."

"What should you say to cocks and hens, Peggy? There are to be fresh eggs there, aren't there? And chickens sometimes. I rather think they take eggs and chickens to market, don't they?"

"Oh yes, I'm sure they do. How stupid I am! Of course the little wooden house is for cocks and hens. You're making it lovelily, mamma. What is it like inside, and who lives in it? I do so want to know."

"Inside?" said mamma. "I'm almost afraid you might be disappointed, Peggy, if you've never been in a real cottage. There are so many that look very pretty outside and are not at all pretty inside. But at least we may think it is neat and clean. There are only two rooms, Peggy — a kitchen which you go straight into, and another room which opens out of it. The kitchen is very bright and pleasant; there is a table before the window with some flower-pots on it, in which both winter and summer there are plants growing. There is a large cupboard of dark old wood standing against the wall, and a sort of sofa that is called a settle with cushions covered with red cotton, standing near the fireplace. There are shelves, too, on which stand some dishes and two or three shining pots and pans, the ugly black ones are kept in a little back kitchen where most of the cooking is done, so that the front kitchen should be kept as nice as possible."

"That makes another room, mamma dear. You said there was only two."

"Oh, but it's so very tiny you couldn't call it a room. The second room is a bedroom, but the best pieces of furniture are kept there. There is a nice chest of drawers and a rocking-chair, and there is a very funny wooden cradle, standing right down on the floor, not at all like Baby's cot. And in this cradle is a nice, fat, bright-eyed little baby."

" A baby," said Peggy, doubtfully.

" Yes, to be sure. There's always a baby in a cottage, unless you'd rather have a very old couple whose babies are grown-up men and women, out in the world."

" No," said Peggy, "I don't want that. A very old woman in a cottage would be *razer* like a witch, or else it could make me think of Red Riding-Hood's grandmother, and that is *so* sad. No, I don't mind the baby if it has a nice mamma — but only one baby, pelease, mamma dear. I don't want *lots*, like the children at the back, they're always tumbling about and sc'eaming so."

"Oh no, we won't have it like that. We'll only have one baby — a very contented nice baby, and its mamma is very nice too. She's got quite a pretty rosy face, and she stands at the door every morning to see her husband go off to his work, and every evening to watch for him coming back again, and she holds the baby up in her arms and it laughs and crows."

"Yes," said Peggy, "that'll do. And the eggs and the chickens, mamma?"

"Oh yes, she takes great care of the cocks and hens, and never forgets to go outside the garden to feed them on the hill, and in the evening they all come home of themselves through the little door in the wall. There's a very nice cat in the cottage too; it sits purring on the front steps on fine days, as if it thought the cottage and garden and everything else belonged to it. And—"

But suddenly the clock struck. Up started mamma.

"Peggy, darling, I had no idea it was so late. And I have to go out the moment after luncheon, and I have still two letters to write. I am a greater baby than any of you! Run off, dear, and tell nurse I want to speak to her before I go out."

"And to-morrow," said Peggy, "to-morrow, will you tell me some more about the white cottage, mamma? It *is* so nice — I don't think you're a baby at all, mamma. A baby couldn't make it up so lovelily."

And Peggy set off upstairs in great content. The

white spot would give her more pleasure than ever, now that she knew what sort of *real* fancies to have about it.

"And to-morrow," she said to herself, "to-morrow mamma will tell me more, lots more. If I say my lessons very goodly, p'raps mamma will tell me some more every day. And p'raps Hallie would like those kinds better than about fairies, and wouldn't call *them* nonsense stories."

Poor little Peggy — "to-morrow" brought news which put her pretty fancies about the white cottage out of her head for a while.

She gave her mother's message to nurse, and after dinner nurse went downstairs. When she came up again she looked rather grave, and Peggy thought perhaps she was unhappy about Hal, who was still cross and had bright red spots on his cheeks.

"Does you think poor Hallie is ill, nurse?" asked Peggy in a low voice, for Hal not to hear.

"No, my dear, it's only his teeth. But they'll make him fractious for a while, I'm afraid, and he's not a very strong child, not near so strong as Baby and the big boys."

"Poor Hallie," said Peggy, with great sympathy. "I'll be very good to him even if he is very cross, nurse."

Nurse did not answer for a minute, and she still looked very grave.

"Why do you look so sad, nurse, if it isn't about Hal?" asked Peggy, impatiently.

"Did I look sad, Miss Peggy? I didn't know it. I was thinking about some things your mamma was speaking of to me."

"Oh!" said Peggy, "was it about our new frocks? Mamma and you is always very busy when we need new frocks, I know."

"Yes, dear," said nurse, but that was all.

Then Peggy and Hal and nurse and Baby went out for a walk. They did not go very far, for it was what nurse called a queer-tempered day. Between the gleams of blue sky and sunshine there came sharp little storms and showers. It was April weather, though April had not yet begun.

"Which way are we going?" Peggy asked, as they set off, she and Hal hand-in-hand, just in front of nurse and the perambulator. She *hoped* nurse would say "up Fernley Road," because Fernley Road led straight on towards the hills — so at least it seemed to Peggy. Their street ran into Fernley Road at one end, so that Fernley Road was what is called at right angles with it, and Peggy felt sure that if you walked far enough along the road you *could* not but come to "the beginning of the hills."

But to-day Peggy was to be disappointed.

"We can't go far, Miss Peggy, and we must go to Field's about Master Hal's new boots. It looks as if it might rain, so perhaps we'd better go straight there. You know the way, Miss Peggy? — right on to the end of this street and then turn to the left."

Peggy gave a little sigh, but trotted on quietly. Hal began grumbling.

"What is I to have new boots for?" he said. "I doesn't want new boots."

"Oh, Hal," said Peggy, "I think it's very nice indeed to have new boots. They shine so, and sometimes they do make such a lovely squeaking."

But Hal wasn't in a humour to be pleased with anything, so Peggy tried to change the subject.

"Nurse says we are to turn to the left at the end of this street," she said. "Does you know which is the left, Hal? *I* do, 'cos of my pocket in my frock. First I feel for my pocket, and when it's there I say 'all right,' and then I know that's the right, and when it isn't there I *can't* say 'all right,' and so I know the side it isn't at is the left."

Hal listened with some interest, but a slight tinge of contempt for feminine garments.

"Boys has pockets at each sides, so all boys' sides is right," he said.

But Peggy was by this time in the midst of her researches for her pocket, so she did not argue the point.

"Here it is!" she exclaimed, "all right, so the nother side is left. *This* way, Hallie," and very proud to show nurse that she had understood her directions, she led her little brother down the street into which they had now turned.

There were shops in this street, which made it

more amusing than the one in which the children lived, even though they had seen them so often that they knew pretty well all that was worth looking at in the windows — that is to say, in the picture-shops and the toy-shops, and perhaps in the confectioner's. All others were passed by as a matter of course. Field's, the shoemaker's, was not quite so stupid as some, because under a glass shade, in the midst of all the real boots and shoes, were half a dozen pairs of dolls' ones, which Peggy thought quite lovely, though apparently no one else was of her opinion, as the tiny things stayed there day after day without a single pair being sold. Peggy herself could remember them for what seemed to her a very long time, and Baldwin, who owned to having admired them when he was "little," assured her they had been there since she was quite a baby; he could remember having "run on" to look at them in the days when he and Terry had trotted in front and nurse had perambulated Peggy behind.

The little boots and shoes came into Peggy's mind just now, partly perhaps because Hal was hanging back so, and she was afraid he would be cross if she asked him to walk quicker.

"Let's run on and look at the tiny shoes in Field's window," she said. "We can wait there till nurse comes up to us. She'll see us."

This roused Hal to bestir himself, and they were soon at the shoemaker's.

"*Isn't* they sweet?" said Peggy. "If I had a gold pound of my very own, Hal, I'd buy some of them."

"Would you?" said Hal, doubtfully. "No, if *I* had a gold pound I'd—"

But just then nurse came up to them and they were all marched into the shop.

CHAPTER V.

THE LITTLE RED SHOES.

" Pif-paf Pottrie, what trade are you ?   Are you a tailor ? "
" Better still ! "   " A shoemaker ? "

Brothers Grimm.

THERE was another reason why the children liked
Field's shop. At the back of it was a sort of little
room railed off by a low wooden partition with cur-
tains at the top, into which customers were shown to
try on and be fitted with new boots or shoes. This
little room within a room had always greatly taken
Peggy's fancy; she had often talked it over with her
brothers, and wished they could copy it in their
nursery. Inside it had comfortable cushioned seats
all round, making it look like one of the large,
square, cushioned pews still to be found in some old
churches, pews which all children who have ever sat
in them dearly love.

There was always some excitement in peeping
into this little room to see if any one was already
there ; if that were the case the children knew they
should have to be " tried on " in the outer shop.
To-day, however, there was no doubt about the
matter — Miss Field, who acted as her father's

shopwoman, marshalled them all straight into the curtained recess without delay; there was no one there — and when Peggy and Hal had with some difficulty twisted themselves on to the seats with as much formality as if they were settling themselves in church, and nurse had explained what they had come for, the girl began operations by taking off one of Hal's boots to serve as a pattern for his size.

"The same make as these, I suppose?" she asked.

"No, miss, a little thicker, I think. They're to be good strong ones for country wear," said nurse.

Peggy looked up with surprise.

"For the country, nursie," she said. "He'll have weared them out before it's time for us to go to the country. It won't be summer for a long while, and last year we didn't go even when summer comed."

Nurse looked a little vexed. Miss Field, though smiling and good-natured, was not a special favourite of nurse's; she was too fond of talking, and she stood there now looking very much amused at Peggy's remonstrance.

"If you didn't go to the country last year, Miss Margaret," said nurse, "more reason that you'll go this. But little girls can't know everything."

Peggy opened her eyes and her mouth. She was just going to ask nurse what was the matter, which

would not have made things better, I am afraid, when
Baby changed the subject by bursting out crying.
Poor Baby — he did not like the little curtained-off
room at all; it was rather dark, and he felt frightened, and as was of course the most sensible thing to
do under the circumstances, as he could not speak,
he cried.

"Dear, dear," said nurse, after vainly trying to
soothe him, " he doesn't like being in here, the poor
lamb. He's frightened. I'll never get him quiet
here. Miss Peggy, love," forgetting in her hurry
the presence of Miss Field, for before strangers
Peggy was always "Miss Margaret" with nurse, " I'll
have to put him back in his perambulator at the
door, and if you'll stand beside him he'll be quite
content."

And nurse got up as she spoke. Peggy slid herself down slowly and reluctantly from her seat; she
would have liked to stay and watch Hal being fitted
with boots, and she would have liked still more to
ask nurse what she meant by speaking of the country
so long before the time, but it was Peggy's habit
to do what she was told without delay, and she
knew she could ask nurse what she wanted afterwards. So with one regretful look back at the snug
corner where Hal was sitting comfortably staring at
his stockinged toes, she trotted across the shop to the
door where Baby, quite restored to good humour,
was being settled in his carriage.

"There now, he'll be quite happy. Nurse will come soon, dear. Just let him stay here in the doorway; he can see all the boots and shoes in the window — that will amuse him."

"Yes," said Peggy, adding in her own mind that she would have a good look at the dear, tiny dolls' ones and fix which she would like to buy if she had the money.

Baby did not interrupt her; he was quite content now he was out in the light and the open air, and amused himself after his own fashion by crowing and chuckling to the passers-by. So Peggy stood still, her eyes fixed on the baby shoes. They were of all colours, black and red and bronze and blue — it was difficult to say which were the prettiest. Peggy had almost decided upon a red pair, and was wondering how much money it would take to buy them, when some one touched her on the shoulder. She looked up; a lady was standing behind her, smiling in amusement.

"What are you gazing at so, my dear? Is this your baby in the perambulator? You had better wheel him a little bit further back, or may I do so for you? — he has worked himself too far into the doorway."

Peggy looked up questioningly in the lady's face. Like many children she did not like being spoken to by strangers in any unceremonious way; she felt as if it were rather a freedom.

"Baby did not interrupt her; he was quite con: tent now he was out in the light and the open air, and amused him: self after his own fashion by crowing and chuckling to the passers-by. So Peggy stood still, her eyes fixed on the baby shoes. They were of all colours, black and red and bronze and blue — it was difficult to say which was the prettiest."

p. 60

But the face that met hers was too kind and bright and pleasant to resist, and though Peggy still looked grave, it was only that she felt rather shy.

"Yes," she said, "he's our baby. I was looking at those sweet little shoes. I didn't see Baby had pushed hisself away. Thank you," as the lady gently moved the perambulator a little farther to one side.

"You and Baby are not alone? Are you waiting for some one?" she asked.

"Nurse is having Hal tried on for new boots," Peggy replied, "and Baby didn't like the shop 'cos it were rather dark."

"And so his kind little sister is taking care of him. I see," said the lady. "And what are the sweet little shoes you like so much to look at? Are they some that would fit Baby?"

"Oh no," said Peggy, "they'd be too little for him. Baby *is* rather fat. Oh no, it's *those* under the glass basin turned upside down," and she pointed to the dolls' shoes. "Aren't they lovely? I've seen them ever since I was quite little — I suppose they'd cost a great lot," and Peggy sighed.

"Which do you think the prettiest?" asked the lady.

"The red ones," Peggy replied.

"Well, I almost think I agree with you," said the lady. "Good-bye, my dear, don't let Baby run himself out into the street." And with a kind smile she went on into the shop.

She passed back again in a few minutes.

"Still there?" she said, nodding to Peggy, and then she made her way down the street and was soon out of sight. Peggy's attention, since the lady had warned her, had been entirely given to Baby, otherwise she might perhaps have noticed a very wonderful thing that had happened in the shop-window. The pair of red dolls' shoes was no longer there! They had been quietly withdrawn from the case in which they, with their companions, had spent a peaceful, but it must be allowed a rather dull life for some years.

In another minute nurse and Hal made their appearance, and Hal had a parcel, which he was clutching tightly in both hands.

"My new boots is *so* shiny," he said, "I do so hope they'll squeak. Does you think they will, nursie? But isn't poor Peggy to have new boots, too? *Poor* Peggy!"

Peggy looked down at her feet.

"Mine isn't wored out yet," she said; "it would take all poor mamma's money to buy new boots for us *all*."

"Never fear," said nurse, who heard rather a martyr tone in Peggy's voice, "you'll not be forgotten, Miss Peggy. But Master Hal, hadn't you better put your boots in the perambulator? You'll be tired of carrying them, for we're not going straight home."

Hal looked as if he were going to grumble at this, but before he had time to say anything, Miss Field came hurrying out of the shop.

"Oh, you're still here," she said; "that's all right. The lady who's just left told father to give this little parcel to missie here," and she held out something to Peggy, who was so astonished that for a moment or two she only stared at the girl without offering to take the tiny packet.

"For me," she said at last.

"Yes, missie, to be sure — for you, as I say."

Peggy took the parcel, and began slowly to undo it. Something red peeped out — Peggy's eyes glistened — then her cheeks grew nearly as scarlet as the contents of the packet, and she seemed to gasp for breath, as she held out for Hal and nurse to see the little red shoes which five minutes before she had been admiring under the glass shade.

"Nursie, Hal," she exclaimed, "see, oh see! The sweet little shoes — for me — for my very own."

Nurse was only too ready to be pleased, but with the prudence of a "grown-up" person she hesitated a moment.

"Are you sure there's no mistake, miss?" she said, anxiously. "Do you know the lady's name? Is she a friend of Missis's, I wonder?"

The girl shook her head.

"Can't say, I'm sure," she replied. "She's a stranger to us. She only just bought a pair of cork soles and these here. There's no mistake, that I'm sure of. She must have seen the young lady was admiring of them."

"Yes," said Peggy, "she asked me which was the prettiest, and I said the red ones."

"You see?" said Miss Field to nurse. "Well, missie, I hope as they'll fit Miss Dolly, and then you'll give us your custom when they're worn out, won't you?"

And with a good-natured laugh she turned back into the shop.

"It's all right, nursie, isn't it? Do say it is. I may keep them; they *is* mine, isn't they?" said Peggy, in very unusual excitement.

Nurse still looked undecided.

"I don't quite know what to say, my dear," she replied. "We must ask your mamma. I shouldn't think she'd object, seeing as it was so kindly meant. And we can't give back the shoes now they're bought and paid for. It wouldn't be fair to the lady to give them back to Field just to be sold again. It wasn't *him* she wanted to give a present to."

"No," said Peggy, trotting along beside the perambulator and clasping her little parcel as Hal was clasping his bigger one, "it was *me* she wanted to please. She's a *very* kind lady, isn't she, nursie? I'm sure they cost a great lot of money — p'raps a pound. Oh! I do so hope mamma will say I may keep them for my very own. Can't we go home now this minute to ask her?"

" We shouldn't find her in if we did," said nurse, "and we've had nothing of a walk so far. But don't you worry, Miss Peggy. I'm sure your mamma will not mind."

Peggy's anxious eager little face calmed down at this; a corner of the paper in which her treasures were wrapped up was torn. She saw the scarlet leather peeping out, and a gleam of delight danced out of her eyes; she bent her head down and kissed the speck of bright colour ecstatically, murmuring to herself as she did so, " Oh, how happy I am ! "

Nurse overheard the words.

"Missis will never have the heart to take them from her, poor dear," she thought. "She'll be only too pleased for Miss Peggy to have something to cheer her up when she has to be told about our going."

And Peggy, in blissful ignorance of any threatening cloud to spoil her pleasure, marched on, scarcely feeling the ground beneath her feet; as happy as if the tiny red shoes had been a pair of fairy ones to fit her own little feet.

Mamma was not at home when they got in, even though they made a pretty long round, coming back by Fernley Road, which, however, Peggy did not care about as much as when they set off by it. For coming back, of course, she could not see the hills without turning round, nor could she have the feeling that every step was taking her nearer to them.

The weather was clearing when they came in; from the nursery window the sky towards the west had a faint flush upon it, which looked as if the sunset were going to be a rosy one.

"Red at night," Peggy said to herself as she glanced out; "nursie, that means a fine day, doesn't it?"

"So they say," nurse replied.

"Then it'll be a fine day to-morrow, and I'll see the cottage, and I'll put the little shoes on the window-sill, so that they shall see it too — the *dear* little sweets," chattered the child to herself.

Hal meanwhile was seated on the floor, engaged in a more practical way, namely, *trying* to try on his new boots. But "new boots," as he said himself, "is stiff." Hal pulled and tugged till he grew very red in the face, but all in vain.

"Oh, Peggy!" he said, "do help me. I does so want to hear them squeak, and to 'upprise the boys when they come in."

Down went kind Peggy on the floor, and thanks to her the boots were got on, though the buttoning of them was beyond her skill. Hal was quite happy, though.

"They do squeak, don't they, Peggy?" he said; "and nurse'll let me wear them a little for them to get used to my feet 'afore we go to the country."

"You mean for your feet to get used to them, Hallie," said Peggy. "But there's lots of time for that. Why, they'll be half wored out before we go to the country if you begin them now."

" 'Tisn't nonsense," said Hal, sturdily. "Nurse said so to that girl in the shop."

Peggy felt very puzzled.

"But, Hal," she was beginning, when a voice interrupted her. It was nurse. She had been down-stairs, having heard the front door bell ring.

" Miss Peggy, your mamma wants you. She's come in. You'll find her in her own room."

"Nursie," she said, " Hal's been saying —"

"You mustn't keep your mamma waiting," said nurse. "I've told her about the little shoes."

"I'll take them to show her — won't she be pleased?" said Peggy, seizing the little parcel which she had put down while helping Hal.

And off she set.

She stopped at her mother's door; it was only half shut, so she did not need to knock.

" Mamma dear, it's me — Peggy," she said.

" Come in, darling," mamma's voice replied.

"I've brought you the *sweet* little red shoes to see," said Peggy, carefully unfolding the paper which held her treasures, and holding them out for mamma's admiration.

" They are very pretty indeed — really lovely little shoes," she said, handling them with care, but so as to see them thoroughly. " It was *very* kind of that lady. I wonder who she was? Of course in a general way I wouldn't like you to take presents from strangers, but she must have done it in such a very nice way. Was she an old lady, Peggy?"

"Oh yes!" said Peggy, "quite old. She was neely as big as you, mamma dear. I dare say she's *neely* as old as you are."

Mamma began to laugh.

"You little goose," she said. But Peggy didn't see anything to laugh at in what she had said, and her face remained quite sober.

"I don't understand you, mamma dear," she said.

"Well, listen then; didn't Hal buy a pair of new boots for himself to-day?" mamma began.

"No, mamma dear. Nurse buyed them *for* he," Peggy replied.

"Or rather *I* bought them, for it was my money nurse paid for them with, if you are so very precise, Miss Peggy. But never mind about that. All I want you to understand is the difference between 'big' and 'old.' Hal's boots are much bigger than these tiny things, but they are not on that account *older*."

Peggy began to laugh.

"No, mamma dear. P'raps Hallie's boots is younger than my sweet little red shoes, for they · has been a great long while in the shop window, and Baldwin and Terry sawed them when they was little."

"Not 'younger,' Peggy dear; 'newer,' you mean.

Boots aren't alive. You only speak of live things as
' young.' "

Peggy sighed.

" It is rather difficult to understand, mamma dear."

"It will all come by degrees," said mamma.
" When I was a little girl I know I thought for
a long time that the moon was the mamma of
the stars, because she looked so much bigger."

" I think that's very nice, mamma, though, of
course, I understand it's only a *fancy* fancy. I
haven't seen the moon for a long time, mamma.
May I ask nurse to wake me up the next time the
moon comes ? "

" You needn't wait till dark to see the moon,"
said mamma. " She can often be seen by daylight,
though, of course, she doesn't look so pretty then, as
in the dark sky which shows her off better. But,
of course, the sky here is so often dull with the
smoke of the town that we can't see her as clearly
in the daytime as where the air is purer."

" Like in the country, mamma," said Peggy. " It's
always clear in the country, isn't it ? "

" Not quite always," said mamma, smiling. " But,
Peggy dear, speaking of the country — "

" Oh yes ! " Peggy interrupted, " I want to tell
you, mamma, what a silly thing Hallie *would* say
about going to the country ; " and she told her
mother all that Hal had said about his boots, and
indeed what nurse had said too ; " and nursie was

just a weeny, teeny bit cross to me, mamma dear," said Peggy, plaintively. "She wouldn't say she'd mistooked about it."

Mamma looked rather grave, and instead of saying at once that of course nurse had only meant that Hal's boots should last till the summer, she took Peggy on her knee and kissed her — kissed her in rather a "funny" way, thought Peggy, so that she looked up and said —

"Mamma dear, why do you kiss me like that?"

Instead of answering, mamma kissed her again, which almost made Peggy laugh.

But mamma was not laughing.

"My own little Peggy," she said, "I have something to tell you which I am afraid will make you unhappy. It is making *me* very unhappy, I know."

"Poor dear little mamma," said Peggy, and as she spoke she put up her little hand and stroked her mother's face. "Don't be unhappy if it isn't anything *very* bad. Tell Peggy about it, mamma dear."

CHAPTER VI.

FELLOW-FEELINGS AND SLIPPERS.

MAMMA hesitated a moment. Then she began.

"You know, Peggy, my pet," she said, "for a good while now I haven't been as strong and well as I used to be — "

"Stop, mamma, stop," said Peggy, with a sort of cry, and as she spoke she threw up her hands and pressed them hard against her ears; " I know what you're going to say, but I can't bear it, no, I can't. Oh mamma, you're not to say you're going to die."

For all answer mamma caught Peggy into her arms and kissed her again and again. For a minute or two it seemed as if she could not speak, but at last she got her voice. And then, rather to Peggy's surprise, she saw that although there were tears in mamma's eyes, and even one or two trickling down her face, she was smiling too.

"My darling Peggy," she said, "did I frighten you? I am so, so sorry. Oh no, darling, it is nothing like that. Please God I shall live to see my

Peggy as old as I am now, and older, I hope. No, no, dear, it is nothing so very sad I was going to tell you. It is only that the doctor says the best way for me to get quite well and strong again is to go away for a while to have change of air as it is called, in some nice country place."

"In the country," said Peggy, her eyes brightening with pleasure. "Oh, how nice! will it perhaps be that country where my cottage is? Oh, dear mamma, how lovely! And when are we to go? May we begin packing to-day? And how could you think it would make me unhappy —" she went on, suddenly remembering what her mother had said at first.

Mamma's face did not brighten up at all.

"Peggy dear, it is very hard for me to tell you," she said. "Of course, if we had all been going together it would have been only happy. But that's just the thing. I can't take you with me, my sweet. Baby must go, because nurse must, and Hallie too. But the friend I am going to stay with can't have more of us than the two little ones, and nurse, and me — it is very, very good of her to take so many."

"Couldn't I sleep with you, mamma dear?" said Peggy in a queer little voice, the tone of which went to mamma's heart.

"My pet, Hallie must sleep with me, as it is. My friend's house isn't very big. And there's another reason why I can't take you — I'm not sure if you could understand —"

" Tell it me, please, mamma."

" The lady I am going to had a little girl just like you — I mean just the same age, and rather like you altogether, I think. And the poor little girl died two years ago, Peggy. Since then it is a pain to her mother to see other little girls. When you are bigger and not so like what her little girl was, I dare say she won't mind."

Peggy had been listening, her whole soul in her eyes.

" I understand," she said. " I wouldn't like to go if it would make that lady cry — if it hadn't been for that — oh mamma, I could have squeezed myself up so very tight in the bed! You and Hallie wouldn't have knowed I were there. But I wouldn't like to make her cry. I am so sorry about that little girl. Mamma, how is it that dying is so nice, about going to heaven, you know, and *still* it is so sorry? "

" There is the parting," said mamma.

" Yes — that must be it. And, mamma, I hope it isn't naughty, but if you were to die I'd be *very* sorry not to see you again just the same — even if you were to be a very pretty angel, with shiny clothes and all that, I'd want you to be my own old mamma."

" I would be your own old mamma, dear. I am sure you would feel I was the same."

" I'm so glad," said Peggy. " Still it is sad to die," and she sighed. " Mamma dear, you won't be very long away, will you? It'll only be a little short parting, won't it?"

"Only a few weeks, dear. And I hope you won't be unhappy even though you must be a little lonely."

"If only I had a sister," said Peggy.

But mamma went on to tell her all she had planned. Miss Earnshaw, a dressmaker who used sometimes to come and sew, was to be with Peggy as much as she could. She was a gentle, nice girl, and Peggy liked her.

"She has several things to make for me just now," said mamma, "and as she lives near, she will try to come every day, so that she will be with you at dinner and tea. And Fanny will help you to dress and undress, and either she or Miss Earnshaw will take you a walk every day that it is fine enough. And then in the evenings, of course, the boys will be at home, and papa will see you every morning before he goes."

"And I dare say he'll come up to see me in bed at night too," said Peggy. Then she was silent for a minute or two; the truth was, I think, that she was trying hard to swallow down a lump in her throat that *would* come, and to blink away two or three tiresome tears that kept creeping up to her eyes.

Two days later and they were gone. Mamma, nurse, Hal, and Baby, with papa to see them off, and two boxes outside the cab, and of course a whole lot of smaller packages inside.

Peggy stood at the front-door, nodding and kissing her hand and making a smile, as broad a one as she possibly could, to show that she was not crying.

When they were gone, really gone, and Fanny had shut the door, she turned kindly to Peggy.

"Now, Miss Peggy, love, what will you do? Miss Earnshaw won't be here till to-morrow. I'll try to be ready so as to take you out this afternoon if it's fine, for it's not a half-holiday. It'd be very dull for you all day alone — to-morrow the young gentlemen will be at home as it's Saturday."

A bright idea struck Peggy.

"Fanny," she said, "did mamma or nurse say anything about soap-bubbles?"

Fanny shook her head.

"No, miss. But I'm sure there'd be no objection to your playing at them if you liked. I can easy get a little basin and some soap and water for you. But have you a pipe?"

Peggy shook her head.

"It isn't for me, Fanny, thank you," she said. "It's for my brothers most. I'd like to make a surprise for them while mamma's away."

"Yes, that would be very nice," said Fanny, who had been charged at all costs to make Peggy happy. "We'll talk about it. But I'd better get on with my work, so as to get out a bit this afternoon."

"Very well. I'll go up to the nursery," said the little girl.

The nursery seemed very strange. Peggy had never seen it look quite so empty. Not only were nurse and the little ones gone, but it seemed as if everything belonging to them had gone too, for nurse had sat up late the night before and got up very early this same morning to put everything into perfect order before leaving. The tidiness was quite unnatural. Peggy sat down in a corner and gave a deep sigh. Just then she did not even care to turn to the window, where the sunshine was pouring in brightly, sparkling on the two little scarlet shoes, standing side by side on the sill, where Peggy placed them every fine morning, that they might enjoy the sight of the white cottage on the hill!

"I almost wish it was raining," she half whispered to herself, till she remembered how very disagreeable a wet day would have been for mamma and the others to travel on. "I hope it will be a sunny day when they come back," she added, as a sort of make-up for her forgetfulness.

And then she got up and wandered into the other room. Here one of Hal's old shoes which had fallen out of a bundle of things to be given away which nurse had taken downstairs just before going, was lying on the floor. Peggy stooped and picked it up. How well she knew the look of Hal's shoes; there was the round bump of his big toe, and the hole at the corner where a bit of his red sock used to peep out! It gave her a strange dreamy feeling as she looked at it. It seemed as if it could not be true that Hallie was far away — "far, far away" by this time, thought Peggy, for she always felt as if the moment people were in the railway they were whizzed off hundreds of miles in an instant. She stroked the poor old shoe lovingly and kissed it. I don't think just then she would have parted with it for any-thing; it would have cost her less to give away the lovely little scarlet ones.

The thought of the old clothes turned her mind to the children at the back.

"I wonder if nurse gave them any of Hal's and Baby's old things," she said to herself.

And she went to the window with a vague idea of looking to see. She had not watched the Smileys or their relations much for some days; she had been busy helping mamma and nurse in various little ways, and her mind had been very full of the going away. She almost felt as if she had neglected her opposite neighbours, though, of course, they knew nothing about it, and she was quite pleased to see them all there as usual, or even more than usual. For it was so fine a day that Reddy and her mother were evidently having a grand turn-out — a sort of spring cleaning, I suppose.

Small pieces of carpet, and one or two mats, much the worse for wear, were hanging out at the open windows. Reddy's head, tied up in a cloth to keep the dust out of her hair, was to be seen every minute or two, as she thumped about with a long broom, and Mary-Hann presently appeared with a pail of soapy water which she emptied at a grid in the gutter. Mary-Hann looked rather depressed, but Reddy's spirits were fully equal to the occasion. Had the window been open, Peggy felt sure she would have been able to hear her shouting to her sister to "look sharp," or to "mind what she was about," even more vigorously than usual.

The rest of the family, excepting, of course, the boys, were assembled on the pavement in front of Mr. Crick the cobbler's shop. He too had opened his window to enjoy the fine day, and in the background he could be dimly seen working, as dingy and leathery as ever. Mrs. Whelan's frilled cap and pipe looked out for a moment and then disappeared again. Apparently just then there was nobody or nothing she *could* scold.

For the poor children on the pavement were behaving very quietly. The Smileys had stayed at home from school to mind the babies, with a view to smoothing the way for the spring cleaning, no doubt, and were sitting, each with a child on her lap, in two little old chairs they had carried down. Crippley was rocking herself gently in her chair beside them, and the last baby but two, as Peggy then thought, was on his knees on the ground, amusing himself with two or three oyster shells and a few marbles. All these particulars Peggy, from her high-up nursery window, could not, of course, see clearly, but she saw enough to make her sigh deeply as she thought that after all, the Smileys were much to be envied.

"I dare say they're telling theirselves stories," she said to herself. "They look so comfable."

Just then the big baby happened to come more in sight, and she saw that one of the things he was playing with was a little shoe — an odd one apparently. He had filled it with marbles, and was pulling it across the stones. Up jumped Peggy from her seat on the window-sill.

"Oh!" she exclaimed, though there was no one to hear, "it must be the nother shoe of this. What a pity! They'd do for Tip, and p'raps they've thought there wasn't a nother. How I would like to take it them! I'll call Fanny and see if she'll run across with it."

Downstairs she went, calling Fanny from time to time as she journeyed. But no Fanny replied; she was down in the kitchen, and to the kitchen Peggy knew mamma would not like her to go. She stood at last in the passage wondering what to do, when, glancing round, she noticed that the back-door opening into the yard was temptingly open. Peggy peeped out — there was no one there, but, still more tempting, the door leading into the small back street — the door just opposite the Smiley mansion — stood open, wide open too, and even from where she was the little girl could catch sight of the group on the other side of the narrow street.

She trotted across the yard, and stood for a minute, the shoe in her hand, gazing at the six children. The sound of their voices reached her.

"Halfred is quite took up with his shoe," said Brown Smiley. "I told mother she moight as well give it he — a hodd shoe's no good to nobody."

"'Tis a pity there wasn't the two of 'em," said Crippley, in a thin, rather squeaky voice. "They'd a done bee-yutiful for — "

"For Tip — yes, that's what *I* were thinking," cried an eager little voice. "Here's the other shoe; I've just founded it."

And little Peggy, with her neat hair and clean pinafore, stood in the middle of the children holding out Hal's slipper, and smiling at them, like an old friend.

For a moment or two they were all too astonished to speak; they could scarcely have stared more had they caught sight of a pair of wings on her shoulders, by means of which she had flown down from the sky.

Then Light Smiley nudged Crippley, and murmured something which Peggy could not clearly hear, about "th' young lady hopposite."

"Thank you, miss," then said Crippley, not quite knowing what to say. "Here, Halfred, you'll have to find summat else to make a carridge of; give us the shoe — there's a good boy."

' "For Tip—yes, that's what I were thinking," cried an eager little voice. "Here's the other shoe; I've just founded it."

And little Peggy, with her neat hair and clean pinafore, stood in the middle of the children holding out Hal's slipper, and smiling at them like an old friend. '

Halfred stopped playing, and still on his knees on the pavement stared up suspiciously at his sister. Brown Smiley, by way of taking part in what was going on, swooped down over him and caught up the shoe before he saw what she was doing, cleverly managing to hold her baby on her knee all the same.

"'Ere it be," she said. "Sarah, put Florence on Lizzie's lap for a minute, and run you upstairs with them two shoes to mother. They'll do splendid for Tommy, they will. And thank the young lady."

Sarah, otherwise Light Smiley, got up obediently, deposited *her* baby on Crippley's lap and held out her hand to Peggy for the other shoe, bobbing as she did so, with a "Thank you, miss."

Peggy left off smiling and looked rather puzzled.

"For Tommy," she repeated. "Who is Tommy? I thought they'd do for Tip. I — "

It was now the sisters' turn to stare, but they had not much time to do so, for Halfred, who had taken all this time to arrive at the knowledge that his new plaything had been taken from him, suddenly burst into a loud howl — so loud, so deliberate and determined, that Peggy stopped short, and all the group seemed for a moment struck dumb.

Brown Smiley was the first to speak.

"Come, now, Halfred," she said, "where's your manners? You'd never stop Tommy having a nice pair o' shoes."

But Halfred continued to weep — he gazed up at

Peggy, the tears streaming down his smutty face, his mouth wide open, howling hopelessly.

"Poor little boy," said Peggy, looking ready to cry herself. "I wish I'd a nother old shoe for him."

"Bless you, miss, he's always a-crying — there's no need to worry," said Crippley, whose real name was Lizzie. "Take him in with you, Sarah, and tell mother he's a naughty boy, that's what he is," and Light Smiley picked him up and ran off with him in such a hurry that Peggy stood still repeating "poor little boy" before she knew what had become of him.

Quiet was restored, however. Peggy, having done what she came for, should have gone home, but the attractions of society were too much for her. She lingered — Crippley pushed Sarah's empty chair towards her.

"Take a seat, miss," she said. "You'll excuse me not gettin' up. Onst I'm a-sittin' down, it's not so heasy."

Peggy looked at her with great interest.

"Does it hurt much?" she asked.

Lizzie smiled in a superior way.

"Bless you," she said again, "*hurt's* no word for it. It's hall over — but it's time I were used to it — never mind about me, missy. I'm sure it was most obligin' of you to bring the shoe, but won't your mamma and your nurse scold you?"

"My mamma's gone away, and so has my nurse," said Peggy. "I'm all alone."

All the eyes looked up with sympathy.

"Deary me, who'd a thought it?" said Brown Smiley. "But there must be somebody to do for you, miss."

"To what?" asked Peggy. "Of course there's cook, and Fanny, and my brothers, and my papa when he comes home."

Brown Smiley looked relieved. She was only a very little girl, not more than three years older than Peggy herself, though she seemed so much more, and she had really thought that the little visitor meant to say she was quite, quite by herself.

"Oh!" she said, "that's not being real alone."

"But it is," persisted Peggy. "It is very alone, I can tell you. I've nobody to play with, and nothing to do 'cept to look out of the window at you playing, and at the nother window at—"

"The winder to the front," said Lizzie, eagerly. "It must be splendid at your front, miss. Father told me onst you could see the 'ills — ever so far right away in Brackenshire. Some day if I could but get along a bit better I'd like fine to go round to your front, miss. I've never seed a 'ill."

Lizzie was quite out of breath with excitement. Peggy answered eagerly.

"Oh I do wish you could come to our day nursery window. When it's fine you can see the mountings

—that's old, no, big hills, you know. And—on one of them you can see a white cottage; it does so shine in the sun."

"Bless me," said Lizzie, and both the Smileys, for Sarah had come back by now, stood listening with open mouths.

"Father's from Brackenshire," said Light Smiley, whose real name was Sarah. She spoke rather timidly, for she was well kept in her place by her four elder sisters. For a wonder they did not snub her.

"Yes, he be," added Matilda, "and he's told us it's bee-yutiful over there. He lived in a cottage, he did, when he were a little lad."

"Mebbe 'tis father's cottage miss sees shining," ventured Sarah. But this time she was not so lucky.

"Rubbish, Sarah," said Lizzie. "There's more'n one cottage in Brackenshire."

"And there's a mamma and a baby—and a papa who goes to work, in my cottage," said Peggy. "So I don't think it could be—" but here she grew confused, remembering that all about the white cottage was only fancy, and that besides the Smileys' father *might* have lived there long ago. She got rather red, feeling somehow as if it was not very kind of her not to like the idea of its being his cottage. She had seen him once or twice; he looked big and rough, and his clothes were old—she could not fancy him ever having lived in her dainty white house.

Just then came a loud voice from the upper story, demanding Sarah.

"'Tis Mother Whelan," said Brown Smiley, starting up. " Rebecca said as how I was to run of an errant for her. It's time I were off."

Peggy turned to go.

" I must go home," she said. " P'raps I'll come again some day. If mamma was at home I'd ask her if you mightn't come to look out of the nursery window," she added, turning to Lizzie.

" Bless you," said the poor girl, " I'd never get up the stairs ; thank you all the same."

And with a deep sigh of regret at having to leave such pleasant company, Peggy ran across the street home.

CHAPTER VII.

A BUN TO THE GOOD.

" The little gift from out our store."

THE yard door was still open; so was the house
door. Peggy met no one as she ran in.

"Fanny's upstairs, p'raps," she said to herself.
But no, she saw nothing of Fanny either on the way
up or in the nursery. She did not feel dull or lonely
now, however. She went to the back window and
stood there for a minute looking at Crippley and
Light Smiley, who were still there with the two babies.
How funny it seemed that just a moment or two ago
she had been down there actually talking to them!
She could scarcely believe they were the very same
children whom for so long she had known by sight.

"I am so glad I found the shoe," thought Peggy.
"I wish, oh I do wish I could have a tea-party, and
'avite them all to tea. I dare say the father could
carry Crippley upstairs — he's a very big man."

The thought of the father carried her thoughts
to Brackenshire and the cottage on the hill, and she
went into the day-nursery to look if the white spot
was still to be seen. Yes, it was very bright and

clear in the sunshine. Peggy gazed at it while a smile broke over her grave little face.

" How I do wish I could go there," she thought. " I wonder if the Smileys' father 'amembers about when he was a little boy, quite well. If he wasn't such a 'nugly man we might ask him to tell us stories about it."

Then she caught sight of the little scarlet shoes patiently standing on the window-sill.

" Dear little shoes," she said, " Peggy was neely forgetting you," and she took them up and kissed them. " Next time I go to see the Smileys," she thought, " I'll take the red shoes with me to show them. They *will* be pleased."

Then she got out her work and sat down to do it, placing her chair where she could see the hills from, the little shoes in her lap, feeling quite happy and contented. It seemed but a little while till Fanny came up to lay the cloth for Peggy's dinner. She had been working extra hard that morning, so as to be ready for the afternoon, and perhaps her head was a little confused. And so when Peggy began telling her her adventures she did not listen attentively, and answered "yes" and "no" without really knowing what she was saying.

" And so when I couldn't find you, Fanny, I just runned over with the 'nother shoe myself. And the poor little boy what was playing with the — the *not* the 'nother one, you know, did so cry, but I think he soon left off. And some day I'm going to ask mamma to let me 'avite them all to tea, for them to see the hills, and — " but here Peggy stopped, " the hills, you know, out of the window."

" Yes, dear; very nice," said Fanny. " You've been a good little girl to amuse yourself so quietly all the morning and give no trouble. I do wonder if the washerwoman knows to come for the nursery things, or if I must send," she went on, speaking, though aloud, to herself.

So Peggy felt perfectly happy about all she had done, not indeed that she had had the slightest misgiving.

The afternoon passed very pleasantly. It was quite a treat to Peggy to go a walk in a grown-up sort of way with Fanny, trotting by her side and talking comfortably, instead of having to take Hal's hand and lugging him along to keep well in front of the perambulator. They went up the Fernley Road — a good way, farther than Peggy had ever been — so far indeed that she could scarcely understand how it was the hills did not seem much nearer than from the nursery window, but when she asked Fanny, Fanny said it was often so with hills — " nothing is more undependable." Peggy did not quite understand her, but put it away in her head to think about afterwards.

And when they came home it was nearly tea-time. Peggy felt quite comfortably tired when she

had taken off her things and began to help Fanny to
get tea ready for the boys, and when they arrived,
all three very hungry and rather low-spirited at the
thought of mamma and nurse being away, it was
very nice for them to find the nursery quite as tidy as
usual — indeed, perhaps, rather tidier — and Peggy,
with a bright face, waiting with great pride to pour
out tea for them.

"I think you're a very good housekeeper, Peg,"
said Terence, who was always the first to say something pleasant.

"Not so bad," agreed Thorold, patronisingly.

Baldwin sat still, looking before him solemnly,
and considering his words, as was his way before *he*
said anything.

"I think," he began at last, "I think that when
I'm a big man I'll live in a cottage all alone with
Peggy, and not no one else."

Peggy turned to him with sparkling eyes.

"A *white* cottage, Baldwin dear; do say a white
cottage," she entreated.

"I don't mind — a white cottage, but quite a tiny
one," he replied.

"Hum!" said Thor, "that's very good-natured, I
must say. There'll be no room for visitors, do you
hear, Terry?"

"Oh yes; p'raps there will sometimes," said Peggy.

"You'll let your poor old Terry come, won't you,
Peg-top?" said Terence, coaxingly.

"Dear Terry," said Peggy.

"Haven't you been very dull all day alone, by the bye?" Terence went on.

"Not very," Peggy replied. "Fanny took me a nice walk, and this morning—" But she stopped short before telling more. She was afraid that Thorold would laugh at her if she said how much she liked the children at the back, and then she had another reason. She wanted to "surprise" her brothers with a present of pipes for soap-bubbles, and very likely if she began talking about the back street at all it would make them think of Mrs. Whelan's, and then they might think of the pipes for themselves, which Peggy did not wish at all. She felt quite big and managing since she had paid a visit to the Smileys, and had a plan for going to buy the pipes "all by my own self."

"To-morrow," said Thorold, "there's to be a party at our school. We're all three to go."

Peggy's face fell.

"It's Saturday," she said. "I thought you'd have stayed with me."

Terence and Baldwin looked sorry.

"*I'll* stay at home," said Terry.

"No," said Thor, "I really don't think you can. They're counting on you for some of the games. Peg won't mind much for once, will you? I'm sorry too."

But before Peggy had time to reply, Baldwin broke in.

"I'll stay at home with Peg-top," he said, in his slow, distinct way. "It won't matter for me not going. I'm one of the little ones."

"And we'll go a nice walk, won't we, Baldwin?" said Peggy, quite happy again. "And I dare say we may have something nice for tea. I'll ask papa," she added to herself. "I'm sure he'll give me some pennies when he hears how good Baldwin is."

Miss Earnshaw came the next morning, and in the interest of being measured for her new spring frock, and watching it being cut out, and considering what she herself could make with the scraps which the young dressmaker gave her, the time passed very pleasantly for Peggy.

Miss Earnshaw admired the red shoes very much, and was interested to hear the story of the unknown lady who had given them to Peggy, and told a story of a similar adventure of her own when she was a little girl. And after dinner she, for Fanny was very busy, took Peggy and Baldwin out for a walk, and on their way home they went to the confectioner's and bought six halfpenny buns with the three pennies papa had given Peggy that morning. At least the children thought there were only six, but greatly to their surprise, when they undid the parcel on the nursery table, out rolled seven!

"Oh dear!" said Peggy, "she's gave us one too many. Must we go back to the shop with it, do you think, Miss Earnshaw? It's such a long way."

"I'll go," said Baldwin, beginning to fasten his boots again.

But Miss Earnshaw assured them it was all right.

"You always get thirteen of any penny buns or cakes for a shilling," she said; "and some shops will give you seven halfpenny ones for threepence. That's how it is. Did you never hear speak of a baker's dozen?"

Still Peggy did not feel satisfied.

"It isn't comfable," she said, giving herself a little wriggle — a trick of hers when she was put out. "Six would have been much nicer — just two for each," for Miss Earnshaw was to have tea with her and Baldwin.

The young dressmaker smiled.

"You *are* funny, Miss Peggy," she said. "Well, run off now and get ready for tea. We'll have Fanny bringing it up in a minute."

Peggy, the seventh bun still much on her mind, went slowly into the night nursery. Before beginning to take off her hat she strolled to the window and looked out. She had seen none of the children to-day. Now, Brown Smiley was standing just in front of the house, a basket on her arm, staring up and down the street. She had been "of an errant" for Mrs. Whelan, but Mrs. Whelan's door was locked; she was either asleep or counting her money, and the little girl knew that if she went on knocking the old woman would get into a rage, so she was

"I can't 'amember your name," she exclaimed, breathlessly, "but I've brought you this," and she held out the bun.

Brown Smiley's face smiled all over. "Lor', miss," she exclaimed. "You are kind, to be sure. Mayn't I give it to Lizzie? She's been very bad to-day, and she's eat next to nought. This 'ere'll be tasty-like."

* * * *

But suddenly a window above opened, and Mother Whelan's befrilled face was thrust out. "What are ye about there then, and me fire burning itself away, and me tea ready, waiting for the bread? What's the young lady chatterin' to the likes o' you for? Go home, missy, darlin', go home."

" waitin' a bit." She liked better to do her waiting in the street, for she had been busy indoors all the morning, and it was a change to stand there looking about her.

Peggy gazed at her for a moment or two. Then an idea struck her. She ran back into the nursery and seized a bun — the odd bun.

" They're all mine, you know," she called out to Baldwin; " but we'll have two each still."

Baldwin looked up in surprise. " What are you going to do with it? " he began to say, but Peggy was out of sight.

She was soon downstairs, and easily opened the back door. But the yard door was fastened; she found some difficulty in turning the big key. She managed it at last, however, and saw to her delight that Brown Smiley was still there.

" Brown," began Peggy, but suddenly recollecting that the Smileys had real names, she stopped short, and ran across the street. " I can't 'amember your name," she exclaimed, breathlessly, " but I've brought you this," and she held out the bun.

Brown Smiley's face smiled all over.

" Lor', miss," she exclaimed. " You are kind, to be sure. Mayn't I give it to Lizzie? She's been very bad to-day, and she's eat next to nought. This 'ere'll be tasty-like."

" Lizzie," repeated Peggy, " which is Lizzie? Oh yes, I know, it's Crippley."

Brown Smiley looked rather hurt.

"It's not her fault, miss," she said. "I'd not like her to hear herself called like that."

Peggy's face showed extreme surprise.

"How do you mean?" she said. "I've made names for you all. I didn't know your real ones."

Brown Smiley looked at her and saw in a moment that there was nothing to be vexed about.

"To be sure, miss. Beg your pardon. Well, she that's lame's Lizzie, and me, I'm Matilda-Jane."

"Oh yes," interrupted Peggy. "Well, you may give her the bun if you like. It's very kind of you, for I meant it for you. I'd like — " she went on, "I'd like to give you more, but you see papa gaved me the pennies for us, and p'raps he'd be vexed."

"To be sure, to be sure, that'd never do," replied Matilda, quickly. "But oh, miss, we've been asking father about Brackenshire, and the cottages. 'Tis Brackenshire 'ills, sure enough, that's seen from your front."

"I knew that," said Peggy, in a superior way.

But Brown Smiley was too eager to feel herself snubbed.

"And oh, but he says it is bee-yutiful there — over on the 'ills. The air's that fresh, and there's flowers and big-leaved things as they calls ferns and brackens."

"And white cottages?" asked Peggy, anxiously.

"There's cottages — I didn't think for to ask if they was all white. My! If we could but go there some fine day. Father says it's not so far; many's the time he's walked over there and back again the next morning when he first comed to work here, you see, miss, and his 'ome was still over there like."

" Yes, in the white cottage," said Peggy. She had made up her mind that it was unkind not to " let it be " that the Smileys' father had lived in that very cottage, for he did seem to be a nice man in spite of his bigness and his dingy workman's clothes. If he wasn't nice and kind she didn't think the children would talk of him as they did.

But she spoke absently; Matilda-Jane's words had put thoughts in her head which seemed to make her almost giddy. Brown Smiley stared at her for a minute.

" How she do cling to them cottages being white," she thought to herself, " but there—if it pleases her! She's but a little one." " White if you please, miss," she replied, " though I can't say as I had it from father."

But suddenly a window above opened, and Mother Whelan's befrilled face was thrust out.

" What are ye about there then, and me fire burning itself away, and me tea ready, waiting for the bread? What's the young lady chatterin' to the likes o' you for? Go home, missy, darlin', go home."

The two children jumped as if they had been shot.

"Will she beat you?" whispered Peggy, looking very frightened. But Brown Smiley shook her little round head and laughed.

"She won't have a chance, and she dursn't not to say beat us — father'd be down on her — but she doesn't think nought of a good shakin'. But I'll push the basket in and run off if she's in a real wax."

"Good-bye, then. You must tell me lots more about the hills. Ask your father all you can," and so saying, Peggy flew home again.

"Where've you been, what did you do with the bun?" asked Baldwin, as soon as she came into the nursery.

"I runned down with it, and gaved it to a little girl I saw in the street," said Peggy.

"Very kind and nice, I'm sure," said Miss Earnshaw. "Was it a beggar, Miss Peggy? You're sure your mamma and nurse wouldn't mind?" she added, rather anxiously.

"Oh no," said Peggy. "It's not a *beggar*. It's a proper little poor girl what nurse gives our nold clothes to."

"Oh," said Baldwin, "one of the children over the cobbler's, I suppose. But, Peggy," he was going on to say he didn't think his sister had ever been allowed to run down to the back street to speak to them, only he was so slow and so long of making up his mind that, as Fanny just then came in with the tea, which made a little bustle, nobody attended to him, and Miss Earnshaw remained quite satisfied that all was right.

The buns tasted very good — all the better to Peggy from the feeling that poor lame Lizzie was perhaps eating hers at that same moment, and finding it " tasty."

" Does lame people ever get quite better?" she asked the young dressmaker.

" That depends," Miss Earnshaw replied. " If it's through a fall or something that way, outside of them so to say, there's many as gets better. But if it's *in* them, in the constitution, there's many as stays lame all their lives through."

Peggy wriggled a little. She didn't like to think about it much. It sounded so mysterious.

" What part's that?" she asked; " that big word."

" Constitootion," said Baldwin, as if he was trying to spell " Constantinople."

Miss Earnshaw laughed. She lived alone with her mother, and was not much used to children. But she was so pleasant-tempered and gentle that she easily got into their ways.

" I shouldn't use such long words," she said. "Our constitution just means ourselves — the way we're made. A strong, healthy person is said to have a good constitution, and a weakly person has a poor one."

Baldwin and Peggy both sat silent for a minute, thinking over what she said.

"I don't see how that's to do with crippling," said Peggy at last. "Does you mean," she went on, "that p'raps lame people's legs is made wrong — by mistake, you know. *In course* God wouldn't do it of purpose, would he?"

Baldwin looked rather startled.

"Peggy," he said, "I don't think you should speak that way."

Peggy turned her gray eyes full upon him.

"I don't mean to say anything naughty," she said. "*Is* it naughty, Miss Earnshaw?"

The young dressmaker had herself been rather taken aback by Peggy's queer speech, and for a moment or two scarcely knew what to say. But then her face cleared again.

"God can't make mistakes, Miss Peggy," she said, "and He is always kind. All the same there's many things that seem like one or the other, I know. It must be that there's reasons for them that we can't see — like when a doctor hurts anybody, it seems unkind, but it's *really* to do them good."

"Like when our doctor cutted poor Baby's tooths to make them come through," said Peggy, eagerly. "They was all *bleeding*, bleeding ever so, Miss Earnshaw. Baby didn't understand, and he was *very* angry. He always sc'eams at the doctor now. I almost think he'd like to kill him."

Baldwin opened his mouth wide at these blood-thirsty sentiments of Baby's. He was too shocked to speak.

"But it is only 'cos he doesn't understand," Peggy went on, placidly. "*I* don't sc'eam at the doctor. I speak to him quite goodly, 'cos, you see, *I* understand."

Baldwin closed his mouth again. He looked at Peggy with admiring respect.

"Yes," agreed Miss Earnshaw, greatly relieved at the turn their talk had taken, "that's just it, Miss Peggy. You couldn't have put it better."

"Peggy," said Baldwin, "when you're big you should be a clergymunt."

CHAPTER VIII.

UNDER THE BIG UMBRELLA.

" As I was going up Pippin Hill,
　　Pippin Hill was dirty,
　　There I met a pretty miss,
　　And she dropped me a curtsey."

OLD NURSERY RHYME.

NOTHING particular happened during the next few days. Peggy's little life went on regularly and peacefully. Miss Earnshaw came every morning, and either she or Fanny took Peggy a walk every afternoon, except twice when it rained, to the little girl's great disappointment.

The second of these wet days happened to be Friday. Peggy stood at the front nursery window that morning looking out rather sadly. There were no hills — no white spot to be seen, of course.

" I wonder what the Smileys do when it rains all day," she said to herself. " I think I'll go to the back window and look if I can see any of them."

She had scarcely caught sight of her neighbours for some days. Only now and then she had seen the little ones tumbling about on the pavement, and once or twice the elder girls had brought their chairs down and sat there sewing. Lizzie had never come out. Peggy feared she must be still ill, and perhaps that made the others extra busy. It was not likely any of them would come out to-day, as it was raining so; but *sometimes* she was able to see their faces at the window. And on a rainy day some of the little ones at least would perhaps be looking out.

She turned to go to the other nursery when Miss Earnshaw spoke to her.

"I wouldn't be so vexed at its being wet to-day, Miss Peggy, if I was you," she said. "It'll be much worse if it's wet to-morrow, for it's your brothers' half-holiday."

"Is to-morrow Saturday?" asked Peggy.

"To be sure it is. And I'm afraid I can't possibly stay here in the afternoon. I've got to go to see a lady some way off about some work. I wish she hadn't fixed for Saturday. If it's fine it won't matter so much. Fanny and I were saying you could all go a nice walk — the young gentlemen and you, with her. But if it's wet I don't know however she'll manage you all in the house."

Suddenly Peggy's eyes began to sparkle.

"Miss Earnshaw," she said, "I've thought of something. If you'll ask Fanny, I'm sure she'll say we can; we've not had them for such a long time, and I've got my four pennies and a halfpenny — that'll get six, you know, in case any's brokened."

Miss Earnshaw looked at her and then began to laugh.

"Miss Peggy dear, you must tell me first what you mean," she said. "Your thoughts come so fast that they run ahead of your words. What is it you mean to get six of — not buns?"

"Buns!" repeated Peggy. "You can't blow bubbles with buns. No, of course I meant pipes. Nice white pipes to blow soap-bubbles."

"Oh, to be sure," said Miss Earnshaw. "That's a very good idea, Miss Peggy, in case to-morrow afternoon's wet, and I shouldn't wonder if it was."

"And you'll ask Fanny?"

"Of course; you can ask her yourself for that matter. I'm sure she's the last to grudge you anything that'd please you and the young gentlemen. And even if soap-bubbles are rather messy sometimes, it's easy to wipe up. It's not like anything dirty."

"Soap must be clean, mustn't it?" said Peggy, laughing. "But don't tell the boys, pelease, dear Miss Earnshaw. I do so want to 'apprise them. I can get the pipes to-morrow morning. I know where to get them," and quite happy, Peggy trotted off to take out her money-box and look to be quite sure that the three pennies and three halfpennies were there in safety, where for some weeks they had been waiting.

"Bless her heart," said the young dressmaker. "She is the sweetest little innocent darling that ever lived."

After looking over her pennies Peggy turned to

the window. No, none of the Smileys were to be seen.

"Never mind," said Peggy to herself. "I'll p'raps see them to-morrow when I go for the pipes. I almost hope it'll be a wet day. It will be so nice to blow soap-bubbles. Only," and she sighed a little, "it does seem such a very long time since I sawed the white cottage."

To-morrow *was* rainy, very rainy, with no look of "going to clear up" about it. The boys grumbled a good deal at breakfast at the doleful prospect of a dull half-holiday in the house.

"And papa's going away to-day till Monday," said Thorold; "so there'll be no going down to the dining-room to sit beside him while he's at dinner for a change."

"Poor papa," said Peggy, "he'll get very wet going such a long way."

"Nonsense, you little goose," said Thor, crossly. "People don't get wet in cabs and railway carriages."

"I forgot," said Peggy, meekly.

"You shouldn't call her a goose, Thor," said Terence. "It's very disagreeable to travel on a very rainy day. I've often heard people say so."

"I wish I was going to travel, rainy or not, I know that," grumbled Thorold. "Here we shall be mewed up in this stupid nursery all the afternoon with nothing to do."

"There's lots of things to do," said Baldwin. "I

think I'll write a letter to mamma for one thing. And I want to tidy my treasure-box and — ”

“ You're a stupid,” said Thorold. “ You're too fat and slow to have any spirit in you.”

“ Now, Thorold, I say that's not fair,” said Terry. “ Would it show spirit to grumble? You'd be down upon him if he did. There's no pleasing you.”

“ *I* know something that would please him,” said Peggy, who was trembling between eagerness to tell and determination *not* to tell her “ surprise.”

“ What?” said Thor, rather grumpily still.

“ I'm not going to tell you till you come home. And it'll only be if it's a rainy afternoon,” said Peggy.

Terence and Baldwin pricked up their ears.

“ Oh, do tell us, Peg-top,” they said.

But the little girl shook her head.

“ No, no,” she replied. “ I've promised myself — . *quite* promised not.”

“ There's a reason for you,” said Thor. But his tone was more good-natured now. He felt ashamed of being so cross when the little ones were so kind and bright.

“ I'll really, *truly* tell you when you come back from school,” said Peggy, and with this assurance the boys had to content themselves.

Miss Earnshaw arrived as usual, or rather not as usual, for she was dripping, poor thing, and had to leave her waterproof downstairs in the kitchen,

"What weather, Miss Peggy," she said, as she came in. "I thought it would be a wet day, but not such a pour. It is unfortunate that I have to go so far to-day, isn't it? And I'm sorry to leave you children alone too."

"Never mind," said Peggy, cheerily; "we'll be quite happy with the soap-bubbles. I've got my money quite ready. Mayn't I go and get the pipes now?"

"Out, my dear? In such weather!" exclaimed Miss Earnshaw.

"Oh, but it's *quite* near," said Peggy. "Just hop out of the door and you're there. The boys always buy their pipes there, and mamma goes there herself sometimes to see the old woman."

"Well, wait a bit, anyway. It can't go on raining as fast as this all the morning surely. It's real cats and dogs."

Peggy looked up in surprise.

"Cats and dogs, Miss Earnshaw?" she repeated.

"Oh, bless you, my dear, it's only a way of speaking," said the dressmaker, a little impatiently, for she was not very much accustomed to children. "It just means raining *very* hard."

Peggy went to the window to look out for herself. Yes indeed it was raining very hard. The little girl could not help sighing a little as she gazed at the thick even gray of the clouds, hiding like a curtain every trace of the distant hills she was so fond of.

"I won't put out the little red shoes to-day," she said to herself, "there's nothing for them to see."

.Then other thoughts crept into her mind.

"I wonder if it's raining at the white cottage too," she said to herself. And aloud she asked a question.

"Miss Earnshaw, pelease, does it ever rain in the country?" she said.

"Rain in the country! I should rather think it did. Worse than in town, you might say — that's to say, where there's less shelter, you'll get wetter and dirtier in the country, only of course it's not the same kind of really black sooty rain. But as for mud in country lanes! I shall see something of it this afternoon, I expect."

"Oh, I'm so sorry," said Peggy. "I thought it never rained in the country. I thought it was always quite pretty and lovely," and she sighed deeply. "I wonder what people who live in little cottages in the country do all day when it rains," she said.

"Why, my dear, much the same as other folk, I should say. They have their rooms to clean, and their dinner to cook, and their children to look after. Still I dare say it'd be a bit drearier in the country of a right-down wet day like this, even than in town. I've never lived there myself, except for a week at a time at most, but mother was all her young days in the country."

"Everybody's fathers and mothers lived there," said Peggy, rather petulantly. "Why don't peoples let their children live there now?"

Miss Earnshaw laughed a little. Peggy did not like her to laugh in that way, and she gave herself a little wriggle, though poor Miss Earnshaw certainly did not mean to vex her.

"There are plenty of children in the country too, Miss Peggy," she said. "Mother's youngest sister has twelve."

"Twelve," repeated Peggy, "*how* nice! at least if there's lots of sisters among them, and no very little babies. Do they live over in that country?" she went on, pointing in the direction of the invisible hills, "that country called Brack— You know the name."

"Brackenshire," said Miss Earnshaw, "no, my mother comes from much farther off. A very pretty place it must be by what she says. Not but what Brackenshire's a pretty country too. I've been there several times with the Sunday school for a treat."

"And did you see the hills and the white cottages?" asked Peggy breathlessly.

"Oh yes, the hills are beautiful, and there's lots of cottages of all kinds. They look pretty among the trees, even though they're only poor little places, most of them."

"The white ones is the prettiest," said Peggy, as if she knew all about it.

"Yes, I dare say," said Miss Earnshaw, without paying much attention; she had got to rather a difficult part of the sleeve she was making.

"Did you ever walk all the way there when you was a little girl?" Peggy went on.

"Oh yes, of course," Miss Earnshaw replied, without the least idea of what she was answering.

"Really!" said Peggy, "how nice!" Then seeing that the dressmaker was absorbed in her work: "Miss Earnshaw," she said, "I'm going for the pipes now. It isn't raining *quite* so fast, and I'll not be long."

"Very well, my dear," Miss Earnshaw replied, and Peggy went off to fetch her pennies from the drawer in the other nursery where she kept them. She had a new idea in her head, an idea which Miss Earnshaw's careless words had helped to put there, little as she knew it.

"If I see the Smileys," thought Peggy, "I'll tell them what she said."

She glanced out of the window, dear me, how lucky! There stood Brown Smiley looking out at the door, as if she were hesitating before making a plunge into the dripping wet street. It did seem at the back as if it were raining faster than in front. Peggy opened the cupboard and took out her little cloak which was hanging there.

"I won't put on my hat," she thought, "'cos nurse says the rain spoils the feavers. I'll get a numbrella downstairs, and then I *can't* get wet, and here's my pennies all right in my pocket. I do hope Brown Smiley will wait till I get down."·

She made all the haste she could, and found, as she expected, an umbrella in the stand downstairs. It was not very easy to open, but she succeeded at last, then came, however, another difficulty, she could not get herself and the umbrella through the back door together.

"Dear me," thought Peggy, "I wonder how people does with their numbrellas. They *must* open them in the house, else they'd get wet standing outside while they're doing it. I never looked to see how nurse does, but then we almost never go out when it's rainy. I 'appose it's one of the hard things big peoples has to learn. Oh, dear! *won't* it come through?"

No, she couldn't manage it, at least not with herself under it. At last a brilliant idea struck Peggy; anything was better than closing the tiresome thing now she *had* got it opened — she would send it first and follow after herself. So the umbrella was passed through, and went slipping down the two or three steps that led into the yard, where it lay gaping up reproachfully at Peggy, who felt inclined to call out "Never mind, poor thing, I'm coming d'reckly."

And as "d'reckly" as possible she did come, carefully closing the door behind her, for fear the rain should get into the house, which, together with the

picking up of the umbrella, far too big and heavy
a one for a tiny girl, took so long that I am afraid
a good many drops had time to fall on the fair
uncovered head before it got under shelter again.

But little cared Peggy. She felt as proud as
a peacock, the umbrella representing the tail, you
understand, when she found herself outside the yard
door, which behaved very amiably, fairly under
weigh for her voyage across the street. She could
see nothing before her; fortunately, however, no
carriages or carts ever came down the narrow back
way.

Half-way over Peggy stopped short — she had
forgotten to look if Brown Smiley was still standing
there. It was not easy to get a peep from under
the umbrella, without tilting it and herself backwards on to the muddy road, but with great care
Peggy managed it. Ah dear, what a disappointment! There was no little girl in front of the
cobbler's window, but glancing to one side, Peggy
caught sight of the small figure with a shawl of
" mother's " quaintly drawn over the head, trotting
away down the street. With a cry Peggy dashed
after her.

" Oh, Brown Smiley," she called out, " do come
back. I'm too frightened to go to buy the pipes
alone," for what with her struggles and her excitement, the little damsel's nerves were rather upset.
"Oh, Brown Smiley — no — no, that's not her

"But an umbrella rolling itself about on the pavement, an umbrella from which proceeds most piteous wails, an umbrella from underneath which, when you get close to it, you see two little feet sticking out, and by degrees two neat black legs, and then a muddle of short skirts, which by rights should be draping the legs, but have somehow got all turned upside down like a bird's feathers ruffled up the wrong way — such an umbrella, or perhaps I should say an umbrella in such circumstances, may certainly be called a strange sight, may it not?"

p. 111, 112

name, oh what *is* your name, Brown Smiley?" and on along the rough pavement behind the little messenger she rushed, if indeed poor Peggy's toddling, flopping from one side to another progress, could possibly be called " rushing."

It came to an end quickly — the paving-stones were rough and uneven, the small feet had only " my noldest house-shoes " to protect them, and the " numbrella " was sadly in the way; there came suddenly a sharp cry, so piercing and distressful that even Matilda-Jane, accustomed as she was to childish sounds of woe of every kind and pitch, was startled enough to turn round and look behind her.

"Can it be Halfred come a-runnin' after me?" she said to herself. But the sight that met her eyes puzzled her so, that at the risk of Mother Whelan's scoldings for being so long, she could not resist running back to examine for herself the strange object. This was nothing more nor less than an umbrella, and an umbrella in itself is not an uncommon sight. But an umbrella rolling itself about on the pavement, an umbrella from which proceeds most piteous wails, an umbrella from underneath which, when you get close to it, you see two little feet sticking out and by degrees two neat black legs, and then a muddle of short skirts, which by rights should be draping the legs, but have somehow got all turned upside down like a bird's feathers ruffled up the wrong way — *such* an umbrella, or perhaps

I should say an umbrella in such circumstances, certainly may be called a strange sight, may it not?

Matilda-Jane Simpkins, for that was Brown Smiley's whole long name, thought so anyway, for she stood stock still, staring, and the only thing she could collect herself enough to say was, " Lor'!"

But her state of stupefaction only lasted half a moment. She was a practical and business-like little person; before there was time for another cry for help, she had disentangled the umbrella and its owner, and set the latter on her feet again, sobbing piteously, and dreadfully dirty and muddy, but otherwise not much the worse.

Then Matilda-Jane gave vent to another exclamation.

" Bless me, missy, it's *you!* " she cried. " Whatever are you a-doing of to be out in the rain all alone, with no 'at and a humbrella four sizes too big for the likes of you, and them paper-soled things on yer feet? and, oh my! ain't yer frock muddy? What'll your folk say to you? Or is they all away and left you and the cat to keep 'ouse?"

" I was running after you, Brown Smiley," sobbed Peggy. She could not quite make out if Matilda-Jane was making fun of her or not, and, indeed, to do Matilda justice, she had no such intention. " I was running after *you*," Peggy repeated, " and you *wouldn't* stop, and I couldn't run fast 'cos of the numbrella, and so I felled down."

"Never mind, missy dear, you'll be none the worse, you'll see. Only, will they give it you when you go home for dirtying of your frock?"

"Give it me?" repeated Peggy.

"Yes, give it you; will you get it — will you catch it?" said Matilda, impatiently.

"I don't know what you mean," Peggy replied.

Matilda wasted no more words on her. She took her by the arm, umbrella and all, and trotted her down the street again till they had reached the Smiley mansion. Then she drew Peggy inside the doorway of the passage, whence a stair led up to Mrs. Whelan's, and to the Simpkins's own rooms above that again, and having shut up the umbrella with such perfect ease that Peggy gazed at her in admiration, as she tried to explain her meaning.

"Look 'ere now, miss," she said, "which'll you do — go straight over-the-way 'ome, just as you are, or come in along of *huz* and get yerself cleaned up a bit?"

"Oh, I'll go in with you, pelease," sobbed Peggy. "P'raps Miss Earnshaw wouldn't scold me. She let me come, and I didn't fell down on purpose. But I *know* she wouldn't let me come out again — I'm sure she wouldn't, and I do so want to get the pipes my own self. You'll take me to Mrs. Whelan's, won't you, dear Brown Smiley?"

"I'll catch it when she sees I haven't done her errant," said Matilda. " But never mind; she'll not

be so bad with you there, maybe. Come up with
me, missy, and I'll get Rebecca to wipe you a bit,"
and she began the ascent of the narrow staircase,
followed by Peggy.

CHAPTER IX.

THE OPPOSITE HOUSE.

" There was an old woman that lived in a shoe,
She had so many children she didn't know what to do."
NURSERY RHYMES.

IN spite of her misfortunes, Peggy could not help feeling very pleased at finding herself at last inside the house she had watched so often from the outside. It was certainly not a pretty house — a big person would probably have thought it a very poor and uninteresting one; but it was not dirty. The old wooden steps were scrubbed down once a week regularly, so there was nothing to strike the little girl as disagreeable, and it seemed delightfully queer and mysterious as she climbed the steep, uneven staircase, which grew darker and darker as they went on, so that but for Brown Smiley's voice in front, Peggy would not have had the least idea where she was going.

"There's Mother Whelan's door," Matilda said in a half whisper, as if afraid of the old woman's pouncing out upon them, and Peggy wondered how she knew it, for to her everything was perfectly dark; " but we'll go upstairs first to Rebecca," and on they climbed.

Suddenly, what seemed for a moment a blaze of brilliant light from the contrast with the darkness where they were, broke upon them. Peggy quite started. But it was only the opening of a door.

"Is that you, Matilda-Jane? My, but you have been sharp. I should think old Whelan 'ud be pleased for onst."

The speaker was Reddy; she stood in the doorway, her bare red arms shining, as they always did, from being so often up to the elbows in soap and water.

"Oh, Rebecca, don't say nothin', but I've not been of my errant yet. Now, don't ye begin at me — 'tweren't of my fault. I was a-'urryin' along when I saw miss 'ere a-rollin' in the wet with her humber-ellar, and I 'ad to pick her up. She's that muddy we were afeared they'd give it her over the way — her mar's away. So I told her as you'd tidy her up a bit. Come along, missy. Rebecca's got a good 'eart, has Rebecca; she'll clean you nicely, you'll see."

For at the sound of Rebecca's sharp voice poor Peggy had slunk back into the friendly gloom of the staircase. But she came creeping forward now, so that Reddy saw her.

"Lor'!" said the big girl, "little miss from the hopposite winder to be sure."

This quite restored Peggy's courage.

"Have you seen me at the window?" she said. "How funny! I've looked at you lotses and lotses of times, but I never thought of you looking at me."

To which both sisters replied with their favourite exclamation, " Lor' ! "

Just then came a voice from inside.

" Shut the door there Rebecca, can't you ? If there's one thing I can't abide, and you might know it, it's a hopen door, and the draught right on baby's head."

Rebecca took Peggy by the hand and drew her into the room, and while she was relating the story of little missy's misfortunes to her mother, little missy looked round her with the greatest interest.

It was a small room, but oh, how full of children ! Dinner was being got ready " against father and the boys coming home," Matilda said, but where father and the boys could possibly find space to stand, much less to sit, Peggy lay awake wondering for a long time that night. She counted over those already present, and found they were all there except Lizzie, the lame girl. And besides the two babies and Alfred, whom she knew by sight, she was amazed to see a fourth, a very tiny doll of a thing — the tiniest thing she had ever seen, but which they all were as proud of as if there had never been a baby among them before. At this moment it was reposing in the arms of Mary-Hann ; Light Smiley, whose real name was Sarah, you remember, was taking charge of the two big babies in one corner, while Reddy and her mother were busy at the fire, and " Halfred " was amusing himself quietly with some marbles, apparently his natural occupation.

What a lot of them! Peggy began to feel less sure that she would like to have as many sisters as the Smileys. Still they all looked happy, and their mother, whom Peggy had never seen before, had really a very kind face.

"I'll see to the pot, Rebecca," she said; "just you wipe missy's frock a bit. 'Twill be none the worse, you'll see. And so your dear mar's away, missy. I 'ope the change'll do her good."

"Yes, thank you," said Peggy. "She's gone to the country. Did you ever live in the country? And was it in a white cottage?"

Mrs. Simpkins smiled.

"No, missy, I'm town-bred. 'Tis father as knows all about the country; he's a Brackenshire man."

"Oh yes," said Peggy, "I forgot. It's Miss Earnshaw's mother I was thinking of."

"But father," said Matilda, "*he* can tell lots of tales about the country."

"I wish he was at home," said Peggy. "But I must go, now my frock's cleaned. Some day p'raps I'll come again. Thank you, Reddy," at which Rebecca, who had been vigorously rubbing Peggy's skirts, stared and looked as if she were going to say "Lor'!" "I'm going to buy soap-bubble pipes at Mrs. Whelan's," Peggy went on, for she was losing her shyness now; "that's what I comed out in the rain for. We're going to play at soap-bubbles this afternoon, 'cos it's too wet to go out a walk."

All the Smileys listened with great interest.

" Mayn't Brown — I mean Matilda-Jane — come with me, pelease? " said Peggy. " I'm *razer* frightened to go to buy them alone; sometimes that old woman does look so cross."

" She looks what she is then," said Reddy, " 'cept for one thing; she's awful good to Lizzie. She's a-sittin' down there this very minute as is, is Lizzie, to be out o' the way like when mother and me's cleaning, you see, miss."

Brown Smiley's face had grown grave.

" I dursn't let Mother Whelan see as I've not gone," she said, " but if missy doesn't like to go alone — not as she'd be sharp to the likes of you, but still — "

" *I'll* go," said little Sarah, Light Smiley, that is to say. " Jest you see to the childer will ye, Mary-Hann? " she shouted to the deaf sister. " I won't be harf a minute."

" And you, Matilda-Jane, off with you," said Rebecca, which advice Brown Smiley instantly followed.

Sarah took Peggy's hand to escort her down the dark staircase again. Light Smiley was, of all the family perhaps, Peggy's favourite. She was two years or so older than her little opposite neighbour, but she scarcely looked it, for both she and Brown Smiley were small and slight, and when you came to speak to them both, Sarah seemed a good deal younger than Matilda; she was so much less managing and decided in manner, but on the present occasion Peggy would have preferred the elder Smiley, for to tell the truth her heart was beginning to beat much faster than usual at the thought of facing Mrs. Whelan in her den.

"Isn't you frightened, Light Smiley?" asked the little girl when the two stopped, and Peggy knew by this that they must be at the old woman's door.

"Oh no," Sarah replied. "'Tisn't as if we'd been up to any mischief, you see. And Lizzie's there. She's mostly quiet when Lizzie's there."

So saying she pushed the door open. It had a bell inside, which forthwith began to tinkle loudly, and made Peggy start. This bell was the pride of Mrs. Whelan's heart; it made such a distinction, she thought, between her and the rest of the tenants of the house, and the more noisily it rang the better pleased she was. Sarah knew this, and gave the door a good shove, at the same time pulling Peggy into the room.

"What's it yer afther now, and what's become of Matilda-Jane?" called out the old woman, not, at the first moment, catching sight of Peggy.

"It's little missy from over-the-way," Sarah hastened to explain; "she's come to buy some pipes of you, Mother Whelan."

Mrs. Whelan looked at Peggy where she stood behind Sarah, gravely staring about her.

"To be sure," she said in her most gracious tone. 'Tis the beauti- ful pipes I have. And 'tis proud I am to say the purty young lady," and on she went with a long flattering speech about Peggy's likeness to her "swate mother," and inquiries after the lady's health, all the time she was reaching down from a high shelf an old broken cardboard box, containing her stock of clay pipes. '

p 121

" To be sure," she said in her most gracious tone. " 'Tis the beautiful pipes I have. And 'tis proud I am to say the purty young lady," and on she went with a long flattering speech about Peggy's likeness to her " swate mother," and inquiries after the lady's health, all the time she was reaching down from a high shelf an old broken cardboard box, containing her stock of clay pipes.

Peggy did not answer. In the first place, thanks to the old woman's Irish accent and queer way of speaking, she did not understand a quarter of what she said. Then her eyes were busy gazing all about, and her nose was even less pleasantly occupied, for there was a very strong smell in the room. It was a sort of mixed smell of everything — not like the curious " everything " smell that one knows so well in a village shop in the country, which for my part I think rather nice — a smell of tea, and coffee, and bacon, and nuts, and soap, and matting, and brown holland, and spices, and dried herbs, all mixed together, but with a clean feeling about it — no, the smell in Mrs. Whelan's was much stuffier and snuffier. For joined to the odour of all the things I have named was that of herrings and tobacco smoke, and, I rather fear, of whisky. And besides all this, I am very much afraid that not only a spring cleaning, but a summer or autumn or winter cleaning, were unknown events in the old woman's room. No wonder that Peggy, fresh from the soft-soap-and-water smell of the Simpkins's upstairs, sniffed uneasily and wished Mrs. Whelan would be quick with the pipes; her head felt so queer and confused.

But looking round she caught sight of a very interesting object; this was Lizzie, rocking herself gently on her chair in a corner, and seeming quite at home. Peggy ran — no she couldn't run — the room was so crowded, for a counter stood across one end, and in the other a big square old bedstead, and between the two were a table and one or two chairs, and an old tumble-down chest of drawers — made her way over to Lizzie.

" How do you do, Crip — Lizzie, I mean? I hope your pains aren't very bad to-day? "

" Not so very, thank you, miss," said the poor girl. " It's nice and quiet in here, and the quiet does me a deal o' good."

Peggy sighed.

" I don't like being very quiet," she said. " I wish you would come over to the nursery; now that Hal and baby and nurse are away it's dreffully quiet."

" But you wouldn't care to change places with me, would you, missy? " said Lizzie. " I'm thinking you'd have noise enough if you were upstairs sometimes. My — it do go through one's head, to be sure."

Peggy looked very sympathising.

" Aren't you frightened of *her?* " she whispered, nodding gently towards Mrs. Whelan.

"Not a bit of it," said Lizzie, also lowering her voice; "she's right down good to me, is the old body. She do scold now and then and no mistake, but bless you, she'd never lay a finger on me, and it's no wonder she's in a taking with the children when they kicks up a hextra row, so to say."

Peggy's mouth had opened gradually during this speech, and now it remained so. She could not understand half Lizzie's words, but she had no time to ask for an explanation, for just then Light Smiley called to her to come and look at the pipes which were by this time waiting for her on the counter.

They were the cleanest things in the room — the only clean things it seemed to Peggy as she lifted them up one by one to choose six very nice ones. And then she paid her pennies and ran back to shake hands with Lizzie and say good-bye to her — she wondered if she should shake hands with Mrs. Whelan too, but fortunately the old woman did not seem to expect it, and Peggy felt very thankful, for her brown wrinkled hands looked sadly dirty to the little girl, dirtier perhaps than they really were.

"I like your house much better than hers," said Peggy, when she and Light Smiley were down at the bottom of the stairs again; "it smells much nicer."

"Mother and Rebecca's all for scrubbing, that's certing," replied Sarah, with a smile of pleasure — of course all little girls like to hear their homes praised

—"but she's not bad to Lizzie, is old Whelan," as if that settled the whole question, and Peggy felt she must not say any more about the dirty room.

Light Smiley felt it her duty to see "missy" safe across the street. Peggy's hands were laden with the precious pipes, and Sarah carried the big umbrella over the two of them. They chattered as they picked their way through the mud and stood for a minute or two at the yard-door of Peggy's house. Light Smiley peeped in.

"Lor'," she said, expressing her feelings in the same way as her sisters, "yours must be a fine house, missy. All that there back-yard for yerselves."

"You should see the droind-room, and mamma's room; there's a marble top to the washing-stand," said Peggy, with pride.

"Lor'," said Sarah again.

"Some day," Peggy went on, excited by Sarah's admiration, "*some* day when my mamma comes home, I'm going to ask her to let me have a tea-party of you all — in the nursery, you know. The nursery's nice too, at least I dare say you'd like it."

"Is that the winder where you sees us from?" asked Sarah. "Matilda-Jane says as how we could see you too quite plain at it if you put your face quite close to the glass."

"I can't," said Peggy. "There's the toilet-table close to the window — at least, it's really a chest of drawers, you know, but there's a looking-glass on the top and a white cover, so it's like a toilet-table for nurse, though its too high up for me. I have to stand on a chair if I want to see myself popperly."

"Dear!" said Sarah sympathisingly.

"And I can only see you by scrooging into the corner, and the curting's there. No, you couldn't ever see me well up at the window. But that's not the nursery where we'd have tea. That's only the night nursery. The other one's to the front; that's the window where you can see the hills far away."

"In the country, where father used to live. Oh yes, I know. I heerd Matilda-Jane a-asking 'im about it," said Sarah.

"Oh, and did he tell you any more? Do ask him if it's really not far to get there," said Peggy, eagerly.

Sarah nodded.

"I won't forget," she said; "and then, missy, when you axes us to the tea-party, I'll be able to tell you all about it."

She did not mean to be cunning, poor little girl, but she was rather afraid Peggy might forget about the tea-party, and she thought it was not a bad plan to say something which might help to make her remember it.

"Yes," Peggy replied, "that would be lovely. Do make him tell all you can, Light Smiley. Oh, I do wish mamma would come home now, and I'd ask her about the tea-party immediately. I'm sure

she'd let me, for she likes us to be kind to poor
people."

Sarah drew herself up a little at this.

"We're not — not to say *poor* folk," she said, with
some dignity. "There's a many of us, and it's hard
enough work, but still — "

"Oh, don't be vexed," said Peggy. "I know
you're not like — like beggars, you know. And I
think *we're* rather poor too. Mamma often says papa
has to work hard."

Sarah grew quite friendly again.

"I take it folks isn't often rich when they've a lot
of children," she began, but the sound of a window
opening across the street made her start. "Bless
me," she said, "I must run. There's Rebecca a-going
to scold me for standing talking. Good-bye, miss,
I'll not forget to ask father."

And Sarah darted away, carrying with her the
umbrella, quite forgetting that it was Peggy's.
Peggy forgot it too, and it was not raining so fast
now, so there was less to remind her. She shut the
door and ran across the yard. The house door still
stood open, and she made her way up to the nursery
without meeting any one.

CHAPTER X.

"SOAP-BUBBLING."

" And every colour see I there."
The Rainbow. — CHARLES LAMB.

THERE was no one upstairs. Miss Earnshaw had gone down to the kitchen to iron the seams of her work, without giving special thought to Peggy. If any one had asked her where the child was she would have probably answered that she was counting over her money in the night nursery. So she was rather surprised when coming upstairs again in a few minutes she was met by Peggy flying to meet her with the pipes in her hand.

"I've got them, Miss Earnshaw; aren't they beauties?" she cried. "And I don't think my frock's reely spoilt? It only just looks a *little* funny where the mud was."

"Bless me!" exclaimed the young dressmaker, "wherever have you been, Miss Peggy? No, your frock'll brush all right; but you don't mean to say you've been out in the rain? You should have asked me, my dear."

She spoke rather reproachfully; she was a little vexed with herself for not having looked after the child better, but Peggy was one of those quiet "old-fashioned" children, who never seem to need looking after.

"I did ask you," said Peggy, opening wide her eyes, "and you said, 'Very well, my dear.'"

Miss Earnshaw couldn't help smiling.

"I must have been thinking more of your new frock than of yourself," she said. "However, I hope it's done you no harm. Your stockings aren't wet?"

"Oh no," said Peggy; "my slippers were a weeny bit wet, so I've changed them. My frock wouldn't have been dirtied, only I felled in the wet, Miss Earnshaw, but Brown — one of the little girls, you know, that lives in the house where the shop is — picked me up, and there's no harm done, is there? And I've got the pipes, and won't my brothers be peleased," she chirruped on in her soft, cheery way.

Miss Earnshaw could not blame her, though she determined to be more on the look-out for the future. And soon after came twelve o'clock, and then the young dressmaker was obliged to go, bidding Peggy "Good-bye till Monday morning."

The boys came home wet and hungry, and grumbling a good deal at the rainy half-holiday. Peggy had hidden the six pipes in her little bed, but after dinner she made the three boys shut their eyes while she fetched them out and laid them in a row on the table. Then, "You may look now," she said; "it's my apprise," and she stood at one side to enjoy the sight of their pleasure.

"Hurrah," cried Terry, "pipes for soap-bubbles! Isn't it jolly? Isn't Peggy a brick?"

"Dear Peggy," said Baldwin, holding up his plump face for a kiss.

"Poor old Peg-top," said Thor, patronisingly. "They seem very good pipes; and as there's six of them, you and I can break one a-piece if we like, Terry, without its mattering."

Peggy looked rather anxious at this.

"Don't try to break them, Thor, pelease," she said; "for if you beginned breaking it might go on, and then it would be all spoilt like the last time, for there's no fun in soap-bubbling by turns."

"No, that's quite true," said Terry. "You remember the last time how stupid it was. But of course we won't break any, 'specially as they're yours, Peggy. We'll try and keep them good for another time."

"Did you spend all your pennies for them?" asked Baldwin, sympathisingly.

"Not quite all," said Peggy. "I choosed them myself," she went on, importantly. "There was a lot in a box."

"Why, where did you get them? You didn't go yourself to old Whelan's, surely?" asked Thor, sharply.

"Yes, I runned across the road," said Peggy. "You always get them there, Thor."

" But it's quite different. I can tell you mamma won't be very pleased when she comes home to hear you've been so disobedient."

Poor Peggy's face, so bright and happy, clouded over, and she seemed on the point of bursting into tears.

" I weren't disobedient," she began. " Miss Earnshaw said, ' Very well, dear,' and so I thought — "

" Of course," interrupted Terry; " Peggy's never disobedient, Thor. We'll ask mamma when she comes home; but she won't be vexed with you, darling. You won't need to go again before then."

" No," said Peggy, comforted, " I don't want to go again, Terry dear. It doesn't smell very nice in the shop. But the *children's* house is very clean, Terry. I'm sure mamma would let us go *there*."

" Those Simpkinses over old Whelan's," said Terry. " Oh yes, I know mother goes there herself sometimes, though as for that she goes to old Whelan's too. But we're wasting time; let's ask Fanny for a tin basin and lots of soap."

They were soon all four very happy at the pretty play. The prettiness of it was what Peggy enjoyed the most; the boys, boy-like, thought little but of who could blow the biggest bubbles, which, as everybody knows, are seldom as rich in colour as smaller ones.

" I like the rainbowiest ones best," said Peggy. " I don't care for those 'normous ones Thor makes. Do you, Baldwin ? "

"They were soon all four very happy at the pretty play. The prettiness of it was what Peggy most en: joyed the most; the boys, boy- like, thought little but of who could blow the biggest bubbles, which, as everybody knows, are seldom as rich in colour as smaller ones."

p. 130

Baldwin stopped to consider.

" I suppose very big things aren't never so pretty as littler things," he said at last, when a sort of grunt from Terry interrupted him. Terry could not speak, his cheeks were all puffed out round the pipe, and he dared not stop blowing. He could only grunt and nod his head sharply to catch their attention to the wonderful triumph in soap-bubbles floating before his nose. There was a big one, as big as any of Thorold's, and up on the top of it a lovely every-coloured wee one, the most brilliant the children had ever seen — a real rainbow ball.

They all clapped their hands, at least Peggy and Baldwin did so. Thorold shouted, "Hurrah for Terry's new invention. It's like a monkey riding on an elephant." But Peggy did not think that was a pretty idea.

" It's more like one of the very little stars sitting on the sun's knee," was her comparison, which Baldwin corrected to the moon — the sun was too yellow, he said, to be like a no-colour bubble.

Then they all set to work to try to make double-bubbles, and Thor actually managed to make three, one on the top of the other. And Terry made a very big one run ever so far along the carpet without breaking, bobbing and dancing along as he blew it ever so gently.

And as a finish-up they all four put their pipes into the basin and blew together, making what they called " bubble-pudding," till the pudding seemed to get angry and gurgled and wobbled itself up so high that it ended by toppling over, and coming to an untimely end as a little spot of soapy water on the table.

"Pride must have a fall, you see," said Thor.

"It's like the story of the frog that tried to be as big as an ox," said Terence, at which they all laughed as a very good joke.

Altogether Peggy's pipes turned out a great success, and the rainy afternoon passed very happily.

The Sunday that came after that Saturday was showery, sunny, and rainy by turns, like a child who having had a great fit of crying and sobbing can't get over it all at once, and keeps breaking into little bursts of tears again, long after the sorrow is all over. But by Monday morning the world — Peggy's world, that is to say — seemed to have quite recovered its spirits. The sun came out smiling with pleasure, and even the town birds, who know so little about trees, and grass, and flowers, and all those delightful things, hopped about and chirruped as nicely as could be. The boys set off to school in good spirits, and while Fanny was taking down the breakfast-things Peggy got out the little red shoes, and set them on the window-sill, where they had not been for several days.

"There, dear little red shoes," she said, softly, "you may look out again at the pretty sun and the sky, and the fairy cottage up on the mounting. You can see it quite plain to-day, dear little shoes. The clouds is all gone away, and it's shinin' out all white and beautiful, and I dare say the mamma's standin' at the door with the baby — or p'raps," Peggy was never very partial to the baby, "it's asleep in its cradle. Yes, I think that's it. And the hens and cocks and chickens is all pecking about, and the cows moo'in. Oh, *how* I do wish we could go and see them all, don't you, dear little shoes?"

She stood gazing up at the tiny white speck, to other eyes almost invisible, as if by much gazing it would grow nearer and clearer to her; there was a smile on her little face, sweet visions floated before Peggy's mind of a day, "some day," when mamma should take her out "to the country," to see for herself the lovely and delightful sights that same dear mamma had described.

Suddenly Fanny's voice brought her back to present things. Fanny was looking rather troubled.

"Miss Peggy, love," she said, "cook and I can't think what's making Miss Earnshaw so late this morning. She's always so sharp to her time. I don't like leaving you alone, but I don't know what else to do. Monday's the orkardest day, for we're always so busy downstairs, and your papa was just saying this morning that I was to tell Miss Earnshaw to take you a nice long walk towards the country, seeing as it's so fine a day. It will be right down tiresome, it will, if she don't come."

"Never mind, Fanny," said Peggy. "I don't mind much being alone, and I dare say Miss Earnshaw will come. I *should* like to go a nice walk to-day," she could not help adding, with a longing glance out at the sunny sky.

"To be sure you would," said Fanny, "and it stands to reason as you won't be well if you don't get no fresh air. I hope to goodness the girl will come, but I doubt it — her mother's ill maybe, and she's no one to send. Well, dear, you'll try and amuse yourself, and I'll get on downstairs as fast as I can."

Peggy went back to the window and stood there for a minute or two, feeling rather sad. It did seem hard that things should go so very "contrarily" sometimes.

"Just when it's such a fine day," she thought, "Miss Earnshaw doesn't come. And on Saturday when we *couldn't* have goned a walk she did come. Only on Saturday it did rain very badly in the afternoon and she didn't stay, so that wasn't a pity."

Then her thoughts went wandering off to what the dressmaker had told her of having to go a long way out into the country on Saturday afternoon, and of how wet and muddy the lanes would be. Peggy sighed; she *couldn't* believe country lanes could ever be anything but delightful.

"Oh how *very* pretty they must be to-day," she said to herself, "with all the little flowers coming peeping out, and the birds singing, and the cocks and hens, and the cows, and — and — " she was becoming a little confused. Indeed she wasn't *quite* sure what a "lane" really meant — she knew it was some kind of a way to walk along, but she had heard the word "path" too, — were "lane" and "path" quite the same? she wondered. And while she was wondering and gazing out of the window, she was startled all of a sudden by a soft, faint tap at the door. So soft and faint that if it had been at the window instead of at the door it might have been taken for the flap of a sparrow's wing as it flew past. Peggy stood quite still and listened; she heard nothing more, and was beginning to think it must have been her fancy, when again it came, and this time rather more loudly. "Tap, tap." Yes, "certingly," thought Peggy, "there's somebody there."

She felt a little, a *very* little frightened.

Should she go to the door and peep out, or should she call "Come in"? she asked herself. And one or two of the "ogre" stories that Thorold and Terry were so fond of in their "Grimm's Tales," *would* keep coming into her head — stories of little princesses shut up alone, or of giants prowling about to find a nice tender child for supper. Peggy shivered. But after all what was the use of standing there fancying things? It was broad, sunny daylight — not at all the time for ogres or such-like to be abroad. Peggy began to laugh at her own silliness.

"Very likely," she thought, "it's Miss Earnshaw playing me a trick to 'apprise me, 'cos she's so late this morning."

This idea quite took away her fear.

"It's you, Miss Earnshaw, I'm quite sure it's you," she called out; "come in quick, you funny Miss Earnshaw. Come in."

But though the door slowly opened, no Miss Earnshaw appeared. Peggy began to think this was carrying fun too far.

"Why don't you come in quick?" she said, her voice beginning to tremble a little.

The door opened a little farther.

"Missy," said a low voice, a childish hesitating voice, quite different from Miss Earnshaw's quick bright way of speaking. "Missy, please, it's me, Sarah, please, miss."

And the door opened more widely, and in came, slowly and timidly still, a small figure well known to Peggy. It was none other than Light Smiley.

Peggy could hardly speak. She was so very much astonished.

"Light Smiley — Sarah, I mean," she exclaimed, "how did you come? Did you see Fanny? Did she tell you to come upstairs?"

Sarah shook her head.

"I don't know who Fanny is, missy. I just comed in of myself. The doors was both open, and I didn't meet nobody. I didn't like for to ring or knock. I thought mebbe your folk'd scold if I did — a gel like me. Mother knows I've comed; she said as how I'd better bring it myself."

And she held up what Peggy had not noticed that she was carrying — the big umbrella that had caused so much trouble two days before.

"The numbrella," cried Peggy. "Oh thank you, Sarah, for bringing it back. I never thought of it! How stupid it was of me."

"Mother told me for to bring it to the door and give it in," Sarah went on. "I didn't mean to come upstairs, but, the door was open, you see, miss, and I knowed your nussery was at the top, and — I 'ope it's not a liberty."

"No, no," said Peggy, her hospitable feelings awaking to see that her little visitor was still standing timidly in the doorway, "I'm *very* glad you've comed. You don't know how glad I am. It's so lonely all by myself — Miss Earnshaw hasn't come this morning. Come in, Light Smiley, do come in. Oh now nice! I can show you the mountings and the little white cottage shining in the sun."

She drew Sarah forwards. But before the child looked out of the window, her eyes were caught by the tiny red slippers on the sill.

"Lor'," she said breathlessly, "what splendid shoes! Are they for — for your dolly, missy? They're too small for a baby, bain't they?"

"Oh yes," said Peggy, "they're too small for our baby, a great deal. But then he's very fat."

" They'd be too small for ours too, though she's not a hextra fine child for her age. She were a very poor specimint for a good bit, mother says, but she's pickin' up now she's got some teeth through. My — but them shoes is neat, to be sure! They must be for a dolly."

" *I've* no doll they'd do for," said Peggy, " but I like them just for theirselves. I always put them to stand there on a fine day; they like to look out of the window."

Sarah stared at Peggy as if she thought she was rather out of her mind! — indeed the children at the back had hinted to each other that missy, for all she was a real little lady, was very funny-like sometimes. But Peggy was quite unconscious of it.

" Lor'," said Sarah at last, " how can shoes see, they've no eyes, missy? "

" But you can *fancy* they have. Don't you ever play in your mind at fancying? " asked Peggy. " I think it's the nicest part of being alive, and mamma says it's no harm if we keep remembering it's not real. But never mind about that — do look at the hills, Sarah, and oh, *can* you see the white speck shining in the sun? *That's* the cottage — I call it my cottage, but *p'raps*," rather unwillingly, " it's the one your papa lived in when he was little."

" D'ye really think so? " said Sarah, eagerly. " It's Brackenshire over there to be sure, and father's 'ome was up an 'ill — deary me, to think as it might be the very place. See it — to be sure I do, as plain as plain. It do seem a good bit off, but father he says it's no more'n a tidy walk. He's almost promised he'll take some on us there some fine day when he's an 'oliday. I axed 'im all I could think of — missy — all about the cocks and 'ens and cows and pigses."

"Not pigs," interrupted Peggy. "I don't like pigs, and I won't have them in my cottage."

"I wasn't a-talking of your cottage," said Sarah, humbly. "'Twas what father told us of all the things he seed in the country when he were a boy there. There's lots of pigses in Brackenshire."

"Never mind. We won't have any," persisted Peggy. "But oh, Light Smiley, do look how splendid the sky is — all blue and all so shiny. I never sawed such a lovely day. I would so like to go a walk."

"And why shouldn't you?" asked Sarah.

"There's no one to take me," sighed Peggy. "It's Monday, and Fanny's very busy on Mondays, and I told you that tiresome Miss Earnshaw's not comed."

Sarah considered a little.

"Tell you what, missy," she said, "why shouldn't we — you and me — go a walk? I'm sure mother'd let me. I've got my 'at, all 'andy, and I did say to mother if so as missy seed me I might stop a bit, and she were quite agreeable. I'm a deal older nor you, and I can take care of you nicely. Mother's training me for the nussery."

Peggy started up in delight. She had been half sitting on the window-sill, beside the shoes.

"Oh, Light Smiley," she said, "how lovely! Of course you could take care of me. We'd go up Fernley Road, straight up — that's the way to Brackenshire, you know, and p'raps we might go far enough to see the white cottage plainer. If it's not a very long way to get there, we'd be sure to see it much plainer if we walked a mile or two. A mile isn't very far. Oh, do let's go — quick! quick!"

But Sarah stopped her.

"You'd best tell your folks first, missy," she said. "They'll let you go and be glad of it, I should say, if they're so busy, and seein' as they let you come over to our 'ouse, and your mar knowin' us and all."

"It was Miss Earnshaw that let me go," said Peggy, "and then she said she didn't know I'd goned. And Thor said — oh no, he only said I shouldn't have goned to the shop. But I'll ask Fanny — I'll tell you what I'll do. I'll put on my boots and my hat and jacket — you shall help me, Sarah, and then we'll go down and I'll call to Fanny from the top of the kitchen stairs and ask her if I may go out with you, Sarah, dear. I'm sure she'll say I may."

So the two little maidens went into the night nursery, where Light Smiley was greatly interested

in looking at her own dwelling-place from other
people's windows, and quite in her element too, seeing that she was being trained for the nursery, in
getting out Peggy's walking things, buttoning her
boots, and all the rest of it.

CHAPTER XI.

"But the way is long and toilsome,
And the road is drear and hard ;
Little heads and hearts are aching,
Little feet with thorns are scarred."
THE CHILDREN'S JOURNEY.

LIGHT SMILEY kept looking round the room with great satisfaction.

"It is nice in 'ere and no mistake," she said at last. "Your 'ats and coats and frocks all in a row, as neat as neat, and these little white beds a sight to be seen. I should love for Rebecca and Matilda-Jane to see it."

"They will," said Peggy, "when I avite you all to a tea-party, you know."

Sarah drew a deep breath. A tea-party in these beautiful nurseries seemed almost too good ever to come true.

"Is there a many nusseries as nice as this 'un, do you think, missy? I do 'ope as I'll get into a nice one when I'm big enough. One 'ud take a pride in keeping it clean and tidy."

"I don't think this is at all a *grand* one," Peggy replied. "Mamma's was much grander when she was little, I know. But, of course, she's very per-tickler, and so's nurse, about it being very tidy."

And then, Peggy being ready, the quaint pair of friends took each other's hands and set off to the top of the kitchen stairs.

"Should we take the humberellar?" said Sarah, suddenly stopping at the foot of the first little flight of stairs. "I don't think it looks any ways like rain, still one never knows, and I can carry it easy."

In her heart she hoped Peggy would say yes. For to Sarah's eyes the clumsy umbrella was a very "genteel" one indeed, and she felt as if it would add distinction to their appearance.

Peggy, not looking at it from this point of view, hesitated.

"P'raps it would do to keep the sun off us," she said. "My parasol's wored out, so I can't take it. Mamma's going to get me a new one."

Sarah ran back and fetched the umbrella.

When they got to the door at the top of the kitchen stairs, Peggy opened it and called down softly, "Fanny, are you there? Can you hear me?" for she was not allowed to go down to the kitchen by herself.

But no one answered. Fanny was busy washing in the back kitchen with both doors shut to keep in the steam, and the cook had gone out to the butcher's.

"Fanny," called Peggy again.

Then a voice came at last in return.

"Is it anything I can tell the cook when she comes

in, please, miss?" and a boy came forward out of the kitchen and stood at the foot of the steep stone stairs. "I'm the baker's boy, and I met cook and she told me to wait; she'd be back with change to pay the book in a minute. There's no one here."

Peggy turned to Sarah in distress.

" Fanny must be out too," she said.

"Well, it'll be all right if the boy 'ull tell her, won't it, missy? 'Tisn't the cook," she went on, speaking to the boy herself, "'tis t'other one. Jest you tell her when she comes in that miss has gone out a little walk with me — Sarah Simpkins — she'll know. I'll take good care of missy."

"All right," said the boy, with no doubt that so it was, and thinking, if he thought at all, that Sarah Simpkins must be a little nurse-girl, or something of the kind about the house, though certainly a small specimen to be in service! He whistled as he turned away, and something in the cheerful sound of his whistle helped to satisfy Peggy that all *was* right!

" He's a nice boy," she said to Sarah. " He won't forget, will he?"

"Not he," Sarah replied. " He'll tell 'em fast enough. And as like as not we'll meet 'em along the street as we go. Is Webb's your butcher, missy —'tis just at the corner of Fernley Road?"

Peggy shook her head.

"I don't know," she said, feeling rather ashamed of her ignorance; "but I'd like to meet Fanny, so, pelease, let us go that way."

And off the two set, by the front door this time, quite easy in their minds, though, as far as they knew, the baker's boy was the only guardian of the house.

They trotted down the street in the sunshine; it was very bright and fine — the air, even there in the smoky town, felt this morning deliciously fresh and spring-like.

"How nice it is," said Peggy, drawing a deep breath; "it's just like summer. I'd like to go a quite long walk, wouldn't you, Sarah?"

Light Smiley looked about her approvingly.

"Yes," she said, "I does enjoy a real fine day. And in the country it must be right-down fust-rate."

"Oh, the country!" said Peggy; "oh dear, how I do wish we could go as far as the country!"

"Well," said Sarah, "if we walk fast we might come within sight of it. There's nice trees and gardings up Fernley Road, and that's a sort of country, isn't it, missy?"

They were at the corner of the road by this time, but there was no sign of Fanny or cook. "Webb's" shop stood a little way down the other side, but as far as they could see it was empty.

"P'raps your folk don't deal there," said Sarah, to which Peggy had nothing to say, and they stood looking about them in an uncertain kind of way.

"We may as well go on a bit," said Sarah at last, "that there boy's sure to tell."

Peggy had no objection, and they set off along Fernley Road at a pretty brisk pace.

They had not very far to go before, as Sarah said, the road grew less town-like; the houses had little gardens round them, some of which were prettily kept, and after a while they came to a field or two, not yet built upon, though great placards stuck up on posts told that they were waiting to be sold for that purpose. They were very towny sort of fields certainly, still the bright spring sunshine made the best of them as of everything else this morning, and the two children looked at them with pleasure.

"There's nicer fields still, a bit farther on," said Sarah. "I've been along this 'ere road several times. It goes on and on right into the country."

"I know," said Peggy, "it goes on into the country of the mountings. But, Sarah," she said, stopping short, and looking rather distressed, "I don't think we see them any plainer than from the nursery window, and the white cottage doesn't look even as plain. Are you sure we're going the right way?"

"We couldn't go wrong," answered Sarah, "there's no other way. But we've come no distance yet, missy, and you see there's ups and downs in the road that comes between us and the 'ills somehow. I suppose at the window we could see straightforward-like, and then we was 'igher up."

"Yes, that must be it," said Peggy; "but I would like to go far enough to see a *little* plainer, Sarah, wouldn't you? I've got the red shoes in my pocket, you know, and when we come to a place where we can see very nice and clear I'll take them out and let them see too."

" Lor'," said Sarah, " you *are* funny, missy."

But she smiled so good-naturedly that Peggy did not mind.

After a bit they came to a place where another road crossed the one they were on. This other road was planted with trees along one side, and the shade they cast looked cool and tempting.

" I wish we could go along that way," said Peggy, " but it would be the wrong way. It doesn't go on to the mountings."

Sarah did not answer for a minute. She was trying to spell out some letters that were painted up on the corner of a wall, which enclosed the garden of a house standing in the road they were looking down.

" ' B, R, A,' " she began, " ' B, R, A, C, K :' it's it, just look, missy. Bain't that Brackenshire as large as life? 'Brackenshire Road.' It must be this way," and she looked quite delighted.

" But how can it be ?" objected Peggy. " This road *doesn't* go to the hills, Sarah. They're straight in front."

" But maybe it slopes round again after a bit," said Sarah. " Lots of roads does that way, and runs the same way really, though you wouldn't think so at the start. It stands to reason, when it's got the name painted up, it must lead Brackenshire way;" and then suddenly, as a man with a basket on his arm appeared coming out of one of the houses, she darted up to him.

"Please, mister, does this road lead to Brackenshire?" she asked.

The man did not look very good-natured.

"Lead to where?" he said, gruffly.

"To Brackenshire — it's painted up on the wall, but we want to be sure."

"If it's painted up on the wall, what's the sense of askin' me?" he said. "If you go far enough no doubt you'll get there. There's more'n one road to Brackenshire."

Sarah was quite satisfied.

"You see," she said to Peggy, running back to her, "it's all right. If we go along this 'ere road a bit, I 'specs it'll turn again and then we'll see the 'ills straight in front."

Peggy had no objection. Fernley Road was bare and glaring just about there, and the trees were very tempting.

"It's really getting like the country," said Peggy, as they passed several pretty gardens, larger and much prettier than the small ones in Fernley Road.

"Yes," Light Smiley agreed, "but though gardings is nice, I don't hold with gardings anything like as much as fields. Fields is splendid where you can

race about and jump and do just as you like, and no
fears of breakin' flowers or nothink."

"Do you think we shall come to fields like that
soon?" said Peggy. "If there was a very nice one
we might go into it p'raps and rest a little, and look
at the mountings. I wish we could begin to see the
mountings again, Sarah, it seems quite strange without them, and I'm getting rather tired of looking at
gardens when we can't go inside them, aren't you?"

Sarah was feeling very contented and happy.
She was, though a little body for her age, much
stronger than Peggy, as well as two years older, and
she looked at her companion with surprise when she
began already to talk of "resting."

"Lor', missy, you bain't tired already," she was
beginning, when she suddenly caught sight of something which made her interrupt herself. This was
another road crossing the one they were on at right
angles, and running therefore in the same direction
as Fernley Road again. "'Ere's our way," she cried,
"now didn't I tell you so? And this way goes
slopin' up a bit, you see. When we get to the top
we'll see the 'ills straight 'afore us, and 'ave a
beeyutiful view."

Peggy's rather flagging steps grew brisker at this,
and the two ran gaily along the new road for a little
way. But running uphill is tiring, and it seemed to
take them a long time to get to the top of the slope,
and when they did so, it was only to be disappointed.

Neither mountains nor hills nor white cottage were to be seen, only before them a rather narrow sort of lane, sloping downwards now and seeming to lead into some rather rough waste ground, where it ended. Peggy's face grew rather doleful, but Sarah was quite equal to the occasion. A little down the hill she spied a stile, over which she persuaded Peggy to climb. They found themselves in a potato field, but a potato field with a path down the middle; it was a large field and at the other end of the path was a gate, opening on to a cart track scarcely worthy the name of a lane. The children followed it, however, till another stile tempted them again, this time into a little wood, where they got rather torn and scratched by brambles and nettles as they could not easily find a path, and Sarah fancied by forcing their way through the bushes they would be sure to come out on to the road again.

It was not, however, till they had wandered backwards among the trees and brambles for some time that they got on to a real path, and they had to walk a good way along this till they at last came on another gate, this time sure enough opening into the high road.

Sarah's spirits recovered at once.

"'Ere we are," she said cheerfully, "all right. 'Ere's Fernley Road again. Nothink to do but to turn round and go' ome if you're tired, missy. *I'm* not tired, but if you'd rayther go no farther — "

Peggy did not answer for a moment; she was staring about her on all sides. The prospect was not a very inviting one; the road was bare and ugly, dreadfully dusty, and there was no shade anywhere, and at a little distance some great tall chimneys were to be seen, the chimneys of some iron-works, from which smoke poured forth. There were a good many little houses near the tall chimneys, they were the houses of the people who worked there, but they were not sweet little cottages such as Peggy dreamed of. Indeed they looked more like a very small ugly town, than like rows of cottages on a country road.

"This isn't a pretty road at all," said Peggy at last, rather crossly I am afraid, "it is very nugly, and you shouldn't have brought me here, Sarah. I can't see the mountings; they is quite goned away, more goned away than when it rains, for then they're only behind the clouds. This isn't Fernley Road, Light Smiley. I do believe you've losted us, and Peggy's so tired, and very, very un'appy."

It was Peggy's way when she grew low-spirited to speak more babyishly than usual; at such times it was too much trouble to think about being a big girl. Poor Sarah looked dreadfully distressed.

"Oh, missy dear, don't cry," she said. "If it bain't Fernley Road, it's *a* road anyway, and there's no call to be frightened. We can ax our way, but I'd rayther not ax it at the cottages, for they might think I was a tramp that'd stoled you away."

"And what would they do then?" asked Peggy, leaving off crying for a minute.

"They'd 'av me up mebbe, and put us in the lock-ups."

"What's that?"

"The place where the pl'ice leaves folk as they isn't sure about."

"Prison, do you mean?" said Peggy, growing very pale.

"Well, not ezackly, but somethin' like."

Peggy caught hold of Sarah in sudden terror.

"Oh come along, Light Smiley, quick, quick. Let's get back into the fields and hide or anything. Oh come quick, for fear they should catch us." And she tugged at Sarah, trying to drag her along the road.

"Stop, missy, don't take on so; there's no need. We'll just go along quietly and no one'll notice us, only you stop crying, and then no one'll think any 'arm. We'll not go back the way we came, it's so drefful thorny, but we'll look out for another road or a path. I 'spects you're right enough — this 'ere bain't Fernley Road."

Peggy swallowed down her sobs.

"I don't think you look quite big enough to have stolened me, Sarah," she said at last. "But I would like to get back into the fields quick. If only we could see the mountings again, I wouldn't be quite so frightened."

They had not gone far before they came upon a gateway and a path leading through a field where there seemed no difficulties. Crossing it they found themselves at the edge of the thorny wood, which they skirted for some way. Peggy's energy, born of fear, began to fail.

"Sarah," she said at last, bursting into fresh tears, "Peggy can't go no farther, and I'm so hungry too. I'm sure it's long past dinner-time. You must sit down and rest; p'raps if I rested a little, I wouldn't feel so very un'appy."

Sarah looked at her almost in despair. She herself was worried and vexed, very afraid too of the scolding which certainly awaited her at home, but she was not tired or dispirited, though very sorry for Peggy, and quite aware that it was she and not "missy" who was to blame for this unlucky expedition.

"I'd like to get on," she said, "we're sure to get back into a road as'll take us 'ome before long. Couldn't I carry you, missy?"

"No," said Peggy, "you're far too little. And I can't walk any more without resting. You're very unkind, Light Smiley, and I wish I'd never seen you."

Poor Sarah bore this bitter reproach in silence.

She looked about for a comfortable seat in the hedge, and settled herself so that Peggy could rest against her. The sunshine, though it had seemed hot and glaring on the bare dusty road was not really very powerful, for it was only late April, though a very summerlike day. Peggy left off crying and said no more, but leant contentedly enough against Sarah.

"I'm comf'able now," she said, closing her eyes. "Thank you, Light Smiley. I'll soon be rested, and then we'll go on."

But in a moment or two, by the way she breathed, Sarah saw that she had fallen asleep.

" Bless us," thought the little guardian to herself, "she may sleep for hours. Whatever 'ull I do? She's that tired — and when she wakes she'll be that 'ungry, there'll be no getting her along. She'll be quite faint-like. If I dared leave her, I'd run on till I found the road and got somebody to 'elp carry her. But I dursn't. If she woked up and me gone, she'd be runnin' who knows where, and mebbe never be found again. Poor missy — it'll be lock-ups and no mistake, wusser I dessay for me, and quite right too. Mother'll never say I'm fit for a nussery after makin' sich a fool of myself."

And in spite of her courage, the tears began to trickle down Sarah's face. Peggy looked so white and tiny, lying there almost in her arms, that it made her heart ache to see her. So she shut her own eyes and tried to think what to do. And the thinking grew gradually confused and mixed up with all sorts of other thinkings. Sarah fancied she

"And at last, though she was really so anxious
and distressed, the quiet and the mild air, and
the idleness perhaps, to which none of the Simp:
kins family were much accustomed, all joined
together and by degrees hushed poor Light
Smiley to sleep, her arms clasped
round Peggy as if to protect
her from any possible
danger.." p. 155

heard her mother calling her, and she tried to answer, but somehow the words would not come.

And at last, though she was really so anxious and distressed, the quiet and the mild air, and the idleness perhaps, to which none of the Simpkins family were much accustomed, all joined together and by degrees hushed poor Light Smiley to sleep, her arms clasped round Peggy as if to protect her from any possible danger.

It would have been a touching picture, had there been any one there to see. Unluckily, not merely for the sake of the picture, but for that of the children themselves, there was no one.

CHAPTER XII.

THE SHOES-LADY AGAIN.

"I'll love you through the happy years,
   Till I'm a nice old lady."

POEMS WRITTEN FOR A CHILD.

WHEN they woke, both of them at the same moment it seemed, though probably one had roused the other without knowing it, the sun had gone, the sky looked dull, it felt chilly and strange. Peggy had thought it must be past dinner-time before they had sat down to rest; it seemed now as if it must be past tea-time too!

Sarah started up, Peggy feebly clinging to her.

"Oh dear, dear," said Sarah, "I shouldn't have gone to sleep, and it's got that cold!" She was shivering herself, but Peggy seemed much the worse of the two. She was white and pinched looking, and as if she were half stupefied.

"I'm so cold," she said, "and so hungry. I thought I was in bed at home. I do so want to go home. I'm sure it's very late, Light Smiley; do take me home."

"I'm sure, missy, it's what I want to do," said poor Sarah. "I'm afeared it's a-going to rain, and

156

whatever 'ull we do then? You wouldn't wait 'ere a minute, would you, while I run to see if there's a road near?"

"No, no," said Peggy, "I won't stay alone. I'm very, very frightened, Light Smiley, and I think I'm going to die."

"Oh Lor', missy, don't you say that," said Sarah, in terror. "If you can't walk I'll carry you."

"I'll try to walk," said Peggy, picking up some spirit when she saw Sarah's white face.

And then the two set off again, dazed and miserable, very different from the bright little pair that had started up Fernley Road that morning.

Things, however, having got to the worst, began to mend, or at least were beginning to mend for them, though Peggy and Sarah did not just yet know it. Not far from the edge of the field where they were, a little bridle-path led into a lane, and a few yards down this lane brought them out upon Fernley Road again at last.

"I see the mountings," cried Peggy, "oh Light Smiley, Peggy sees the mountings. P'raps we won't die, oh, p'raps we'll get home safe again."

But though she had been trying to be brave, now that she began to hope again, it was too much for her poor little nerves — Peggy burst into loud sobbing.

"Oh, dear missy, try not to cry," said Sarah. "There — there — where's your hankercher?" and she dived into Peggy's pocket in search of it. And as she pulled it out, out tumbled at the same time the two little scarlet shoes, falling on the ground.

"Oh Light Smiley, my red shoes. They'll be all spoilt and dirtied," said Peggy, as well as she could, for Sarah was dabbing the handkerchief all over her face.

Sarah stooped to pick them up; both children were too much engaged to notice the sound of wheels coming quickly along the quiet road. But the sight of a speck of dirt on one of the shoes set Peggy off crying again, and she cried for once pretty loudly. The wheels came nearer, and then stopped, and this made Sarah look round. A pony-carriage driven by a lady had drawn up just beside them. The groom, sitting behind, jumped down, though looking as if he he did not know what he was to do.

"What is the matter, little girls?" said the lady.

"It's, please 'm — we've lost our road — it's all along o' me, mum — but I didn't mean no 'arm, only missy's that wore out 'm, and —" but before Sarah could get farther, she was stopped by a sort of cry from both the lady and Peggy at once.

"Oh, oh," called out Peggy, "it's the shoes-lady — oh, pelease, pelease, take me home," and she seemed ready to dart into the lady's arms.

"I do believe," *she* said, "I do believe it's the little girl I saw at the bootmaker's, and — yes, of course it is — there are the shoes themselves! My dear child, whatever are you doing to be so far from home — at least I suppose you live in the town? — and what have you got the dolly's shoes with you for?"

"I brought them for them to see the mountings and the white cottage," sobbed Peggy; "but I'm so cold and hungry, pelease take me home, oh, pelease, do."

The lady seemed rather troubled. Even if she had not remembered Peggy, she would have seen in a moment that she was a little lady, though Peggy looked miserable enough with her torn clothes, and scratched and tear-stained face.

"Poor child," she said, "tell me your name, and where you live."

"I'm Peggy, but I don't 'amember my nother name, 'cos I'm tired and it's very long," she said.

The lady looked at Sarah. Sarah shook her head.

"No, mum, I don't know it neither, but I knows the name of the street. 'Tis Bernard Street 'm — off Fernley Road, and their back winders looks over to us. We're Simpkinses 'm, and missy's mar knows as we're 'speckable, and mother she never thought when she told me to take back the humberellar, as I'd lead missy sich a dance. I'll never do for the nussery, no never. I'm not steady enough," and here Light Smiley gave signs of crying herself.

It was not easy for the lady to make out the story,

but by degrees, with patience she did so. But while talking she had lifted Peggy into the carriage beside her, and wrapped her up in a shawl that lay on the seat, Peggy nestling in, quite contentedly.

"Now," said the lady, "you get in too, Sarah Simpkins, and I'll drive you both home. I was on my way home out into the country, but I can't leave you here on the road. This is Fernley Road, but it's quite four miles from the town."

In scrambled Sarah, divided between fear of her own and Peggy's relations' scoldings when they got home, and the delight and honour of driving in a carriage! The groom would have liked to look grumpy, I am quite sure, but he dared not. Peggy, for her part, crept closer and closer to the lady, and ended by falling asleep again, so that it was a good thing Light Smiley was sitting on the other side, to keep her from falling out.

The four miles seemed very short to Sarah, and as they got into the outskirts of the town her face grew longer and longer.

"I'm more'n half a mind to run away, I 'ave," she said to herself, quite unaware she was speaking aloud. "It'll be more'n I can stand, mother and Rebecca and all on 'em down on me, for I didn't mean no 'arm. I'd best run away."

The lady turned to her, hitherto she had not taken much notice of Sarah, but now she felt sorry for the little girl.

"What are you saying, my dear?" she said gently, though all the same her voice made Sarah jump. "Are you afraid of going home? You have not done anything naughty, exactly, as far as I understand. It was only thoughtless. I will go with you to your home if you like, and explain to your mother how it was."

"Oh thank you, mum," said Sarah, eagerly, her spirits rising again at once; "you see, mum, I do so want to be in the nussery onst I'm big enough, and I was so afeared mother'd never think of it again. I only wanted to please little missy, for she seemed so lonely like, her mar and all bein' away and no one for to take her a walk. She's a sweet little missy, she is, but she's only a baby, so to say; she do have such funny fancies. 'Twas all to see the cottage on the 'ills she wanted to come up Fernley Road so badly."

" The cottage — what cottage?" asked the lady.

Sarah tried to explain, and gradually the lady got to understand what little Peggy had meant about bringing the red shoes "to see the mountings and the cottage."

"She's always a-talking of the country, and father lived there when he was a boy, and missy had got it in her 'ead that he lived in a white cottage, like the one she fancies about," Sarah went on.

"I would like to take her out into the real country, poor little pet," said the lady, looking tenderly at the sweet tiny face of the sleeping child. She loved all children, but little girls of Peggy's age were especially dear to her, for many years before she had had a younger sister who had died, and the thought of her had come into her mind the first time she had seen Peggy at the door of the shoe shop. "If I can see any of her friends I will ask them to let her spend a day with me," she went on, speaking more to herself than to Sarah.

As they turned into Bernard Street a cab dashed past them coming very fast from the opposite direction. It drew up in front of the house which Sarah was just that moment pointing out to the lady as Peggy's home, and a gentleman, followed by a young woman, sprang out. The door was opened almost as soon as they rang, and then the three, the other servant who had answered the bell, the young woman and the gentleman, all stood together on the steps talking so anxiously and eagerly that for a moment or two they did not notice the pony-carriage, and though the groom knew the whole story by this time and had jumped down at once, he was far too proper to do anything till he had his lady's orders.

"Ask the gentleman to speak to me," said the lady, "and you jump out, little Sarah. I think he must be Peggy's father."

He had turned round by this time and came hurrying forward. The moment the lady saw him she knew she had guessed right. He was so like Peggy

— fair and gray-eyed, and with the same gentle expression, and very young looking to be the father not only of Peggy, but of *big* little boys like Thor and Terry. His face looked pale and anxious, but the moment he caught sight of the little sleeping figure leaning against the lady it all lighted up and a red flush came into his cheeks.

"Oh — thank God," he exclaimed, "my little Peggy! You have found her! How good of you! But — she is not hurt? — she is all right?"

"Yes — yes — only cold and hungry and tired," said the lady eagerly, for Peggy did look rather miserable still. "Will you lift her out?" and as he did so, she got out herself, and turned to Sarah. "May I bring this other child in for a moment," she said, "and then I can explain it all?"

Sarah followed gladly, but a sudden thought struck her, "Please 'm," she said, bravely, though the tears came to her eyes as she spoke, "p'raps I'd best run 'ome; mother'll be frightened about me."

"But I promised you should not be scolded," said the lady; "stay," and she turned to Fanny, "she lives close to, she says."

"At the back — over the cobbler's," said Sarah, readily.

"Can you let her mother know she's all right, then? And say I am coming to speak to her in a moment," said the lady, and Fanny went off. She had been so terrified about Peggy, and so afraid that

she would be blamed for carelessness, that she dared
not wait, though she was dying with curiosity to
know the whole story and what one of the Simpkins
children could have had to do with it.

Peggy awoke by the time her father had got her
into the dining-room, where cook had made a good
fire and laid out Peggy's dinner and tea in one to
be all ready, for the poor woman had been hoping
every instant for the last few hours that the little
girl would be brought home again. It had been
difficult to find Peggy's father, as he was not at his
office, and Fanny had been there two or three times
to fetch him.

"Oh dear papa," were Peggy's first words, "I'm
so glad to be home. I'll never go up Fernley Road
again; but I did so want to see the cottage and the
mountings plainer. And it wasn't Light Smiley's
fault. She was very good to me, and I was very
cross."

This did not much clear up matters. Indeed
Peggy's papa was afraid for a minute or two that his
little girl was going to have a fever, and that her
mind was wandering. But all such fears were soon
set at rest, and when the lady went off with Sarah,
she left Peggy setting to work very happily at her
dinner or tea, she was not sure which to call it.

"And you will let her come to spend the day
with me to-morrow?" said the lady, as she shook
hands with Peggy's father. "I shall be driving this

way, and I can call for her. I should not be happy not to know that she was none the worse for her adventures to-day."

Then the lady took Sarah by the hand and went round with her to her home in the back street, telling the groom to wait for her at the corner.

It was well she went herself, for otherwise I am afraid poor Light Smiley would not have escaped the scolding she dreaded. Her mother and sisters had been very unhappy and frightened about her, and when people — especially poor mothers like Mrs. Simpkins, with "so many children that they don't know what to do" — are anxious and frightened, I have often noticed that it makes them very cross.

As it was, however, the lady managed to smooth it all down, and before she left she got not only Sarah's mother, but Rebecca and Mary-Hann and all of them to promise to say no more about it.

"'Tisn't only for myself I was feelin' so put about, you see, ma'am," said Mrs. Simpkins, "but when I sent over the way and found the little missy was not to be found it flashed upon me like a lightenin' streak — it did that, ma'am — that the two was off together. And if any 'arm had come to the little lady through one of mine, so to say, it would 'ave gone nigh to break my 'art. For their mar is a sweet lady — a real feelin' lady is their mar."

" And a kind friend to you, I dare say," said the stranger.

"Couldn't be a kinder as far as friendly words and old clotheses goes," said Mrs. Simpkins. "But she's a large little fam'ly of her own, and not so very strong in 'ealth, and plenty to do with their money. And so to speak strangers in the place, though she 'ave said she'd do her best to get a place in a nice fam'ly for one of my girls."

The lady glanced at the group of sisters.

"Yes," she said, "I should think you could spare one or two. How would you like to be in a kitchen?" she added, turning to Rebecca.

The girl blushed so that her face matched her arms, and she looked more "reddy" than ever. But she shook her head.

"I'm afraid —" she began.

"No, ma'am, thank you kindly, but I couldn't spare Rebecca," the mother interrupted. "If it were for Mary-Hann now — Matilda-Jane's coming on and could take her place. Only, for I couldn't deceive you, ma'am, she's rather deaf."

"I shouldn't mind that," said the lady, who was pleased by Mary-Ann's bright eyes and pleasant face. "I think deaf people sometimes work better than quick-hearing ones, besides, it may perhaps be cured. I will speak about her to my housekeeper and let you know. And you, Sarah, you are to be in the nursery some day."

Sarah grinned with delight.

"Not just yet," said Mrs. Simpkins; "she 'ave a

deal to learn, 'ave Sarah. Schooling and stiddiness to begin with. She don't mean no 'arm, I'll allow."

"No; I'm sure she wants to be a very good girl," said the lady. "She was very kind and gentle to little Miss Peggy. So I won't forget you either, Sarah, when the time comes."

And then the lady said good-bye to them all, and Mrs. Simpkins's heart felt lighter than for long, for she was sure that through this new friend she might get the start in life she had been hoping for, for her many daughters.

Peggy slept off her fatigue, and by the next morning she was quite bright again and able to listen to and understand papa's explanation of how, though without meaning to be disobedient, she had done wrong the day before in setting off with Sarah Simpkins as she had done. Two or three tears rolled slowly down her cheeks as she heard what he said.

"I meant to be so good while mamma was away," she whispered. "But I'll never do it again, papa. I'll stay quiet in the nursery all alone, even if Miss Earnshaw doesn't come back at all."

For a message had come from the dressmaker that her mother was very ill, as Fanny had feared, and that she was afraid she would not be able to leave her for several days.

"It won't be so bad as that, dear," said her father. "Mamma will be back in five days now, and I don't think you are likely to be left alone in the nursery

—certainly not to-day;" and then he told her about the lady having asked her to spend the day out in the country with her, and that Peggy must be ready by twelve o'clock, not to keep her new friend waiting.

Peggy's eyes gleamed with delight.

"Out into the country?" she said. "Oh, how lovely!   And oh, papa, do you think *p'raps* she lives in a white cottage?"

Papa shook his head.

"I'm afraid it's not a cottage at all where she lives," he said. "But I'm sure it is a very pretty house, and let us hope it is a white one."

"No," said Peggy, "you don't understand, papa— not as well as mamma does. I don't care what colour it is if it's only an 'ouse."

And she couldn't understand why papa laughed so that he really couldn't correct her. "I'm afraid, Peggy," he said, "you've been taking lessons from little Miss Simpkins. It's time mamma came home again to look after you."

"Yes, I wish mamma was come home again," said Peggy.   "We can't do without her, can we, papa?"

But when the dear little pony carriage came up to the door, and Peggy got in and drove off with her kind friend, she was so happy that she had not even time to wish for mamma.

And what a delightful day she had!   The lady's house was very pretty, and the gardens and woods in which it stood even prettier in Peggy's opinion.

And though it was not a cottage, there were all the country things to see which Peggy was so fond of — cocks and hens, and cows, and in one field lots of sheep and sweet little lambkins. There were pigs too, which Peggy would not look at, but ran away to the other end of the yard as soon as she heard them "grumphing," which amused the lady very much. And in the afternoon she went a walk with her friend through the village, where there were several pretty cottages, but none that quite fitted Peggy's fancy. When they came in again Peggy stood at the drawing-room window, which looked out towards Bracken-shire, without speaking.

"You like that view, don't you, dear?" said the lady. "You can see the hills?"

"Yes," said Peggy, "I can see the mountings, but not the white cottage. It's got turned wrong some-how, from here. I can only see *it* from the nursery window at home," and she gave a very little sigh.

"Some day," said the lady, "some day in the sum-mer when the afternoons are very long, I will drive you right out a long way among the hills, and perhaps we'll find the cottage then. For I hope your mamma will often let you come to see me, my little Peggy."

"Yes," said Peggy, "that would be lovely. I *wonder* if we'd find the white cottage."

No, they never did! The sweet long summer days came, and many a bright and happy one Peggy spent with her kind friend, but they never found the white cottage on the hill. Peggy knew it so well in her mind, she felt she could not mistake it, but though she saw many white cottages which any one else *might* have thought was it, she knew better. And each time, though she sighed a little, she hoped again.

But before another summer came round Peggy and her father and mother, and Thor, and Terry, and Hal, and Baldwin, and Baby had all gone away — far away to the south, many hours' journey from the dingy town and the Fernley Road, and the queer old house in the back street where lived the cobbler and old Mother Whelan and Brown Smiley and Light Smiley and all the rest of them. Far away too from the hills and the strange white speck in the distance which Peggy called her cottage.

So it never was more than a dream to her after all, and perhaps — perhaps it was best so? For nothing has ever spoilt the sweetness and the mystery of the childish fancy — she can see it with her mind's eye still — the soft white speck on the far-away, blue hills — she can see it and think of it and make fancies about it even now — now that she has climbed a long, long way up the mountain of life, and will soon be creeping slowly down the other side, where the sun still shines, however, and there are even more beautiful things to hope for than the sweetest dreams of childhood.

THE END.